BROCK
A HOPE CITY NOVEL

KRIS MICHAELS
BOOK ONE

Copyright © 2020 by Kris Michaels

All rights reserved. No part of this book may be reproduced or transmitted in any form or by any means, electronic or mechanical, including photocopying, recording, or by any information storage and retrieval system without the written permission of the author, except where permitted by law.

If you are reading this book and did not purchase it, then you are reading an illegal pirated copy. Make sure that you are only reading a copy that has been officially released by the author.

This book is a work of fiction. Names, characters, places, and incidents either are products of the author's imagination or are used fictitiously. Any resemblance to actual persons, living or dead, events, or locales is entirely coincidental.

❦ Created with Vellum

CHAPTER 1

"Detective King, there is a report of a warehouse fire with a dead body off of Livingston in the old warehouse district. Patrols are on scene, and a cordon has been established." The dispatcher's voice was far too fucking perky for 1:00 a.m.

He blinked hard and tried to bring the light fixture and fan on the ceiling into focus. It wasn't working too well. He closed his eyes again and mumbled, "Roger that. Send the address to my phone. Have you notified Detective Whitt?"

"I called him first, sir. He told me to remind you he's with Vice tonight."

Crap that's right. He glanced at the clock. He'd

just fallen asleep. Thirty-five minutes ago, to be exact. "Fuck."

"Sir?"

"Sorry. Never mind. Text me the address. Tell the responding patrols I'm on my way." He flipped the blanket back and headed to the bathroom. Two minutes later he made a quick detour into the kitchen. He had two coffee pots, one of the drip-brew big boys that made a pot the size of the Titanic, and a different machine that made coffee quickly, by the cup. He used three coffee pods, enough cream to sink the aforementioned Titanic, and a fuck-ton of sugar to fill his travel tankard before he headed downstairs to his truck. The three-minute delay waiting for his coffee was a necessity. The general public needed him awake when he drove, and the dead body wasn't going to get... deader. *Damn, it was going to be a long night.*

The tires of his old truck crunched against the scattered gravel on the patchwork asphalt as he came to a stop outside the charred remnants of what once was a warehouse. Now it was a fucking shell, a huge husk burned and purged empty of any contents. Thanks to the lack of sleep he'd tallied over the last three weeks, he felt a strange kinship to the hollow, gutted structure. The outsides were still present, the insides? Desolate, charred and unusable. Fuck, he *was* tired. When the morbid comparisons started rolling it was well past time to get a few hours of uninterrupted sleep. If only the fucking criminals who worked overtime in Hope City would read that memo. He rolled his shoulders and groaned when the vertebrae in his neck and back popped.

He focused on the building. The outer structure of the warehouse still smoldered in places. While the rest of the responding firemen were busy emptying hoses and replacing them on the trucks, a hotshot crew scrambled, hunting down unextinguished embers. He glanced at the number on the side of the hook and ladder truck—his baby brother's battalion. He had no idea if Blay was on shift or not. That was a moot point because right now, he had a dead body to meet and a death scene to process; there was no time for catching up with his brother.

It wasn't difficult to find where he needed to be. Instead of the flashing red lights of the fire trucks, the slow-rolling blue strobes of the responding patrol units heralded the position of the body as if a lighthouse's million-watt beam cutting through the grayness of a fog bank. He took his time walking up to the crime scene. It was his habit to take in the entirety of the area prior to approaching the body. He needed to get a feel for the location and any circumstance on the outside that could contribute to what he was about to see inside.

This warehouse was on the outer edges of the Inner Harbor, a few miles and a couple lifetimes from the classy shops, high-dollar restaurants, and upscale bars that had taken over what used to be run down fisheries, storage warehouses, an old cannery, and a plethora of failed businesses in Hope City, Maryland. Young, eager money flowed into the Inner Harbor now. This area of the city was being revitalized, if you believed the hype in the *Hope City Journal*.

He put his hands on his hips and looked away from the building, absorbing the oppressiveness of the outer edges of his city. *Revitalization*. Not from where he stood. In his district, he worked amongst the poorest of the poor, people who had no hope, people who didn't have a way out. Crime, hell, that was *the* constant for his people. For the ones who lived in his district, crime equaled income. As money flowed into Hope City, crime became a lucrative investment. Drugs, prostitution, illegal gun sales, smuggling, and larcenies had all taken notice of new money and had bumped up the crime rates for his district.

His attention centered on the shadowy images of old, vacant warehouses that lay further from the smoldering ruins where he now stood. His job had taken him there in the past. A large homeless population had settled just beyond those warehouses. They lived scattered among the desolation and decay of better times.

A strong wind blew, lifting his father's old, green field jacket away from his body. Fall was slipping into winter. Brock closed his eyes. The annual coat and blanket drive organized by the Hope City Humanitarian Alliance should be wrapping up. He prayed the organization got enough donations this year. Far too many died last year due to exposure to the cold. There weren't enough shelters to hold all the people who had nowhere to go. Life on his side of the city was brutal.

He turned away from his thoughts and faced the charred walls of the warehouse. The yellow crime scene tape flickered and snapped in the brisk, cold wind. Careful to avoid any of the debris surrounding the building, he picked his way through the rubble that littered his path.

Carrying the duffle that held his crime scene kit, he rounded the corner, entered the warehouse, and stopped short. A small smile spread across his face. "Well, if you're here, why the fuck am I? Someone said this was a homicide."

Sean McBride's head snapped up. "About time you showed up, King." His best friend of damn near thirty years stood and carefully backed away from whatever he studied on the wall. The latex gloves Sean wore snapped off and Brock was enveloped in a hug a heartbeat later. "How have you been, man?"

"Not bad. How're your mom and dad?" He slapped Sean's back a couple times before they broke apart. He shoved his hands into his jacket pockets, feeling more than a little guilty about not going home lately. He hadn't been by to see his parents or Colm and Sharon McBride in far too long. Life had a way of becoming complicated, busy, and downright unpleasant. It was the unpleasant he tried to keep from his family and friends, though they were well acquainted with life in law enforcement.

"They're good. Hey, did you hear Rory and Erin are getting out of the military?" Sean mimicked Brock's position as they stared at the dead body.

Neighbors their entire life, the King and McBride clans were practically family. Erin and Rory were Sean's younger brother and sister. Twins. It seemed to be a rite of passage in both families that almost all the children had served in the armed forces. "No. I hadn't heard. Are they coming home, or are they spreading their wings and conquering the world outside of Hope City?"

"They're home. Erin's just out and moved in with Mom and Dad until she knows what she wants to do. Rory was discharged last month. In fact, he's already volunteering with the same fire battalion that Blayze works for while studying to be an EMT. We need to have dinner and drinks and catch up—" Sean motioned to the dead body not more than fifteen feet from them "—but I think both of us may be busy for the foreseeable future."

The dead body they stared at was the reason he'd been called from his warm, seldom used bed. The victim wasn't the toasted remnants of a homeless person trying to stay warm. The man in front of them wore designer clothes. Barely a scratch marred the soles of his shoes, although there were a few tiny scuffs on the toes. His hair was styled with product. The slacks he wore were obviously expensive. The fall of blood from the man's severed neck coated the front of the man's chest, a stark difference from the pristine white of the shirt's sleeves and cuffs. That material shimmered in the headlights of the patrol cars and the temporary lighting Sean had set up by the scorched wall.

Brock took out the pair of latex gloves he carried in his jacket pocket. He set his duffle down and filled his jacket pockets with what he would need before he snapped the latex barrier over his hands. He bent down to get at eye level with his victim. A gaping wound, deep with straight edges. Powerful person... unless they were hopped up on drugs, or hell, in a fit of rage, but he'd state with confidence this wasn't a tentative hack job. The angle of the cut was hauntingly familiar. He'd seen several of these types of wounds during his deployments overseas when his team had found villagers executed. He leaned down farther to get a better look at the wound. Due to the angle and the depth, and based on the blood spatter, his initial guess was the killer was taller than his victim, but he'd wait for the ME's report before he'd consider his early theory a probable fact.

The muscles in his jaw tightened as he ground his back teeth together. A fucking waste. What had this guy been involved in that he ended up here, like this? *What's your story? Who did this to you?* He made a quick scan of the evidence markers Sean and the patrols had set in place before he stood, repositioned, and withdrew his digital camera from his kit bag. He inserted a new memory card and took a slew of pictures of the scene.

Brock shifted and called to the patrolman behind him. "What's the ETA on the medical examiner and crime scene technicians, and was the photographer called?"

"The medical examiner will be here in less than five. There was a discussion as to whose jurisdiction the scene fell into." The officer glanced at Sean before he crossed his arms and rocked back on his heels. "I was told the arson investigator was the lead in this case."

He rolled his head and looked at Sean. He didn't outright laugh at his friend, although it was a close thing. "So, do you consider this death a result of the arson?"

"Fuck you, man. This fire falls into the parameters of several of my open cases. Yes, I told your patrols I was lead investigator, which I am, as far as the arson is concerned. This guy? Not so much. Let me gather the evidence I need. I promise not to fuck up your investigation as long as you don't mess with mine. You can call in your crime scene technicians anytime."

An arsonist? That would add some seriously fucked up elements to the investigation. "You think this homicide is tied into your serial arsonist?"

Sean's brow furrowed and he shook his head. "I don't know. First impressions say not, but I never go on first impressions."

That was where he and his best friend differed. He'd learned to trust his gut as it was generally right, but Sean was one hell of an investigator. He'd bet his last dollar his friend would catch whoever was nuking buildings in Hope City.

Sean motioned toward the far side of the room. "What I need is over there. Looks like an accelerant of some kind was used, however, it's crucial to determine if it was cast on this side of the wall or the other. Besides that, the scene is yours. Just make an annotation I was here. I've already marked in my notes where the body was located. I'm assuming the Fire Department did a check to make sure he was dead."

As responding detectives, they were not medical professionals and the body was off limits until the ME arrived. Any personal effects left on the body would have to be requested as evidence. The wading pool of blood the man lay in, in conjunction with the nearly decapitating wound across his neck, made the MO pretty fucking obvious. "Dude, he's definitely dead."

"No shit, asshole. I'm not a homicide detective, but I figured that out. Proper procedure dictates when you find a body on scene, you check for signs of life." Sean bristled at Brock's teasing. His friend was easy to rile up, and he'd gleefully indulged since they were kids.

"Always a stickler for procedure. A rule-follower from way back." He ducked the slug to the shoulder headed his way. Damn, he missed spending time with Sean. Their careers tended to suck up any free time, but they did need to get together. He'd make time. Somehow.

"Following the rules saved our asses more than once." Sean cuffed him on the shoulder, this time connecting. "Now let me work, and for the love of God please take care of... him." His best friend waved toward the dead body and threw him a smirk before he sauntered over to the charred remains of the interior wall.

His attention once again centered on the victim in front of him. "Did you get any ID?" He looked over at the officer standing by the hole in the wall they'd used as an entrance.

The guy shook his head. "Your friend wouldn't let me touch shit."

"Yeah, well my friend is a damn good investigator —" The blaring of the officer's radio interrupted his comment. The medical examiner had arrived on scene. He nodded at the officer. "Have the guy on the perimeter go around to the front of the building and help them drive the van back here. They're going to need the wagon, and we don't want to parade a DB through the lookie-loos or any press the fire might have attracted." The officer acknowledged him with a head tilt and stepped out.

He raised his small digital camera again and changed angles. He always took his own crime scene photos. He could access these photos when he couldn't sleep at night. Dragging cases files home from the office was frowned upon, plus bringing work home was just a royal pain in the ass. The crime scene techs were effective and efficient, but they didn't look at the scene the way he did. Needing to get closer to the victim, he reached in his pocket and retrieved new protective booties. He covered the soles of his boots with the protective liner so he wouldn't contaminate the crime scene as he approached the dead body.

Brock angled his camera and snapped pictures as he walked and then squatted down in front of the man. The victim's watch, wedding ring, and cufflinks remained untouched. He made sure to get all those items in a shot. Oh, happy day, a wallet had fallen onto the cement next to him. *That* he could collect as evidence. He used the ass end of his ballpoint pen to lift the wallet. *Bingo*. He took several photos, added a marker, and then took three additional photos. Diligent not to touch or move the body in any way, he carefully picked the wallet up from its location in the congealed blood. The vic's blood had seeped around the wallet, but the leather had shielded what was inside.

He flipped the slim wallet open and examined the contents before he snapped a string of photos. No cash, or credit cards, but a picture of a beautiful blonde woman, a driver's license, several receipts, and laundry tickets. He cataloged and annotated each item on the evidence tag. The driver's license was issued to... Samuel Treyson. Brock entered the name on the evidence tag and then shot a glance at his vic. Oh shit. *Fuck him standing.* If this guy was related to *the* Treysons, his case was about to explode.

He palmed his phone and did a quick search of the internet. *Damn it.* The face on the *Forbes* magazine cover was the same one that stared back at him on the driver's license. He dipped his head and took a damn good look at the victim. Yeah, this case was going to suck on an epic level.

He glanced over his shoulder at his best friend. "Get ready for one hell of a ride, Sean."

His friend rose from whatever fire-bug stuff he was doing by the far wall. "What's up?"

"The deceased is one Samuel Treyson."

His friend narrowed his eyes as realization dawned and glared across the space. "If you're fucking with me, I'm going to kick your ass."

"Not even in the slightest." He flashed his phone toward Sean, displaying the magazine cover.

"You realize the can of worms that opens up, right?" Sean placed his hands on his hips. His chest expanded before he blew an exasperated huff of air. "I need to call my Captain, who really doesn't like to talk to people at two in the morning, and your dad needs a heads up. I wouldn't want to be in your shoes. The brass and the press will be crawling up your ass as soon as this breaks. Criminal Proctology 101, my friend."

Great. Just what he needed—a media circus. Well, hopefully they could get the body processed and to the morgue before the vultures started circling. Bringing the medical examiner's van to the rear of the building was the right call. He dropped Treyson's wallet into an evidence bag. He sealed the bag with tamper resistant tape, attached the initial bare-bones inventory sheet, interrupted Sean to initial the tag as a witness, and initialed it himself to start the chain of custody. Covering his ass started now. He'd go over the inventory of the contents again when the property officer was available to witness the accounting. Carefully stepping away from the victim to an open area, Brock palmed his cell. His Lieutenant needed a heads up before he tapped his old man on the shoulder and whispered in his ear.

CHAPTER 2

He'd bet his last paycheck that the fucking stairs were steeper today than yesterday. Pulling his dog-tired ass up the six flights of stairs to the corner of the building homicide had claimed as home, he yawned at the top of the stairs until his entire body shook. He'd passed fucking exhausted a couple days ago. Sleep and he weren't on speaking terms on the best of days. He'd suffered from insomnia for years and had done everything to try to combat it except drugs and a consistent sleep hygiene regiment. His doctors insisted a routine that would signal his body it was time to shut down would help immensely. Only life as a homicide detective never ran nine to five, and this year, he could count on one hand the times he'd been home in time to watch the five o'clock evening news. So, he slept when he could, for as long as he could. The ever-present exhaustion was just a fact of his life that he managed.

Trudging up the stairs, his over-tired mind flicked through the events of the last four hours. Of course, once he'd made his notifications, the big boys had shown up on scene. Right on the brass' heels had come the press. So much for keeping things under wraps. The feeding frenzy was because of the last name of the man zipped in the body bag. This would guarantee a three-ring circus. What had Samuel Treyson been doing there?

A contingent of blue suits had kept the bastards at bay, while the crime scene techs had erected a visual barrier, also known as a tarp, which allowed everyone to finish their jobs. Thank God there was still a roof over this portion of the warehouse otherwise the helicopters he heard outside would have been able to get graphic photos.

The brass had held to the perimeter of the crime scene and talked among themselves. They didn't help, but at least they hadn't hindered the job either. It was important this case was handled correctly. He got that. As lead detective, he called all the shots and the powers-that-be had respected his authority over the scene.

The Treyson family owned half the city. He was actually surprised the case hadn't been taken from him. It would make sense to transfer it to the homicide detectives assigned to the Briar Hill precinct. The brass would want the case where they could monitor it, and his dad's office was in Briar Hill. He shoved open the stairwell door as he worried the specifics of the case like a dog gnawing on a steak bone. He kinda-sorta hoped the Briar Hill Precinct would take this one because he had a feeling dealing with the elite in Briar Hill was going to become a hemorrhoid of biblical proportions. Yep, a hemorrhoid. Big, ugly, irritating as fuck, and no way to make it go away. Besides, the two murders he was currently working were enough to keep both he and his partner busy. Let the Briar Hill detectives deal with the political nightmare. He'd be good with that... or at least that's what he kept telling himself. Damn it, what was Treyson doing in his district? Why in the hell was he in that abandoned warehouse? They hadn't found any signs of struggle, even after they'd set up lighting when the crime scene tech arrived. *Why were you there, Samuel?*

What were you involved with that got you killed? Why didn't you fight?

Instead of heading straight to his desk, he hung a hard right into the break room. Coffee made up at least ninety percent of the liquid in his body, what would a few more gallons of caffeine matter? He grabbed his massive thermos mug from the shelf above the coffee pot and poured half the carafe into the insulated jug. Six heaping spoons of sugar and a couple of glugs of creamer later and he was in business.

"You're going to die of diabetes, son."

Brock chuckled as he brought his coffee mug to his lips. *Nirvana.* He chugged three burning gulps and turned to look at his father, the Commissioner of Hope City's Police Force. The job fit his old man as well as the three-piece suits he wore. Chauncey King was two inches shorter than the six feet, seven inches he'd given Brock, and he carried more muscle than his father ever had, but the resemblance between them was uncanny. His old man was still as strong as a team of mules, and the guy had a mustache Tom Selleck would envy, plus a smile that could disarm a small army, or a seething handful of Hope City politicos.

"If I die of diabetes, at least I won't have to

suffer through this case." Brock rolled his head and popped his neck. "Did you see the swarm outside or were you able to avoid them?"

"Dealing with the press is in my job description." His father gave him a quick smile. "Did you make it through the crush unscathed?"

"I kept my head down and said nothing. I mean, hello, we just caught this case. Do I have any suspects? Ah... yeah, the entire city at this fucking point. What a shit storm." He shook his head and examined his cup. "Dad, I gotta ask, why didn't you pull it from me and put someone from the Briar Hill district on the case? With you being the Commissioner of Police and I your son, the press is going to make something of me being the lead detective. Hell, I don't have the Briar Hill detectives' connections or their... tact, to handle the fake ass people over on your side of town."

His father looked over his shoulder and nudged the door shut with his foot. "Fisher and Jeremiah will be available to you should you need their assistance, but this is your case. It was your call. It's your case; you follow it through to the end. Besides, it'll be good for you. You can play nice; I know you can." There was determination in his father's eyes.

When his old man accepted the job as police commissioner, the entire force had been riddled with corruption. When the press realized that both he and his brother Brody were on the force too, the headlines read, 'Corruption Sweep Nets Nepotism Boon.'

"I'm gonna ruffle feathers, Pops. Hell, I might end up killing a golden goose or two in the process." Brock took another gulp of his life sustaining hot bean juice. God did a good thing the day he poofed the coffee bean into existence.

"I have a feeling there are one or two geese over in Briar Hill this city could do without. Just make sure you color within the lines. I need you to sort this case as quickly as possible. Pressure is coming from way up. I've had seventeen calls already this morning from the governor on down. You and Jordan are a formidable team. If you need to sluff off the other case files on your desk, do it. Lieutenant Davidson already knows this one has priority." His father walked across the room to the coffee pot and poured himself a Styrofoam cup full.

Jordan Whitt, his more charming and more socially acceptable partner, was the counter point on his compass. Where he was sharp edges, blunt conversation, and couldn't be bothered with social niceties, his partner was polite, disarming, and could get people to talk to him. Which sucked. Well, not really. Jordan handled all the non-hostile witness interactions. Jordan was the pretty boy who could sweet-talk a fucking snake out of a tree. He had a resting bitch face that scared women and children, but they had a great system in place. He was damn good at becoming a statue when people were talking to Jordan. His height and bulk tended to intimidate just about everyone, so if imitating a piece of granite advanced their investigations, he froze and let Jordan work.

However, *he* conducted all suspect interviews. It wasn't a case of good cop-bad cop. Brock's military training and experience made him damn good at reading people and he had a built-in lie detector that rarely failed him. He'd keep hammering away until he got to the truth. His techniques were… inventive and sometimes skimmed the lines of legal, but never crossed them.

"Jordan is supposed to be loaned to the Feds for the task force they're building."

"Shit, that's right. The Grappelli disaster."

"Unfortunately, he's the expert on the fucker."

His partner had worked undercover for two

years getting close to the guy before he busted him. Too bad the Feds couldn't keep the slimy son of a bitch in custody. Now that murderous bastard was on the loose, and the Feds were pulling his partner back into the mess. As it stood now, the finger pointing and hysterics at the Federal level were the only thing keeping his partner in Hope City. When they fucking pulled their heads out of their asses, Jordan would be gone, and God only knew how long the Feds would keep him.

"I'll make sure you get a partner with experience."

"I'd rather work alone." Breaking in a new partner, even for the short-term, sent fucking nails down his mental chalkboard.

"Tough." His father tossed the comment over before he lifted his coffee to his lips. "I have just the person. Comes highly recommended from people I trust."

He narrowed his eyes at his old man and chose to ignore the fact he'd have a new partner before long. Instead he zoned in on his dad drinking coffee. "I thought you were supposed to be giving up caffeine?" He watched his father as the man took a long drink. His dad had a health scare last year. High blood pressure, which was now under control, but his mother hovered like a fucking Blackhawk helicopter. She'd topple the best of them with her machine guns of guilt, motherly-wifely love, and yes, intimidation. He'd seen her lock and load those sons of bitches and then fire with relentless precision if she thought anyone in her family wasn't toeing the line. She should've been an investigator, not a legal aid worker.

"As far as your mother knows, I have." He shrugged, spun, and leaned against the counter. "The Treyson Empire is breathing down everyone's neck. Samuel Treyson was the anointed one. The old man has three more sons, but they're still kids. Samuel was being groomed to take over for Sebastian Treyson. According to one of his lawyers, the old man is flying back from Switzerland as we speak. Samuel's wife has arranged a time to identify his body."

He nodded. "I stopped by the Treyson residence prior to coming here. I was met at the door by no less than four attorneys and a pack of reporters shouting questions so damn loud I could hardly hold a conversation. They 'scheduled' a time for Mrs. Treyson to speak to me." He shook his head and took another sip of coffee. "So, until three-thirty this afternoon, Jordan and I will be working Samuel Treyson's last hours." He smiled into his coffee cup.

"Oh, son, I've seen that look before. What do you have that Treyson's lawyers don't know you have?"

"The less you know the better. Plausible deniability would be a good thing." He waggled his eyebrows at his father. He was screwing with his old man. He'd never put him in a bad light.

"Answer one question for me." His father turned to face him.

"Sure."

"What you have, it's legal and admissible, right?" His father poured the remainder of his coffee into the small break room sink.

Although that question hurt, Brock kept his expression blank as he stared at his father. "That stung."

His old man scrubbed his face and then sighed, "Fuck. I'm sorry. The pressure on this one is mighty heavy. I trust you with my life and, incidentally it would seem, my livelihood."

"Believe me, I understand. I'm doing this by the book. I don't want to be the stumbling block in this case." It wasn't like he'd be violating Treyson's fourth amendment rights. The man was dead after all. He'd call his contact Cliff, at the District Attorney's office, to validate his actions before he pressed forward with his investigation, but he was on solid ground. He frowned as he thought about the phone he'd just dropped off at evidence. *Damn it.* That meant he had to go back downstairs and get it after Cliff gave his official blessing. The GPS hits off cell phone towers when the phone was active would be the easiest way to trace the man's last twenty-four, and those were always critical when investigating a homicide.

There wasn't a security code, and after the crime scene technicians had dusted it for prints, he'd been able to access everything on the man's cell. He would use the man's apps to his advantage. After he called Cliff and made it legal, he'd direct the techies in cybercrimes to download all the information they could from the phone. There were volumes of emails and texts. From past cases, he knew he could access them, but he could never use anything he found in court. They'd have to get a warrant to keep it admissible. Cliff should be able to find a judge not intimidated by the Treyson name. *He hoped.*

His father's hand landed on his shoulder. "Make sure it's airtight. If you get anything from those leads, we need to ensure the evidence and procedure is rock solid." Apparently, his father had been thinking the same thing.

"I haven't lost a suspect due to shoddy police work, yet," Brock reminded his father.

His old man chuckled. "I know that. You're one of the best detectives I have. I just worry. It's a father's prerogative. Oh, and you're coming to dinner Sunday. Your mother, bless her heart, wants all her children at the dinner table every Sunday. You've missed the last three months. I don't care what you have on your plate here at work, make time for your mother." His dad headed toward the break room door.

"Damn, old man, you're good at the guilt trip, thing. Was it Gramma Thompson or Mom who taught you that?" Brock teased as the man reached for the door.

"I'm good at a lot of things, none of which your grandma or mother taught me." His father leveled a stare at him and jacked up a single eyebrow.

The smirk his father added took his mind to a place it never needed to go. *Ever.* He squeezed his eyes shut. He dropped his mug to the counter and slapped his hand over his ears. "TMI, Dad." The rumble of his father's laughter still made it past his hastily erected barriers.

Slowly he allowed one eye to ease open. He relaxed when he realized his father wasn't in the break room any longer. After a full body shiver, he grabbed his coffee mug and poured the rest of the pot into his mug. It took him less than a minute to start another pot of coffee. In this precinct, everyone followed "the code". A person never took the last cup of coffee without making another pot. God help the person who decided to test it. Coffee was the lifeblood of any building inhabited by police officers.

He rolled his shoulders, grabbed his mug, and headed to his desk. Treyson's body would be at the front of the queue in the morgue. So, minus the toxicology and histology reports, the autopsy report should be ready tomorrow. It didn't matter how much money you had; those damn tests took time. Real life didn't work like the television crime shows where the reports were done as soon as the medical examiner had finished the autopsy. True, money had a way of making shit happen more rapidly, but it couldn't make chemicals process any faster than nature allowed.

The amount of money the Treysons had could

also make shit disappear. The hunt to find Samuel's killer needed to be quick and efficient, especially if Samuel Treyson had enemies. Which led to the question–who would want Samuel Treyson dead? Between now and 3:30 this afternoon, he and Jordan were going to try to find out.

He maneuvered through the homicide bullpen. Actually, it wasn't much of a pen, more a conglomeration of mismatched desks pushed together in the center of the large room. There were currently four whiteboards being used. He and Jordan had moved one board next to their desks and were using both sides. One side displayed the facts they had for the murder of an eighteen-year-old prostitute. The other side tracked the case of a gang related drive-by shooting. An APB had been issued for their primary suspect in the drive-by. Rival gangs and known players made investigations like this a common event. He and Jordan were well known to all the gangs who resided and fought over territory in the area of town designated as The Desert. Commission Street acted as a border for the largest gangland rivalry in the city. Destitution, hardship, and low-paying jobs highlighted those two neighborhoods. The good people who could, had already moved. The ones who couldn't afford to move were paying the price. Unfortunately, more times than not, it was with their lives. Samuel Treyson and his ilk didn't frequent The Desert. The shoes the man wore probably cost more than most of these people earned, legal or not, in months. Samuel Treyson did not belong in that warehouse. Why had he been there?

His cell phone rang as he stood looking at the murder boards that stood as sentinels in the early morning quiet of the precinct. He palmed it without looking at the caller ID. "King."

"Hey, Brock, we've got the initial swabs back and were able to confirm my findings against Jonas'." Brock had seen Sean's partner working in the warehouse, but he hadn't had a chance to talk to him after the atom bomb also known as Samuel Treyson had detonated.

"What's that mean to me? Was this the work of your arsonist?"

"It was arson, *but not* our serial arsonist. This was amateur hour compared to the guy we are tracking. I'm sending off the accelerant, but I think it is primarily gasoline. I'll let you know if they come back with anything different."

"So, our killer is probably trying to get rid of evidence and the body with an inept arson attempt. Nukes the building but not the body." Inept was right.

"Yeah, that is what we're thinking."

"All right got it. Tell Jonas I said hey, and we really do need to get together." He turned at the sound of someone else coming into the bullpen via the stairs. He dipped his chin and acknowledged another detective who headed into the break room.

"We do. I'll send what I get back on the accelerant. Be safe."

"You too." He ended the call, dropped into his chair, and picked up the receiver on his desk phone. Punching the scratched plastic button that accessed an outside line, he punched the sequence of numbers he knew by heart.

"Assistant District Attorney Clifford Sand's office. This is Miranda, may I help you?" As it always did, the soft low voice of Cliff's longtime secretary greeted him.

"Hey Miranda, is he in?" He leaned back in his chair and propped his feet on his desk.

"Oh, hey Brock, he's just left for a meeting. Can I have him give you a call? I know he wants to talk to you."

"How do you know that?" He threw one of his

many stress balls into the air and caught it as it came down. Somehow, he'd become a collector of the squishy toys.

"Because he asked me to remind him to call you after his meeting." The "duh" was implied.

"Yeah, okay. I'll be here at my desk for the foreseeable future." He sighed the last comment. The stacks of paperwork on his desk that needed to be completed for the ongoing cases pretty much guaranteed that.

"It's called job security," Miranda teased.

"I'd gladly switch jobs if it meant dead bodies stopped popping up all over the place."

"Ain't that the truth, honey. He shouldn't be too long. Maybe thirty minutes or so."

"Okay, say hi to Doug for me." Brock liked Miranda's husband and he was one hell of a mechanic. He owned a big shop, Alston Repair and Towing, on Belmont Avenue.

Grabbing his coffee cup, he hit the stairwell and trudged down to the basement to retrieve Treyson's cell phone and an assortment of random receipts and business cards from his wallet.

"That was quick." Sergeant Timmons, or "Pops" as he was known to the officers around the 13th, signed him into the evidence room by swiping his badge through the system.

"Yeah. Needed to clear my plan of action with the lawyers before I stepped off. Where is the inventory for the case?" The evidence intake desk was pristine. Pops was one anal son of a bitch, but that was why he lived down here in the hole.

"Processed and filed. What do you think I am, a slacker?" Pops called up the electronic version of the inventory with a few strokes of his fingers. "Tell me what you need, I'll have it removed, get the chain of custody tags signed off and have it delivered to you."

"Fuck, I think I'm in love with you, Pops." He grabbed an available mouse and ticked the boxes next to the evidence he wanted to go over with Jordan before the man was pulled away from him and the case.

"Mrs. Timmons would be upset if I drifted from my lane." The old guy gave him a wink.

"Yeah but think of the fun." He laughed at Pops' horrified expression and elevated his badge, swiping himself out of the room. The door buzzed open, and he headed back up the six flights of stairs.

After a pit stop at the break room for a warmup

on his go-juice, heavy on the cream and sugar, he dropped his ass at his desk and leaned forward to grab the paper file compiled on the young prostitute. The cover snapped back, and he once again examined her sophomore high school picture, one of two pictures they had of Caitlyn Eliason, aka Star. His vision shifted to the whiteboard and fixed on the grainy, enhanced duplicate of her high school picture taped next to the crime scene photo of her corpse lying bloody and beaten in a filthy alley. Her pimp was the primary suspect, but as of now, several of his girls were covering for him. Jordan had been working last night with a couple of the guys from Vice trying to apply pressure. The working girls were terrified of Gino and with good reason. They didn't want to end up dead like Star. "Being used, abused, and treated like shit is better than being dead." Yeah, those words actually came out of the mouth of one of Gino's working girls.

Which reminded him. He grabbed the middle desk drawer and yanked it. Damn it. Nothing happened. He grabbed the right top desk drawer, violently strong-armed it, and then shoved it back in. The desk moved several inches away from Jordan's, but it popped the middle drawer open. He reached back and patted around until he felt the stack of business cards he wanted and reloaded his jacket with the cards. Tara McBride, Sean's sister, was a social worker. She didn't necessarily handle prostitutes, but if he could get the women to call her, she could plug them into programs. It was better to try to help than to do nothing and admit defeat like the women who worked the streets. He shoved the remaining stack back into the drawer and closed it before he reached for the folder on the drive-by.

His phone vibrated. He grabbed it and groaned. He thumbed the slide on the face of the phone. "Hi, Mom."

"I saw you on the news this morning. You looked tired. You've lost weight. What's wrong? Have you been sick?" Hannah King's questions fired as rapidly as machine gun bullets.

"I look tired because I was called out at midnight last night, and I was wearing a coat, so you can't tell if I've lost weight. Which I haven't."

"Your face is thinner, and they say television puts ten pounds on you. If you had a woman in your life, you'd look more relaxed. I wouldn't have to worry that you look like a walking skeleton. What did you have for breakfast?"

"Mom, please. I gotta get back to work." He scrubbed his neck and sent a furtive glance around to make sure no one was overhearing this conversation. Several detectives were staring at him with shit-eating grins. *Fuck him standing.* His mother, he loved her, but damn...

"Fine, but I want to see you, in person, not on the television."

"I'm coming over for dinner on Sunday."

His mom tsked. "I've heard that before."

"Mom, I'll be there as long as the case permits. If you've seen the news, then you know this one is going to be difficult." He leaned forward and stared at the coffee ring on his calendar, trying hard not to hear the snorts and chuckles around him.

"I miss you, sweetheart. It's been forever since we've talked. I need to know you're okay. You may be my oldest, but you will always be my baby. Please come see me."

God. He dropped his head to the desk. "I know, Mom. I'll try. It's the best I can do."

"All right honey. Be safe. I love you."

"Love you too, Mom." He hung up and dropped his phone, his head still on the desk.

"Yo, King, you die over there? Should we call your mom?"

His arm elevated over his head, and he flipped the detective across the pen the finger. The entire room erupted in laughter. *Fucking bastards.*

He sat up and buried himself in the specifics of requesting a task force to go into The Desert to search for their shooter when his phone rang. He picked it up without looking at the caller ID. His mom had never struck twice in one day. "King."

"Miranda said you called?" Cliff's gravelly voice cut across the connection. His old Recon commander was the toughest son of a bitch he'd ever met. No, strike that, second toughest man he'd ever met. His dad had the first slot firmly cemented.

"Yes, and she said you wanted to talk to me. How about you go first?" Brock closed his eyes and massaged the bridge of his nose. He needed more coffee.

"I'll get to that in a minute. What did you need?" Cliff's demand was reminiscent of bygone days and barked orders that Brock followed without question.

He exhaled a long stress-filled lungful of air. "I have a dead body. The vic's name is Samuel Treyson. I want to use the information on his phone to determine why the man woke up dead. I went to his residence to speak with his wife but was met at his door by a concrete wall of lawyers. The press was swarming the crime scene. Although his name was never transmitted over the airwaves—we made sure of that—they showed up knowing Samuel Treyson was in that warehouse. I left the crime scene and drove straight to Briar Hills; it was damn early, and it's a quick drive. There was a crowd of press outside Treyson's house. So, number one, I believe there is a leak on the force. Two, I need a warrant so anything I get from these emails and texts can be used in court and three, I need a judge not in the Treysons' pocket. I think that may take a miracle."

Cliff was silent for several long moments. "You have to know the Treysons might have a couple cops in their pocket."

"Yep, figured that." His father hadn't seemed too surprised that Mrs. Treyson had deferred his visit. His father was a straight shooter. Crooked cops were his number one target. He ran a tight ship and had cleaned house when he took over as commissioner, but rats scurry and hide. Sooner or later the remaining vermin would expose themselves and his father would be waiting for them.

"I can get you a warrant. Judge Scottsdale isn't

impressed with wealth as her husband is independently wealthy. However, if Mrs. Treyson's lawyers can find justifiable grounds to contest the warrant, you are back at ground zero."

"What reasons could they possibly have to contest a warrant when all we want to do is solve his murder?"

"They could use the grounds that the information in his emails or his texts is privileged because he owns and operates a business. They could claim proprietary information. I would if I was her lawyer."

Brock grabbed one of his foam balls and squeezed the ever loving shit out of it. "So you're telling me that a judge would limit my ability to conduct a homicide investigation to protect proprietary business information." Son of a bitch, just when he thought he'd seen it all.

Cliff made a noise of agreement. "Look at it from another angle. What apps does he have on his phone? Don't list them off. But seriously, take a look at all his apps including games and the software that comes standard on the phone. I can get you a warrant for all the apps. You can go through the emails and the texts and take note of anything in particular that may assist the investigation.

Should you find anything, then we go for a strategic strike and request a specific warrant for a specific email on a specific date and time."

"That won't fall under the doctrine of 'fruit from the poisonous tree'?" Brock shoved the folder he was working on to the side and stared at the desk blotter. He picked up a pen and doodled around today's date.

"If we were trying Samuel Treyson for crime, then yes it would. However, he's the victim. We need to keep that in front of everybody's eyes. The lawyers can dance to any tune they choose, but we do have a very powerful tool."

"Yeah, and what tool is that?" Brock looked up from his desk blotter and nodded at his partner, who was walking through the bullpen toward him. Jordan was dressed to impress even though he was coming back from a night shift spent with Vice interrogating suspects and looking for witnesses. The guy always turned heads, both male and female. That vibe his partner threw off was potent shit if the action he got was any indication.

"We have the press, which is a huge motivator. People like the Treysons live their life in the court of public opinion. If that information was leaked to the press, it could taint the public's view of this storied family. If we hit resistance, we can use a nondisclosure guarantee to entice them to release what we need."

"You are one devious son of a bitch, Cliff." Brock laughed as his partner sat down across from him.

"I prefer the term tactical."

"Okay, you are one tactical son of a bitch, Cliff."

"Yes, yes, I am. Give me thirty minutes then list those apps and call Judge Scottsdale. She'll approve the warrant." Cliff paused for several moments before he cleared his throat.

Even though his old commander couldn't see him, Brock rolled his eyes. Whatever Cliff wanted from him, he was having a difficult time putting it out there. "Just spit it out, man."

"It's coming up on two years. I was hoping you'd be able to come with Zack and me to the cemetery. I don't know if I'll be able to drive after." His friend's voice broke with emotion. His love for his late wife was still as poignant and tangible as the day he'd watched the man bury his soul mate.

Fuck. He glanced at his desk blotter. Less than two weeks. "You know it man. Just let me know when to be at the house." He'd be there for his former commander. The man had always been there for him.

"I will. Look, I gotta..." His voice trailed off.

"Right man, me too. But you know I'm here, right?"

"Always. Go catch a killer." The line disconnected before he could respond. He returned the phone to the cradle and glanced at his partner, who was messing with his cell phone, pretending not to pay attention to his call. "Did you get anything from Vice?"

Jordan smiled.

He felt a smug slice of satisfaction. "What'd you get?"

"Two of the women in Gino's stable, Mystic and Magic, rolled on the slimy bastard. We got the ladies downstairs. They should be signing their statements about now. Gino is in the holding cell. He's made his one call, so there'll be a lawyer present, but we got him. Both Mystic and Magic claim to have watched him kill Star. They have knowledge of the injuries that we didn't release, and get this, they can place his so-called witnesses on street corners at the time of the murder. Vice is pulling camera footage to corroborate their statements, but it looks like a slam dunk." Jordan leaned back in his chair and tugged at his tie, loosening the knot.

"Have you called the ADA assigned to the case?" He grabbed Star's folder, not sure which ADA was assigned. Getting Gino off the streets would be a major coup for both them and Vice.

"Not yet. We are waiting for the techs in Vice to get the footage that proves Gino's alibi is for shit, and then I'm going down, and we'll make the call together. We wouldn't have been able to advance on this case without Vice's contacts and help." Jordan extended his hand for Star's file. He gratefully handed it over. Any day they could close a murder investigation was a damn good day.

"So, bring me up to speed on the case we caught last night." Jordan reached for his coffee cup and nodded to the break room.

He grabbed his empty coffee mug and followed his partner. "The name Samuel Treyson ring any bells?"

Jordan stopped, his brow furrowed, and he nodded. "Yeah, he's in charge of Treyson Industries, right? Big money, affluent, a couple of mansions over in Briar Hills. Why?"

"Someone killed him last night. HCFD found him in the ass end of a warehouse. Based on the lake of blood the man was lying in, it looks like his throat was slit at that location. No defensive wounds that I could see, and no signs of a struggle; I'm really curious to see the toxicology report. Part of the warehouse went up in flames, but thankfully HCFD did their job before it got a chance to burn up our evidence—what little there is."

"What did the techs find?" Jordan fished around for a new notebook. They both started a new spiral notebook with each new case. Field notes, leads, interview notes, drawings, they all went in new, pristine notebooks. It was a lesson they learned early and fast. Submitting case file notes with other information for other cases scribbled on the margins almost lost them a case as the defense tried to insinuate shit based on those scribbles. Now everything was segmented, and *nothing* went on their phones. *Ever.* Pictures were taken with digital cameras, not cell phones. The SD cards with those pictures were labeled and placed in evidence bags that were attached to the notebooks and filed with the case as evidence. Being a cop was all about crossing the 'T's' and dotting the 'I's'. More crimes were solved by following boring anomalies in evidence than by breaking down doors. He reached beside his desk and into his open duffle, rummaging through and snatching the notebook he'd started last night.

He tossed his notebook to Jordan and continued to talk as the man thumbed through his notes, diagrams, and initial questions the scene had raised. "There wasn't shit not covered in soot or ash. They busted their balls to get what they could. I have a feeling any physical evidence is going to be thin, so we need a solid motive and a strong suspect for this case. We'll start with Samuel's phone, his receipts, and the business cards I found in his wallet.

Jordan looked up from his notebook. His brow furrowed, "Why wasn't this assigned to Briar Hill?"

"My exact question to my father not more than an hour ago. He said Briar Hill would be there to support us, but this is our baby. I need more coffee." They continued to the break room and the coffee pot. He elbowed his way in front of his partner to fill his coffee cup.

"So, the case is ours. If we need assistance from The Hill, Dad suggested we contact Jeremiah or Fisher." They'd worked with those two detectives before, and it didn't totally suck.

"So, we hit Treyson's evidence while I wait for Vice?"

Brock nodded toward the bullpen. "Yeah, and we need to request the Lieutenant put together a task force to shake loose our shooter in The Desert."

"Gino's case is a done deal. Let's see if Kowolski and Edmans will take the drive-by shooting. That way we can focus on Treyson."

"Exactly my plans." Lieutenant Davidson's voice boomed from the break room door, spinning them both.

"Give me the case file on Gino. I'll meet with Vice when they have their end done. Ski and Edmans are waiting for a brief on the drive-by in The Desert. Whitt, the only case you're working until the Feds get off their asses and send for you is Treyson. What time is your meeting with Mrs. Treyson?" Davidson turned and looked directly at him as he spoke.

"3:30. We've got his phone, receipts and business cards that we are going to run down until then." His Lieutenant was a tough fucker and protective as hell of his people.

"Did you clear the use of the information on the phone?"

"I did, but I'm getting a warrant to cover our asses."

"Keep me informed. I'm giving you what cover I can, but you've got to know, your old man is spread and nailed to a cross on this one. The big boys and the press want blood, the killer's or your old man's, it doesn't matter to them; so, let's do everyone a favor and not let the Commissioner be the sacrificial lamb." His Lieutenant's glower landed on them. Ninety-five percent of the cops in this city loved his old man. The other five percent were crooked motherfuckers who preferred the 'good ole boy' system his father had obliterated. Davidson fell firmly on the 'I love your old man' side.

"Will do." He nodded his affirmation. He and Jordan silently watched Davidson leave the breakroom. "Fuck me."

"It would seem your old man has literally put his career in your hands."

His father had alluded as much this morning but hearing it from his Lieutenant and his partner drove the message home with emphasis. A sinking feeling grabbed his gut and held him down as if it was anchored to the weight of the world. "Yeah."

CHAPTER 3

"The man had one hell of a caffeine addiction." Jordan motioned to the coffee shop where one of the many receipts in Samuel's wallet came from.

"Coffee ain't illegal, and seriously, he has just as many dry-cleaning receipts," He grumbled as he put the car into park.

"A clean and pressed caffeine freak," his partner murmured.

"Come on, let's see what they remember." Brock unfolded from the Crown Vic they drove while on duty. He glanced over at the small coffee shop. "What's the time stamp on this one?"

"Ahh... 8:30 a.m."

He flicked his cell phone, waking the home

screen, so he could check the time. The morning crew might still be there. They waited for traffic and then crossed the street. The little bell on the door tinkled above them when they opened the door.

Jordan always made first contact with witnesses, so he drifted to the left to look at the pastries as his partner engaged the young woman behind the counter. He listened to the entire conversation, and tried his damnedest not to glower or hover—Jordan's descriptions, not his.

"I'm sorry, I don't remember the order, but we are always slammed that time of day."

"That's okay, Autumn. Maybe a photo of the guy would help?" Jordan smiled at the young woman, and he could have sworn the girl sighed. His partner produced a photo they'd cropped from an on-line magazine. The picture featured Samuel with a relaxed happy smile.

"Oh, that's Sam. He's in here a couple times a week with Ava. They are regulars. Always together, you don't see one without the other. I must have missed them yesterday, but it was a zoo in here."

"Do you know where Ava or Sam live?"

"Ummm... no. But Ava works over at that store..." The girl held up a finger and turned toward the kitchen and yelled, "What store does Ava work at?"

A disembodied female yell came back through the open door. "Ava who?"

"Ava, tall, long brown hair, killer clothes... ah, extra-large, non-fat, steamed with cinnamon, no sugar, one Splenda."

The disembodied voice answered, "Oh, yeah. The Black Crane, I think."

Autumn turned around and giggled. He rolled his eyes, but Jordan smiled down at the girl. "That's right, she works at the Black Crane. *Very* expensive stuff in there."

Jordan glanced at him. "Are you going to get some of those pastries or just drool?"

"You paying?"

"What day is it?" Jordan glanced at his watch.

"Wednesday, you pay."

The girl behind the counter laughed. "Umm... it's Thursday."

Damn, was it Thursday already? He'd lost a day somewhere. "Thursday." He acknowledged the correct date and smiled at her. Her eyes rounded, and she blushed from the chest up.

"Thursday. You buy." Jordan slapped him on the

back and pointed to a decadent looking cinnamon roll. "Mine."

"Two of those, please, and two of your largest black coffees but leave room for cream and sugar." He'd already found the condiment bar where they could doctor their coffee.

They parked in the parking lot in front of the Black Crane, a high-end retail shop housed in a converted warehouse in the newly gentrified area of the Inner Harbor. He'd driven through this area a couple months ago, six months at the most, and the store hadn't been in operation then, so it had just recently opened its doors. He didn't get over this way much. Most of his days were spent in the bowels of the Southern District. He sniggered to himself watching the well-dressed patrons teeter in on extremely high heels. The one man he saw enter the store wore a suit that probably cost more than his truck. Strike probably. Insert definitely. His truck was older than dirt, but it ran well.

He shoved the last of his cinnamon roll into his mouth and chased it down with a big swig of coffee. Crumpling the bag and using it as a napkin to remove the remnants of cream cheese frosting from his fingers, he pointed at a fancy European vehicle that drove into the lot. "That damn thing cost more than we both make in a year."

Jordan made a polite noise of acknowledgement. He swallowed his food before he spoke, "There is a lot of new money coming into Hope City."

"So it would seem. Shall we go see Miss Ava?"

Jordan grabbed a napkin from the glove box and wiped his fingers, drank the last of his coffee and opened his car door.

Something wasn't lining up in his head. He waited for Jordan to look at him before he said, "Seems a little strange, doesn't it?" Jordan waited for him to come around the vehicle before they started across the parking lot.

"What's that?"

"What is a multimillionaire doing with someone who works at a clothing store? Hell, what is a multimillionaire doing with someone who works, period? And let's take this one step further. What is a *married* multimillionaire doing with a young woman who works at a clothing store?" Brock opened the door and let Jordan go in first.

The air inside the store held a distinct citrus note. The lemony aroma drifted on the same air as the soft classical music playing through the sound system. He snorted when he saw a waiter wearing a tux with tails carrying a silver tray with champagne and glasses piled on top. "Holy fuck. I thought this was a clothing store."

Jordan gave him a look that told him to shut the fuck up. He laughed anyway.

"It is. Only the clothes here aren't on racks." Jordan motioned to the far corner. A stream of reed-thin women paraded past a conversation group. An old, plump, woman at the center of the couch raised a single finger. The model stopped, turned, struck a pose, and then turned again before she exited. "I think she just purchased that outfit." Jordan grabbed his bicep and dragged him away... probably so he didn't say something they'd both regret.

"Dude, I don't think they sell Levi's in here." He trailed his partner as he semi-stared at a god-awful, puffy, silver contraption one woman was wearing.

Jordan laughed at him when he almost tripped over a low couch. "I can't take you anywhere."

"Obviously not," he mumbled and gave up trying to determine what the woman was wearing. Instead, he focused on where they were going. The rich wood tones and jewel color fabrics reminded him of a throne room. Not that he'd ever seen a throne room, but he'd bet royalty would be comfortable in this store.

They approached a low counter where a gentleman in a suit sat, studiously ignoring them. He glanced at Jordan as he reached in his jacket, whipped out his credentials, and shoved a face full of his badge at the man. "We'll talk to your manager, now."

The man withdrew several inches, raised his nose, and scrunched his face, as if he smelled a horrible stench, then his eyes dropped to his identification. He pushed his chair away and stood, pulling delicately on his jacket before he flicked away some invisible lint. "I *am* the manager."

He glanced at Jordan who shrugged. That was his go-ahead to take over the interview move. *Fine by him.* "You have an employee by the name of Ava. We need to speak to her."

The man's eyebrows raised to his hairline. "Ava? She's with a customer at this time. Can you come back?"

He leveled an ice-cold stare at the smaller man. "Now, or I'll put you in cuffs and take you downtown for interfering with a murder investigation." Not that he would ever do that, but the threat was worth the response. The little man almost shit his britches.

The man reached down to the lapel of his jacket and pushed a button on the small mic affixed to it. "Miss Dall, you are required at my location immediately. Miss Simms, please take over for Miss Dall." The man flicked his eyes toward him. "She'll be on her way momentarily. May I show you to a secluded area?"

The man's eyes ran over Jordan before he flicked another disdainful glance in his direction. As much as he'd like a private location to talk to Miss Ava Dall, he got the feeling the manager wanted them hidden from his wealthy clientele.

The sharp click of stiletto heels on hardwood floors drew his attention to the young woman heading their way. He could tell in an instant she wasn't pleased to be taken away from her customers. She slowed when she noticed them; her attitude changed from irritation to curiosity. "How can I help you, Mr. Thorpe?" Ava Dall spoke to her manager but looked at them. Her intelligent eyes swept over them and landed on the bulges under their jackets. She cocked her head and waited.

"Miss Dall, please take these police officers away from the middle of the store and answer their questions. I will be giving Mrs. Davidson's commission to Miss Sims." The little man sniffed as if a fetid odor permeated his presence.

Ava narrowed her eyes at the man and nodded. She turned her pissed off expression to them, and tipped her head toward the back of the store. When they reached the farthest conversation group, Miss Dall sat in one of the massive wing-backed chairs. "What does the Hope City Police Department need from me?"

"Ma'am, you were with Samuel Treyson yesterday morning?" Jordan reached in his pocket for his notebook.

"Yes." She looked from Jordan to him again, her brow furrowed. "Why? What's wrong? Is Sam okay?"

"Ma'am, we regret to inform you that Samuel Treyson is dead."

When Jordan broke the news, he watched the woman's reaction carefully.

Her eyes immediately dilated. She gasped, and her mouth went slack. Her hands clutched to her chest and tears filled her eyes. "Oh my God, how? When? It was that car, wasn't it? I told him he was driving it too fast. Why wouldn't he listen! Has anyone told his wife or the others?"

Whoa, he did not see that coming. Leaning forward he cleared his throat. "Others?"

The woman nodded rapidly. Her tear-filled words were fast and difficult to understand. "I'm Tuesday and Thursday. Chloe is Monday and Wednesday. His wife is Friday, and Garrett has Saturday and Sunday."

"Wait... What do you mean you have certain nights, and they have certain nights?" Jordan interjected the question. Obviously, his partner was just as lost as he was.

She blinked at him as if he was stupid. Nodding her head, she spoke slowly, still crying and hiccupping, but trying to explain, "Sam sleeps with me on Tuesday and Thursday; he sleeps with Chloe on Mondays and Wednesday. On Friday night, he has to do the social obligation things his wife requires. I don't know if he has sex with her or not, and G-Garrett fulfills his needs on Saturday and Sunday." She burst into full on sobs.

"Mr. Treyson was bisexual?" Jordan was writing furiously as he asked.

"Yes." Ava dropped her head into her hands and sobbed before her head popped back up. "I need to be there when you tell Chloey. She's going to be devastated. Out of all of us, she's least capable of dealing with this." Black trails of mascara ran in streaks down the woman's cheeks.

He raised a finger stopping her words. "Wait, you all knew about each other?"

Ava nodded her head again, sucking back heartbroken sobs, trying to speak through her weeping. "Of course, we've been in this relationship for almost four years. We talk to each other because there are times when we have to juggle dates because of important events we want Sam to be at, or when we go on vacation together."

"So last night he should have been with Chloe?"

She nodded, soft sobs coming from behind her hands. He glanced at Jordan, who was still scribbling furiously in his notebook. Looked like they were tag teaming this witness.

The gray matter between his ears probably needed to reboot because, for some reason, he wasn't grasping the totality of the situation. Was he? It would appear that probably the richest man in Hope City was in a polyamorous relationship with three people *and* his wife.

"He takes all of you on vacation together with his wife?" Brock reached over and snagged a sterling silver rectangle that enclosed a two-dollar box of tissue and handed it to the woman.

She gratefully grabbed several puffs of tissue from the heavy silver box and swabbed at her tears. She shook her head and blew her nose before she spoke, "No, just the three of us and Sam would go on vacation. His wife went on her own vacation with her lover. They had an open relationship, but they maintained a traditional front for the public." She lurched upright. "Oh my God, you're not going to let the media know about this, right? You can't do that. It would ruin his reputation. His father would... It wouldn't be good. Not for us and not for Miriam." She grasped at Jordan's arm.

He made sure to clarify, "Miriam Treyson, Samuel's wife?"

"Yes. Sam's father is a real jerk. If he found out, we'd all end up dead."

"Isn't that a little dramatic?" Jordan smiled at the woman.

She stared at him. Rivers of black mascara pooled under her eyes before they streaked and smudged across her once perfect makeup. She shook her head. "Maybe. But you don't know the horror stories Sam has told us about growing up with that man. If half of what Sam relayed was true, that man would do anything to protect his reputation. Anything."

Jordan nodded and patted her hand. "I assure you everything you tell us will be kept in the strictest confidence. This is an ongoing murder investigation; we aren't very forthcoming with information."

"Wait, what? *Murder?*" The woman's shriek echoed in the vastness of the store. Her eyes could have passed for teacup saucers and she paled, losing all color from her face. She turned her head to stare at him. "Somebody *murdered* Sam?" She shook her head and held up a hand as if the motion would stop his partner's words. "No, that's impossible. Sam is the kindest, sweetest man on the face of the earth. He wouldn't hurt a bug. I mean, seriously. He made me get the spiders out of the bathtub and set them loose outside! He wouldn't hurt a soul. Why would anyone kill Sam? I thought you meant he died in a traffic accident or something. No. No. No, you… you must have this wrong."

She broke down then, and the sobs were heart-wrenching. Jordan and he exchanged silent looks as they waited for her to control herself. He mouthed the word *father* and cocked an eyebrow.

Jordan nodded before he soothed, "Ms. Dall, we

are going to need specifics. Names, addresses, telephone numbers, everything you have on Chloey and Garrett."

"Of course. My purse is in the back. It has my phone which has their addresses and their telephone numbers. I haven't memorized a telephone number in years." She mopped at her face, but the tissues were proving ineffective at keeping up.

"That's all right, ma'am. I'll go back with you if that's okay." Jordan stood and offered her his arm.

Chivalrous and caring, that's how Jordan operated. Of course, he was making sure the woman didn't run out the back door. He watched his partner and one of Samuel Treyson's lovers as they left the showroom before he lowered his observation to the tip of his boot. Samuel Treyson was part of a polyamorous relationship. Long-term. His mind flooded with motivations for the crime. Jealous wife, jealous lover, a lover's jealous lover, blackmail, furious father? All plausible and all those suspicions would stay on hold until the evidence led them to those conclusions. Prediction, when used by homicide cops during an investigation, never turned out well.

Hell, right now they had more questions than they had answers. The answers they did have just led to more questions. He leaned forward and placed his elbows on his knees as he waited for Jordan and Ms. Dall. Talking to Mrs. Treyson would be interesting, to say the least. His cell phone vibrated in his jacket. He reached for it, glanced at the face, and read Lieutenant Davidson's text. Fucking fantastic. The Feds had pulled their heads out of their asses. Jordan was being called up to the big leagues, and it looked like he was getting a new partner. Fuck.

CHAPTER 4

K allie Redman sat facing the diner door and stirred her coffee as she watched the precinct house across the street. Her new home, as it were.

A waiter buzzed up to the table. "Are you ready to order?"

In truth, her stomach was not in the mood to wrap itself around anything substantial, but she hadn't eaten all day... nerves were a bitch. All she needed was to go across the street and faint. That would be awkward, especially since she was almost twice the size of a normal female. *Timber*. Splat. Yeah, she didn't need that on top of all the other baggage she was pulling behind her.

"Ma'am?"

She blinked back into the present. "Just a bowl of soup...a hh..." She glanced at the menu. "Clam chowder."

"Excellent. Do you want water or a soda?"

"No, thank you, just another pot of coffee." She indicated the small carafe he'd left about a half hour ago. It was empty.

He chuckled. "Cops and their coffee."

She cocked her head at him and raised an eyebrow. "Did I say I was a cop?"

The waiter smiled. "Nah, didn't have to. My name is Casey. I own this diner, and my mom owned it before me. I've grown up around cops. A person can tell, and after a while it becomes obvious."

"How's that?" She blinked up at him and smiled. He was a nice-looking guy. High and tight haircut indicated prior military, which went along with the strong jawed physique, the anchor and globe tattoo on his right forearm, and the bulldog tat on his left bicep. The guy hovered just over six feet, so Kallie would look him in the eye if she stood up.

"Well, what you did just now, for one. You just sized me up and down with that internal measurement tool all cops seem to have. You have long hair, lots of it, but you have it tugged back tight and wrapped in a braid. You either don't want it to be used against you on the street or you're a librarian, but the shoulder holster and badge you have under your coat would lead me to believe you don't organize the dewey decimal system. You're a nice-looking woman, too, but you're wearing clothes that allow you to move. Your shoes are practical, not heels. Everything about you screams no nonsense allowed, but most of all, you've got that cold, closed off vibe going on."

Kallie wiggled her toes in her black leather lace up boots. They were comfortable and not entirely *unfashionable*, but she'd ruined her fair share of shoes. She'd learned early; fashion had its place, and it wasn't at work.

"Maybe you missed your calling, Casey? Maybe you should be a cop." With his build he'd probably be able to get through basic law enforcement training without much problem, although he was older, maybe thirty or so.

He threw back his head and laughed. "Wait until you taste my clam chowder. You'll see I'm right where I need to be."

"Is that so? I don't know, I've had some mighty fine soup in my day. That is a pretty high bar to reach." She arched an eyebrow in challenge.

"I'll guarantee mine will move that bar way north." He chuckled and grabbed the small thermal-lined coffee pot off her table. His face got serious as he lowered his voice. "Are you joining us here in the Southern Precinct?"

She nodded, interested in his quick change of demeanor.

"Well then you should know I hire ex-cons here. The diner is a part of a work program, and I support a halfway house for those transitioning back into society. For the most part, we have a pretty good success rate, but you'll see prison tats, and a few are still adjusting to being out. It isn't easy on them, especially if my customers have attitudes."

Kallie chuckled. She liked this guy. He was a straight shooter and damned observant. He'd need to be both to run a program for transitioning cons. She could see why he was successful with them. "No attitude from me, unless the soup sucks." She took a drink of her coffee. "But the coffee is good, so I have hope."

"The coffee is awesome. It was good to meet you..." He paused for her to fill in her name.

"Detective Kallie Redman. Homicide." She extended her hand to him. His rough, work-worn palm slid into hers.

"Good to meet you. I'll go get that soup and send Dominque over with more coffee."

She watched him disappear behind the counter and hand her coffee pot to a younger man. The guy smiled and nodded quickly before he beat feet over to the coffee urn. Her phone vibrated. She didn't recognize the number, but the area code was one she recognized. Texas. Houston, to be exact.

"Hello."

"Hey, Kallie, girl. How's life been treating you?" The low rumble of her ex-husband's voice sent a cascade of ice through her veins. Thank God she hadn't answered with her last name. He didn't need to know she'd changed it.

"What do you want, Rich?"

"What? I can't check on my wife?"

"Ex-wife. The divorce was final over four years ago. Are you out?" Her old Captain in Houston had sent her an email and gave her a heads up that Rich was up for parole. It was the only communication she'd had with anyone in HPD since she'd left the city. She'd moved to Atlanta and worked there in private security before she'd gotten her shit together enough to apply for a position in Hope City. She'd done everything she could to delete any trace of Rich from her life.

"As of yesterday. Where are you? Your apartment manager said you'd left years ago without a forwarding address. Why would you do that, baby?"

"I'm not your baby. I left; we're done. Get over it." Her hand shook, but she would be damned if she let her voice tremble.

"But we have unfinished business. You fucking testified *against* me."

"You killed that woman."

"She was going for a gun."

"No, she wasn't. She was unarmed." The victim had held a neon-pink cell phone in her hand. The event played over and over in her mind like a fucking six second meme. Her ex-husband had been undercover for almost a year, and he was strung out, culminating in a massive bust which she and her partner took part in. They were moving across the warehouse toward where Rich was reported to be. She saw it in freeze frame. He looked directly at her and then elevated his weapon and shot the girl. In the back. In cold blood. Her partner claimed to be looking the other direction. Kallie knew he hadn't been, but he wouldn't testify against her husband. She had, and it had cost her everything.

"She was a worthless whore."

"I can't believe you. No life is worthless. None. But be honest for once, would you? Why? Why'd you do it?" She turned her head away from the doors and sightlessly stared past the red leather side panel of her booth. He'd been convicted and sentenced to fifteen years. He'd served five.

"I saw a gun." His story had never changed, but the facts were the facts. He'd pointed his gun and killed the woman. In court it had become apparent that Rich and the woman he'd shot were in a relationship while he'd been undercover. The woman had had a record for aggravated assault. Rich's attorney claimed he'd thought the woman was pulling a weapon to use on *her* as she crossed the warehouse. That was a lie, and she'd told the judge and jury the truth. Then Rich's lawyer had gone after her. He'd made outrageous claims ending with the whopper that she'd been having an affair with her married Lieutenant. It was ridiculous and baseless, yet she was immediately transferred from her precinct, and life went from crispy in a frying pan to smoldering in the fire. No one would work with her. No one would back her up. Her car had been keyed. A lug wrench had been shoved through her radiator; the windshield had been shattered. The last straw was when she'd requested backup for an armed robbery she'd stumbled into at a convenience store on her way home from work. Although the dispatcher's radio traffic had indicated patrols were en route, no one had responded. It resulted in the store clerk being beaten and robbed. She'd been hospitalized for a gunshot through her thigh and one that grazed her arm. The perps had escaped. She'd lost consciousness waiting for someone to respond. Finally, back up rolled up. She'd never forget the words that were said. They'd thought she was dead. "Just what she deserved, the fucking bitch." She'd opened her eyes in time to see them step over her and wave off the responding EMTs. If she hadn't moved her hand to catch the EMT's eyes... She didn't know if she'd be alive today.

"Do you think I can't find you? I got your number, didn't I?" His low question jerked her back from her own personal hell.

"I'm not impressed. How is Lance, by the way?" His brother worked for the NSA. He'd be able to find her. The question was how much information Lance would pull for his brother. If she had to bet, she'd say the telephone number and nothing else. Lance wasn't stupid enough to put his career on the line.

An evil chuckle reached her. "Fine and talented."

"What do you want, Rich?"

"I want to pay you back for all your support and understanding, my lovely wife."

"I'm not your wife."

"Damn straight. Fucking bitch."

She shook her head, keeping silent. Rich was nothing like the man she'd met all those years ago. Something had happened to him during that undercover operation. This wasn't the man she'd married. That man had disappeared when he'd gone under cover. "Why can't you just leave me alone?"

That question was met with a low, nasty, laugh. "You ruined my life."

No, that was his doing, and he'd ruined her life in the process. He'd destroyed everything she'd worked so damn hard to achieve, but she'd do it again. They'd sworn to protect and serve. She'd taken that oath and meant every word. "*You* did that when you killed a defenseless woman."

"I'm going to find you."

"Bring it, Rich, and when you come, *I won't be unarmed.*" She hung up and carefully set down her phone. A glance at the time on the face indicated it had taken less than a minute for him to shred five years' worth of effort to build a life without him in it.

A young man strolled by with her coffee, a basket of warm bread and a plate of butter. "Hi, I'm Dominque. Your soup will be right up. Both the soup and bread are bottomless, so if you want more, just let me know."

She smiled absently and picked up a piece of bread. The warmth felt good in her suddenly cold hands. She focused on the entrance to the precinct across the street. This was her shot to get her life back. Her handlers at Guardian had set up the interview. They knew everything about her past and had hired her anyway. She would have stayed with them if she hadn't gotten the interview here in Hope City. Although the pay was outstanding, and the organization was one of the best in the world, she wasn't fulfilled being a personal security officer. She needed to be back on the streets, as a detective. Her boss told her to let her know if her *'fuck-face of an ex'* became a concern. Jade DeMarco was hell on wheels and didn't sugar coat anything. If Rich made a repeat appearance, she'd consider making that call, but until then, she had a new 'temporary' partner to meet. The man she would be assigned with permanently, a Grant Couch, was due to return soon from a year overseas. Couch was in the Marine Reserves and had been activated for a year-long overseas assignment. She was being placed temporarily with another detective whose partner had been selected to work a Federal Task Force.

The police colonel in charge of Special Investigations had called and asked if she'd report to work early. *Fuck yeah,* she would. Rambling around in her small apartment, she'd managed to bake enough food to stock her freezer for a year. She'd had to join a gym and worked to keep off the weight her boredom-baking put on.

She glanced across the street and watched another television crew set up for a live remote. That made a total of five white media vans staking out the street in front of the precinct building. She hated the media and snarled at the crews across the street. Damn vultures, she'd had to deal with more than her fair share of the bastards when shit went down in Texas.

When Dominque delivered her soup, she glanced at her phone. She had another half hour before she needed to walk in those doors. She was meeting her new Lieutenant and, after that, her temporary partner. God help her, she was nervous.

"Well?"

She jumped at the eager question. Casey pointed to the chowder. "Best you've ever eaten?"

She laughed and sampled a spoonful. The light clam broth was thickened delicately with heavy cream. There was an abundance of minced clams. The seafood was tender, not cooked into rubber bands. A slight onion and garlic background and a hint of butter kissed the offering. It was, in a word, wonderful.

She closed her eyes and moaned. "Perfection."

Casey's smile when she opened her eyes was open, honest and real. "Well then, lunch is on me. Welcome to the Southern District, Kallie Redman."

"Oh, I can't..."

"You don't work there yet, so yeah, you can, and I am picking up the tab. After this you pay just like everyone else. I'll see you around." As Casey headed back into the kitchen, her eyes followed him. She smiled as he waved from behind the pass-through. She really liked this city. Her eyes traveled once again to the precinct across the street. *Please God, let me fit in.*

CHAPTER 5

Jordan extended his hand in goodbye. Brock grabbed his partner and pulled him in for a quick clench. "Don't let those damn Fibbies get you killed, my man."

"I'll try my best. I left my notebook in the car. I'm calling as soon as I can because I want to know what the fuck is happening with this case. I'd give my left nut to be in on the interview with Chloe and the wife, especially with you getting all up in the women's faces." Jordan laughed and ducked a playful jab Brock sent in his direction.

"Hey, I can be empathetic." It was just easier if Jordan played the role.

"I know, man. You've got this. It's just…"

"Fucked," he echoed what he knew his partner

was thinking. He could be gone a long time. Months, maybe even longer.

They stood sheltered behind the precinct in a small walkway that led to the parking lot, neither one inclined to turn and go their separate ways. "You'll probably get shoved onto another team. They won't keep putting you with a slew of temps. Don't let them assign you someone permanently." Jordan shoved his hands in his pockets and looked up at the heavy clouds that hung over them. "It would fucking suck to have to break in a new partner when I get back."

He tipped his eyes up, too. It was going to snow, just a matter of when. He spoke to the clouds, "Never. I don't think anyone else could put up with me."

"Damn straight." He chuckled when his partner immediately agreed.

"Seriously, you take care of yourself. Check in when you can." Because they both knew it would be impossible for him to reach Jordan.

"I guess I'd better go." Jordan glanced toward the parking lot and his car. "You sure you're okay taking care of Fester?"

He shrugged. "Sure. That cat is chill. I'll move him over to mine tonight."

"You have to actually feed him, so you have to leave the damn precinct at least once a day."

"Got it. Feed the cat. He survived me watching him when you went to see your folks."

"That was a week, Brock. This could be… a lot longer."

"Fester and I will be fine." He'd enlist his little sisters to help cat sit if he needed to, but he'd make sure the thing made it through.

"Check on my apartment and car?" Jordan said.

"You know it."

"Okay, so…"

"Yeah." He extended his hand one last time. Jordan took it, and God help him if he didn't feel like they were saying goodbye, not 'so long'. He watched Jordan until he turned the corner before he entered the building. He nodded to people as he passed through the lobby and made his way to the sixth floor. The case and Jordan's departure weighed equally on his mind. He wasn't happy with either situation, but for now his focus had to be on the case. He glanced at his watch. If his new partner wasn't a complete idiot, he could get him up to speed, interview Chloe and maybe Garrett, and make it to Miriam Treyson's home by 3:30. He'd instructed patrol to bring both individuals to the precinct. He'd rather talk to them in their homes, but there was no time to waste. If it turned out his new partner was an idiot, well, he'd just tell the guy to shut his mouth and take notes. He didn't have time to waste on an idiot partner. He had to solve this murder. The stakes were too damn high. His father's career was on the line. Fuck, there wasn't any time to waste.

He did a drive-by and snagged a tankard of coffee before he headed for Lieutenant Davidson's office. The door was closed, so he knuckled the frosted glass and waited. "Enter."

He pushed the door open. "Jordan punched out."

"Ah, King. Come in. This is your new partner, Kallie Redman."

A woman in the corner stood. *Wow.* She was tall and a fucking knock-out punch type of striking, not beautiful in the classic sense, but fuck him, he'd notice her in a crowd. Dark brown hair held away from intelligent brown eyes. He'd describe her vibe as... athletic. No makeup but vibrant and... striking. Oh, yeah, there was a feisty spirit in this lady. He could see the challenge in the way she sized him up. Not an idiot, either. Those eyes were sharp and inquisitive. She extended her hand.

"Brock King." He introduced himself, grasping her hand. The woman had a firm handshake, and she met his eyes. Damn, she struck him as… razor sharp. "Have you been brought up to speed on the case we are working?"

She nodded. "The basics that the Lieutenant had." She nodded at the case file on Davidson's desk.

"Perfect." He turned away from her and addressed Davidson. "We tracked down several key people in Treyson's life. He was in a polyamorous relationship that his wife knew about."

"Jealousy as a motive?" His new partner interjected.

"At this time, we don't believe so. The interview we just had with a Miss Ava Dall suggested the wife has lovers, too. Patrol have brought in two of Treyson's three lovers, and we have an appointment to speak to his wife at 3:30."

His partner blinked twice. "Excuse me? Appointment?"

Oh, fuck, yeah. She was sharp but obviously not from Hope City. An accent was immediately distinguishable. Southern, but not in that twangy backwoods way.

He nodded and then chuckled, "The Treysons own half the city. I tried to talk to the wife this morning after processing the crime scene. Besides the horde of press at the residence, I was met with a wall of lawyers."

"What time was that?" She glanced at her watch.

"About 6:00 a.m."

She glanced at him and narrowed her eyes. "So..." She glanced at the lieutenant and then back at him. She shrugged and finished, "You've got a leak, and someone told wifey that the husband was dead—or she's involved and knew you'd be coming."

Brock smiled. A real, show-your-teeth smile. Fuck, yeah, he'd drawn a winner. "Exactly."

"The file listed the evidence gathered, and I saw the crime scene photos. What about your examination of the scene? Did the fire destroy evidence? Was there any indication as to why this guy was at the warehouse or how he got there?"

"None. Of course, the first responders annihilated any tire tracks around the building. There was little physical evidence on scene. No tracks. The floor was concrete, and it was dry ground. Fingerprints were nonexistent. The arson investigator on scene told me the accelerant used was probably gasoline. The person who torched the warehouse wasn't a professional. More than likely the fire was an attempt to try to hide the crime. The ME has orders to push the tox and histology to the front of the queue, but we have a couple weeks minimum to wait for those. Hopefully, we'll be able to get a ping off of one of his lovers or the wife. We've got the techs downloading his phone information, and we are tracing his moves based on the apps and the receipts in his wallet to build his last twenty-four to forty-eight."

"What does this guy do? Is he a socialite or a businessman? If he is a businessman, does he have enemies?"

"On the list of avenues to travel down and explore. Come on, I'll show you where we work, and then we'll head out and talk to his lovers."

"Perfect, but I'm going to need coffee. How much is the coffee fund, and where did you get that thermos impersonating a mug? I gotta get me one." She nodded at his cup. He glanced at Davidson. "Boss, I like this one."

"Well, she's not yours to keep." Davidson moved a stack of paperwork toward him. "Jordan will be back, and we are finally getting Couch back from deployment. Get out of my office, and find me the bastard who killed this guy. Shut my door on your way out."

He held the door open for her and followed her out. "Coffee is this way." He pointed her to the break room. She grabbed an oversized Styrofoam cup and emptied the pot. Before he could set down his cup, she'd dumped the old grinds and filter. "Grounds and new filter?"

He nodded to the cupboard where they were stored. She filled the filter and slid it back into the slot, flipping the switch to start the water and brewing process.

"You can show me the staplers and paperclips later. All I need is a notebook and pen, which I already have. Which way to interrogation?"

"Down on the second floor." He nodded toward the door and the woman got bonus points when she headed to the stairs.

"What do you know about the lovers?" She asked as they hit the stairs.

He filled her in on the conversation with Ava this morning.

"So… the night Samuel was killed, he was supposed to be with Chloe?"

"Correct."

"And she's here?"

"According to the text I received while you were making coffee, yes. Both of Samuel's lovers are here, waiting in different interview rooms."

"I say we let her wait. If she's involved, she can afford to sweat it out." Kallie took a swig of her coffee.

"Agreed." He nodded at the interview room down the hall. "The man we are meeting now is Garrett Hoftslater. He and Samuel spent the weekends together."

"Man?" She glanced up at him.

He nodded, waiting for her reaction.

"Roger that." She stopped outside the door. "I'm assuming you'll want to take the lead in the questioning."

"Only because I know more about the relationships than you do. Once we get done with this, I'll let you take the lead on Chloe Connors' interview. From what Ms. Dall told me this morning, Chloe is emotional. I don't do the sympathy factor well."

"Fuck. Tears." Kallie rolled her eyes.

Brock smiled at her before he reached for the interview room door. He wiped the smile off his face and opened the door.

The man sitting at the table surprised him. For

some reason he'd been expecting a smaller man. Garrett Hoftslater was big, buff, and bearded. "Mr. Hoftslater, thank you for coming in. I'm Detective King, this is Detective Redman. I'm sorry we couldn't do this at your residence, but time is of the essence in this situation. May I say I'm sorry for your loss." He extended his hand and the big guy took it. "We need to ask you some questions."

"Absolutely. Anything I can do to help. I got to tell you, this just doesn't seem real." Garrett glanced at the ceiling and blinked back emotion before he cleared his throat. "I can't believe he's gone."

"Can you tell me the last time you saw or talked to Samuel Treyson?"

"Monday morning as he left. We spent the weekend together. Saturday was just lounging around. Sunday, we went to the Marauders game. He has a Skybox. We came home afterward."

He flipped open his notebook. "You were in a relationship with Mr. Treyson?"

Garrett nodded. "For the last two and a half years."

"And you knew about Chloe and Ava?"

"And his wife. Yeah."

"You were okay with the division of his attention?"

"Fuck no, but I was the last one added, you know. I hated sharing him. Hated knowing he was with those women, but Sam was upfront when I met him. He told me about them. I gave him something they couldn't. It was… enough. Not ideal by any sense of the imagination, but I loved the guy, you know? I took what he could give."

"You've met his other lovers?"

"Of course. We've gone on vacations together. Ava and Chloe are nice. I'd just rather not share his attention. I'm a selfish prick, but I'm honest about it." The man leaned forward. "When you find who did this, you better put them somewhere I can't get to them. I'd like nothing more than to shred them limb from limb. They took the best part of my life from me."

"I understand your anger, Mr. Hoftslater, but threats like that serve no purpose other than to put you on our scope. Do you know anyone who would have any reason to harm Samuel?"

The man snorted. "Have you talked to his old man? That guy is a class 'A' bastard. He's the only one I could imagine hurting Sam. The guy was so kind and gentle. Everyone liked him. He had a magnetism to him. People were just attracted to him, you know?"

He made a sound of agreement before he continued, "Did he have any conflicts that you were aware of? Anyone that didn't get along with him?"

"No, not to my knowledge..." The guy looked away suddenly.

"What is it?"

"It's nothing really. He told me he'd had an unpleasant conversation with someone about a month ago. Maybe a little more than that."

"Did he say what it was about?"

Garrett shrugged and sighed.

"Mr. Hoftslater, we need to know. Any information you give us can help bring Samuel's killer to justice."

"He was interested in bringing another person into the mix. Said he found someone he could see working with the blend we have now."

"You don't seem too happy about it."

"Would you be? Who was he going to take days away from to add a new person?" The guy pushed back in his chair. "But he said the significant other objected to his advances."

"Would that stop Samuel from pursuing this person?"

"Samuel was a nice guy, but he was rich and used to getting his way. I don't know if he stopped."

"Did you get the person's name?"

The guy gave a snort of disgust. "Ah, that would be a no. I didn't want to know anything else about another lover. We had quite an argument about it."

"So, you were disenfranchised from Samuel?"

This time the man laughed. "Disenfranchised? Fuck no. Make up sex from that argument was amazing. I love… loved that man. I'd have married him in a fucking heartbeat. Did I want to share him? Absolutely not, but I'd never hurt anyone he cared about. That isn't who I am."

"Do you know what he was doing Wednesday night?"

The guy shook his head slowly. "Wednesday nights he's with Chloe. You'd have to talk to her."

"Can I verify your contact information; in case we have any follow up questions?"

"Absolutely." The man rattled off his number, and he jotted it down before he rose from his chair and extended his hand. "Thank you for coming down to talk with us. I'll call you if there are any further questions."

Garrett stood. He paused before he squared up and turned to face him directly. "Detective, he was a good man. I didn't catch the vibe from you, but man, just because he had an alternate lifestyle, he's... he didn't deserve this. Sam, he deserves justice, too."

"Mr. Hoftslater, nobody deserves what happened to Samuel. Who the man had relationships with only factors into the investigation should his lovers have something to hide or something to do with his murder. All my victims deserve justice, and I will do everything I can to ensure they get it."

Garrett's shoulders slumped. "Thank you."

"We'll be in contact. I'll have an officer come escort you out. Do you need a ride home?"

"No, thank you. I'll grab an Uber."

He nodded to the man and opened the door for him to exit. He grabbed a patrol to escort him out before they continued to the next interview. He looked at his new partner. "What do you think?"

"His mannerisms were consistent with the tone of his words. I didn't get the impression he'd been hedging. Did you know about the new mix in the dynamics of the relationship?"

"No. Ava didn't mention it when we spoke with her this morning. Maybe she wasn't aware. Let's see if Chloe knew anything about it." He glanced at his notebook and tapped it with his pen. "It would cut someone's time with him. Jealousy is one hell of a motive."

"Motivation to kill. When you examined the crime scene, did you get the feeling it was a crime of passion?"

He shook his head. "My gut instinct was the man was surprised. No defensive marks, his clothes weren't ripped or torn, his hair wasn't mussed. I think he met someone he knew there, and they killed him. The wound was clean. I didn't see anything that would indicate the person was indecisive."

"How did he get to the warehouse?" They turned and started walking to the interview room where Chloe had been temporarily shelved.

"We're looking for his vehicles. We have all the data off his phone being downloaded, and it should be on our desks when we get done with the witness interviews, but as far as I could tell, the ride share apps on his phone were active. Unfortunately, I didn't see anything for that day. That suggests he drove himself." He stopped at the next interview room door.

Kallie cocked her head. She arched an eyebrow and nodded at the door. "You taking the lead again?"

"Nope. She's yours. Word of warning, the waterworks will be flowing on this one. Ava was a mess this morning, but she said Chloe was going to be the one to take it the hardest."

"No problem." She winked at him and opened the door.

A petite woman lifted her head. Her red-rimmed, puffy eyes glanced up at them. Her nose and face were blotched, and she looked like shit, but there was an elfin beauty under all the emotion. She was, maybe, ninety pounds soaking wet and as thin as a twig.

"Chloe Connors?" The woman nodded her head and hiccupped a shattered breath.

"I'm Detective Redman, this is Detective King. We're looking into Samuel Treyson's murder."

The woman dissolved into sobs again. She said something completely unintelligible and blew her nose.

"I know. Don't worry about it." Kallie reached

over and patted the woman's arm. "Take your time. We know it's a difficult time."

He blinked at his partner. How the hell did she know what was said? Kallie grabbed her notebook and placed her pen beside the paper, waiting until Chloe's tears abated a bit.

"I'm s-so s-sorry." Chloe blew her nose again. "I just c-can't believe h-he's gone."

"I understand, but we need to ask you a couple questions, okay?" Kallie's voice was soft and warm, a soothing balm against the woman's emotional tempest.

"Sure." Chloe ripped another tissue from the almost empty travel pack in front of her.

"The night Mr. Treyson was murdered, he was supposed to be with you? Right?"

She nodded and blew her nose again. "He called me about 6:30 and told me he had a meeting come up suddenly and he'd see me on our next night."

"Was that common?"

"Yes and no. Sammy tried to keep his meetings during the workday, but sometimes things came up."

"Did he say who he was meeting?"

She shook her head. "Sammy didn't tell me anything about work. We blocked out the world when we were together. I don't own a television, and I disable the internet so he can disconnect completely. The pressures of his life were so massive. When he came to me, it was just us."

"Did Mr. Treyson ever mention he wanted to bring another person into your relationship?"

Chloe's big blue eyes jerked up to Kallie and then fired at him. "Who told you about the others? We aren't supposed to tell anyone."

"We've already spoken to Ava and Garrett. Garrett said Mr. Treyson was considering adding another to your group."

She sat up and reached toward Kallie. "You can't say anything. His father will cause trouble."

"We don't release information about ongoing investigations, ma'am." Kallie gave the standard answer. Chloe's eyes shot toward him. He nodded his head, confirming Kallie's statement. Chloe tugged her bottom lip between her teeth and glanced at him again. She shrugged, eventually giving in to the need to talk. "He mentioned he might consider it..."

"Do you know what days this person was going to take?" Kallie's quiet question earned a slow shake of Chloe's head.

"Mr. Treyson didn't say?"

"He said he wanted another with me and Ava. He wanted to watch us. Ava and I doubled a couple times, but there is no chemistry there. It wasn't exciting… for anyone."

"And the new person? Have you met them?"

Chloe shook her head. "Sammy… he hadn't talked about it for a month or so. I'd hoped that I was... That we were enough." She shrugged and sniffed. "It's hard knowing you're not enough to keep the spark in the relationship, you know?"

"Mr. Treyson said that?"

She nodded. "I'm really vanilla. I just loved him. Ava, she's so confident, and she takes charge. I… I just want to be with him, you know? I'd do anything he asked me to do."

"Do you think Ava or Garrett would be upset about bringing another into the relationship?"

She sucked in a shuddering breath. "Ava, she likes multiples. She's the one that talked me into the nights with her. I don't think she'd care. I don't talk to Garrett. He doesn't like us. He barely talks to us when we go on vacation."

"Do you think he'd hurt Samuel?"

"No. Never. Garrett loved him as much as I did." Her tears started to fall again. "How did he die?"

"All we can say is that he was murdered."

"Where?"

Kallie glanced at him and he nodded. She gave a slight nod and answered, "In an abandoned warehouse."

"An abandoned warehouse? Someone made him go then."

"Why do you say that?"

"He despised anything dirty. He absolutely hated anything that wasn't clean. He couldn't tolerate any type of bugs or spiders. If he was there, it was because he was being forced into meeting someone there."

He cleared his throat and both women turned his way. "How did Mr. Treyson travel?"

"He has a car service he sometimes uses, and he owns several cars. We didn't go out, but Ava and he were always doing things on their nights. I don't know about what he did with Garrett."

Kallie took back the interview. "Do you know anyone that would hurt him?"

"You mean besides his dad?" She shook her head. "He was so nice. To everyone."

"Why do you think his father would wish him harm?"

"Sammy told us the stuff his father did when he

was growing up. He'd never win father of the year. I don't know if he'd actually want to hurt Sammy now that he's taken over the business here in Hope City, but if anyone *would*, it would be that horrible man." Chloe dropped her head into her hands. "What am I going to do without him?"

Kallie reached forward once again and laid her hand on Chloe's forearm. "It's moments like this when people discover how strong they actually are. Don't look at the vast amount of time in front of you. Look at the next minute, and get through that. Sometimes the most important parts of our lives are lived with each tick of the second hand. Think of getting through minute by minute, not hour by hour."

Chloe shook her head, her big eyes bright with unshed tears. "Who did you lose?"

A sad smile spread across Kallie's face. "Someone I thought I would have forever to love."

"Then you know what this feels like?"

"I do. Do we have contact numbers?" Kallie shifted her gaze to him. He saw the pain in those big brown eyes. He nodded. She turned back to Chloe. "Can we get you a ride back to your apartment?"

"Please? I... Yes, please."

"Hang tight here, and an officer will come back for you, okay?"

Chloe nodded and sniffed as an answer. They both stood and left the interview room. Neither spoke until they hit the stairway. "The father?" she asked.

"Number one on the list to talk to after the wife."

"When do we talk to her?"

He glanced at his watch. "After we refill with coffee. She lives in Briar Hill."

"You say that as if it means something." Kallie up-ended her coffee cup and downed what remained in her mug as they walked to the stairs.

"Richest neighborhood in the city." They finished the climb in silence. He opened the door to the break room and held it open for her.

Kallie's forehead scrunched in concentration. "Davidson said the Treysons were well connected?"

"Founding family of Hope City. Sebastian Treyson is worth billions. From what we've learned, Samuel was the heir apparent."

"Do we need to look at siblings?"

"I don't think so. The other children are minors. Sebastian Treyson is married to the mother, and they live in Switzerland, not here in the States."

"How did you learn that?"

He took his phone out. "I did a web search this morning while waiting for the crime scene techs to finish up. I also put in for an official background check and snatched a glance at the partial that came back earlier. We'll grab that when we check on the warrant information so you can get up to speed."

"Sounds like a plan." Kallie poured another full cup of coffee and used one of the disposable plastic tops. She watched him doctor his cup. "Holy crap man, how are you not five hundred pounds?"

He laughed and stirred his cream and sugar through the caffeine. "Too much work and not enough sleep."

"Hey, I live at that street corner. Funny I've never met you before."

"Right. Let's grab that info, make sure our warrant information is securely stored and head out."

"After you." Kallie moved and waved him forward. He pushed off and smiled. Maybe being without Jordan for this case wouldn't totally suck.

CHAPTER 6

Brock maneuvered the Crown Victoria sedan he and Jordan, now Kallie, used while working into the driveway of the Treyson Residence. As they approached the mansion, a security guard halted their progress. A huddled mass of reporters shouted questions at the car. Flashes from cameras and cell phones were bright in the grey afternoon hours. Brock gave their names and purpose of visit. The guard removed a metal barrier and they drove through the mob. He stopped the car, shoved the gear selector into Park and leaned back in the seat. The heater blew a steady stream of warm air as sleet pelted the windshield. Kallie leaned toward him to take in the grand manor in front of them until the glovebox door spontaneously dropped on her knees. "You realize this car can be condemned, right?" Kallie shoved the glovebox closed again.

"Push it to the right. It'll catch. She's a damn good car."

"I'll take your word on that. At least the heater works." Kallie put her hands up in front of the dash vent. Her phone vibrated and she glanced at the screen. Her body tensed and she shook her head before she pocketed the phone. Kallie took a deep breath and asked, "So, because I'm curious, at what point in this interview do we plan on bringing up the fact we know about Samuel's polyamorous relationship?" He rolled his eyes toward his new partner. "Can you say awkward?" She crossed her eyes and he chuckled.

"Helluva ace up our sleeve. Let's start with the basics and go from there." He glanced out his window. "Fuck, it looks like it's going to snow for real."

He reached for the keys and turned off the ignition as they exited the car. The exposed brick driveway meandered back toward the massive grand entry for the mansion. White columns held a portico three floors high. Windows with black shutters flanked the immense double oak door. As they approached, the door opened. They reached for their identification, flashing their badges at the individual who opened the door.

Kallie spoke for them. "Detective Redman and Detective King, Hope City homicide. We have an appointment with Ms. Miriam Treyson."

"Yes. Mrs. Treyson is expecting you. She's in the library. Please follow me."

The smallish gentleman trundled across the expansive entryway. He was sure there was a special name for the type of tile he was walking on, but the only thing he registered was... expensive. An enormous crystal chandelier hung over a dining table twice the size of his mother's. A riotous display of flowers sat in the middle. There were probably a thousand dollars worth of petals in that damn thing. What a waste. Not that he minded flowers. Hell, he made sure he sent his mom flowers every year for her birthday and Mother's Day. But this? Talk about overkill.

The little man opened another set of double doors. Mrs. Treyson and five men wearing matching 'I'm important' suits swiveled at their entrance. Once again, he and Kallie flipped up their identification.

He did the introductions this time. "Mrs.

Treyson, Detectives Redman and King. We'd like to talk to you about your husband's murder."

The woman dabbed at her eyes and sniffled as she nodded. One of the men stood and extended his hand toward Kallie. "James Masters, the Treysons' lead attorney. We will be happy to assist you in this investigation. You may ask anything, within reason. All correspondence and requests should be routed through my office, of course."

"Of course," he mumbled under his breath. Kallie sent him a look. She was a sharp one.

"Detectives, please, may we take your coats?" Miriam Treyson looked toward her... hell, he guessed the guy was a butler. Both he and Kallie waved the little guy off. They sat down in the two empty seats across from Mrs. Treyson and her wall of lawyers. They both retrieved their notebooks and leaned forward. Weird that they'd be in sync in their movements and actions already.

"Mrs. Treyson —" Kallie began.

"Please, call me Miriam." The woman reached for another tissue and Brock took the opportunity to inspect the woman in front of him. She was the one in the picture in Samuel's wallet. She was indeed beautiful. However, today, her eyes were swollen and ringed with black circles that her perfectly done makeup couldn't hide.

Her hand shook as she dabbed at the tears in her eyes.

Kallie nodded in response to her request. "Please, tell me, Miriam, where were you last night between the hours of —"

"Don't answer that!" At least three of the five lawyers spoke simultaneously.

He leaned back and chuckled.

"Excuse me, Detective, do you find something funny about the situation?" Mr. Masters hissed.

Brock leaned forward. He should let that question linger without a response, but fuck that. "Yes, Mr. Masters, I do find this situation—" he made a circle with his hand motioning at the lawyers "— comical. What I didn't find comical was examining her husband's dead body. What I still don't find comical is the fact Mrs. Treyson is barricaded behind a wall of lawyers when she's not *yet* a suspect. What I find hilariously offensive is the fact we couldn't ask one question without you stonewalling us. Samuel Treyson deserves justice. We are here to see justice is served. Your client may have information that could help us track down this man's killer. I wouldn't want to be the one to explain to Sebastian Treyson that we can't find his son's killer because his wife's lawyers prevented us from talking to her." He stood. Kallie played along perfectly and mimicked his actions.

Miriam Treyson stood. "Detectives, please do sit down." She glared at her collective stonehedge of lawyers. "Mr. Masters, thank you very much, but I have nothing to hide. I will speak with the detectives. Your interruptions are not welcome. You may remain in the room, but please do not interrupt again." She turned back and motioned toward the chairs.

"Mrs. Treyson, you must rethink this course of action." Mr. Masters ground the words in an apparent warning.

"Mr. Masters, what I must do is answer these detectives' questions." She turned to Kallie and sat down as she said, "I was with another man last night. A longtime lover. I would prefer not to bring him into this investigation; however, he will confirm where I was." She turned her head and looked directly at him. "Detective King, was it?"

He nodded. "Yes, ma'am."

"Like you, I am extremely offended at the scurrying and posturing being done. You should know that my husband and I were in an open relationship. However, we kept the specifics of our love lives from Samuel's family and the public. I would very much appreciate it if details of our relationship were not leaked." She reached forward and plucked another tissue from the box. "You might find this hard to believe, and quite frankly I don't care if you don't believe it, but I loved my husband."

"Ma'am, we are aware of your husband's polyamorous relationship. How long have the two of you had an open relationship?"

"Since the day we were married, fifteen years ago. Neither of us wanted the marriage. It was a merger of convenience for our parents. Over time, we have developed a unique and loving situation both of us would fight to protect. He loved Ava, Chloe, and Garrett, the same way I love Alan and Riley. We have documentation in place, nondisclosure agreements that I'm assuming one of Samuel's lovers ignored. Regardless, the nontraditional relationship worked for us."

"Did your husband have any enemies? Anyone who had a grudge against him?"

"I've been racking my brain, Detective. I can't think of the soul who didn't like Samuel. Except for his father."

Masters exploded from the couch. "Mrs. Treyson! I must object to you casting Sebastian Treyson in this light."

He'd give her credit; the woman didn't back down. A single eyebrow rose. "Do you work for me or Sebastian? I believe I pay your retainer. If there is any conflict of interest, I expect you to recuse yourself immediately." Masters snapped his mouth shut, but, as he planted his ass on the dainty couch, anger flashed in his eyes. Not an unexpected reaction for the rebuke. It was curious that the lawyer's reactions in defense of another were that extreme. He returned his attention to Miriam. "As I was saying, Detective, Sebastian and Samuel didn't get along. However, I do not believe his father had anything to do with this, simply because losing Samuel could mean a loss of income. Samuel ran several entities within Treyson Enterprises efficiently and effectively. Each quarter showed a net gain, and Samuel's business acumen made Sebastian Treyson an even richer man."

"So, there was no business entity or rival who you believe would want to remove him from competition?" Kallie asked to clarify.

"You'd have to talk to Sebastian or perhaps the board of directors at Treyson Enterprises. Samuel and I worked together for our charitable causes. Treyson Enterprises has vast holdings I'm not privy to, nor can I speculate as to his association with those businesses. Detective, I know my husband. He was a good man. He had a kind heart. I believe he was ethical in his business dealings because it was evident when we met those people in a social setting."

"What about his lovers?"

"The last time Samuel and I spoke, they were planning a vacation together. I know Ava and Chloe are probably inconsolable at this point. Garrett? I don't know him as well, he's newer in the relationship."

"So how long have you known his other lovers?" He thumbed back through the notes he'd taken during the interview with Ava Dall.

"Ava was first. Chloe and Samuel started a relationship about six months after he started dating Ava. I believe Ava was the one to suggest Chloe to Samuel. They'd been together for three years before Garrett entered the picture. It took a while for the girls to understand that Samuel needed Garrett as much as he needed them."

"Would there be cause for Ava or Chloe to feel jealousy toward Garrett?" He tapped his notebook with his pen. *If this man was so damn beloved, who the fuck slit his neck?*

"Not that Samuel had mentioned."

"Mrs. Treyson, as Samuel's widow, I assume you stand to inherit his fortune?" Following the money was always a smart move, especially when there didn't seem to be anyone with the next grind.

"You do not need to answer that," Masters growled from the couch.

Mrs. Treyson shook her head and rolled her eyes. "It will soon be a matter of public record, Mr. Masters. What could I possibly gain by not answering that question?" She returned her attention to him and shrugged. "I have a prenup agreement. In the event of Samuel's death, I do stand to inherit a great deal of money from his estate. However, I do know his will specifically indicates his lovers will be taken care of in addition to numerous charities and foundations. Money is nothing to me. I am independently wealthy. I own Beckham-Bennett Pharmaceuticals. I have more money than the Treysons, and I will probably use Samuel's money to feed and clothe the homeless and fund medical research."

"Did you hear from Samuel before he was killed?"

"I spoke to him several times Wednesday. We were coordinating our attendance at the Dempsey Memorial Ball. I called his office twice, and he called me once."

"Did you sense anything was wrong?"

"No, as a matter of fact, he was upbeat. Happy. I poked at him about his good mood. He said things were wonderful, but we changed subjects after that."

"When was the last time you saw him?"

"We spent Friday nights together. Occasionally, a charitable or business event took place on other nights, and we were forced to juggle our personal schedules. You'd have to check with his lovers. Ava usually coordinated Samuel's schedule. I believe they shared an online calendar system."

He leaned back in his chair and stared at the beautiful woman in front of him. There was something he was missing. "What would have happened if Sebastian Treyson discovered your open relationship with Samuel?"

"You're saying that as if Sebastian didn't know." Mrs. Treyson turned a sad smile toward him. "Sebastian Treyson and I were lovers for years, *while* I was married to Samuel. We stopped seeing each other when Sebastian decided to trade me in for a younger model. Literally, a younger model." She shrugged her shoulder.

"Ms. Dall indicated Sebastian Treyson would be angry should he know." Deadly if he recalled her words correctly. And he did.

"I'm sure Samuel told them that in order to keep their relationships quiet. He wouldn't want his father to know about them, and I don't blame him, but there was no worry with the NDA's they had in place." She shook her head and bit her bottom lip. "Perhaps he was open with them about the relationship issues he had with his father because he trusted them."

"You said your husband had an online calendar system. May we please have access to that?"

"Absolutely. But I have been advised by Sebastian's lawyers, and mine, any associated documentation or emails are considered privileged information and exclusive property of Treyson Enterprises. You will need a court order to access those." She smiled tightly and shrugged. It would seem the woman's hands were tied, and it didn't appear she cared for it.

"Thank you, ma'am. Now if we could get the contact information of the individual you were with the night your husband was murdered?"

He scribbled in his notebook and asked a few miscellaneous questions, but for now, the interview with Mrs. Treyson was over. He let Kallie do the nicey-nicey, glad to meet you, thing as he rolled the revelations of the interview through his mind. They had a shit ton of unanswered questions. Samuel Treyson was still an enigma. He didn't have a bead on the man. A successful businessman and all-around good guy with a wife and three full-time lovers, and yet, he ended up in a warehouse with his jugular sliced wide open. They needed to start putting together the pieces of Samuel's last hours. He glanced at his watch. It was going to be another long fucking day.

CHAPTER 7

Kallie unassed her desk chair, and her spine cracked in protest. They'd established their white board. They had the lovers and the wife listed. They'd accessed the man's online calendar, and the warrant had come through for the apps on Samuel's phone. Hope City's crime lab and tech department had printed the information for them. The questions they still had were numerous and daunting. There weren't enough waking hours in the day to get everything done. Right now, it was a matter of waiting for information and completing additional interviews as needed. She'd forgotten how much she really fucking hated waiting.

"Come on." Brock rose and grabbed his green

military field jacket, slipping it on. There was a dress code for homicide detectives, but going by the detectives in this precinct, it was ignored. Jeans and sweaters seemed to be the standard. She was going to love working here.

She didn't question where they were going. She just slipped on her jacket, grabbed her shit, and followed her new partner. It was almost midnight. They'd rehashed the interviews, reviewed the statements, and looked at crime scene photos until she could recite in detail every article found in each photo.

"Detective King, have you made any headway on the case?"

"Detective, is this your partner? Ma'am, what's your name?"

"Detective King, care to comment on the allegations of nepotism, that you're too junior to lead this investigation?"

Kallie kept her head down, hands in her pockets, and followed Brock's wide shoulders through the crowd. Her partner didn't flinch at the attack. Stoic and unbending he moved forward. For fuck's sake, it was the middle of the night and the vultures were still circling.

Her phone vibrated in her pocket. After they

drove away from the station, she clutched it glanced at the text. *Fucking Rich.*

>I have your telephone number. I will find you.

She should have blocked his number, but her gut told her having an eye on his particular brand of crazy would be beneficial in the long run. She could get another number, but then she wouldn't have a way to monitor his insanity. So, she'd deal with the threats and taunts. Rich would be a problem, no matter what steps she took. He had friends on the force before he went to prison. If one of them had contacts, he could eventually track her to Atlanta and from there to here.

"Anything wrong?" Brock asked when she pocketed the phone.

"What? No. Nothing that needs attention right now." Soon, but not now.

Brock maneuvered the Crown Vic into a parallel parking slot in front of a brick building. The two-some exited the vehicle and trudged up four flights of stairs. Brock fished in his pocket for a set of keys and opened the door.

"What are we doing?" Kallie asked as he turned on the light and strode down the hall.

"I need to get Fester before I take you home."

"Who the hell is Fester, and I don't remember asking for a ride home."

Brock swooped down and grabbed a huge cat that wandered over to him. The cat's long orange hair looked like someone had plugged him into an electrical outlet.

"Fester, Kallie. Kallie, Fester. I'm cat sitting until my partner, Jordan, gets back. We need to grab the food and cat litter. I have a box at my apartment."

The cat meowed and clawed Brock's coat, pulling himself up and settling his gnarly-haired body over one shoulder. The poor thing looked like someone had given it a home perm and let it over-process. Its forelegs hung limply over Brock's shoulder, and the cat purred like a motorboat. Brock chuckled, supporting the animal by holding a hand under its rear legs as he headed further into the apartment.

"You know, I have to ask. How the fuck is it that Samuel Treyson is screwing three lovers and a wife, and people like you and me end up cat sitting?" She was tired, but it was a good tired, and damn it, she liked Brock. The man didn't take any shit, and his methods, so far, had been above board.

That... and Brock King was sexy as fuck. With a mental shrug she dismissed the self-inflicted reprimand that usually followed those types of thoughts. He was a temporary partner. They had only this case together. She'd memorized the code of ethics for the organization. Fraternization wasn't illegal in the HCPD. It had to be declared, and the couple couldn't work together, but... she watched the man put the cat on the floor and stretch to pick up a bag of cat food and a bag of cat litter. Oh, yeah, he ticked most of the boxes on her sex-with-this-guy-might-not-be-a-mistake list. He was tall, handsome, sexy, had a great personality, and damned if he wasn't proving to be a nice person and one hell of a cop.

"A billion dollars?" Brock smirked.

"Say what?"

"You asked how Treyson had three lovers."

Oh, shit, she had, hadn't she? "There is that. I don't know about you, but I have given up trying to find *the* one."

He straightened and stared at the ground for a moment. "I can't do that. If I give up hope, then what's left?" He sent her a quick glance almost like he was embarrassed to have spoken so honestly.

Wow. Okay, so time to be real. "I had hope once."

"Sounds like a long story." He lifted a plastic cat carrier off the shelf and turned to look at her.

She shrugged. No sense in lying. "I married someone I thought was 'the one.' He and I were on the force together in Houston. We moved-up from patrol. I worked robbery then homicide. Rich, my former husband, took longer to test up but finally, he passed his exam and worked Vice. He went undercover for–" she blew a lungful of air and leaned against the door, "—hell, just over a year. His assignment ended in a massive takedown, and several of the gang members were killed. My partner and I were there as backup because we were in the vicinity, and it was an all-hands-on-deck-type of take down. I saw him across the warehouse. He wasn't being debriefed, so I headed over to him. My partner tagged along. As we approached, my husband shot and killed a woman in cold blood. I testified against him. My career was tanked, and I was forced to leave. I've been working for Guardian Security, but I missed this. I missed it so damn much."

"Guardian, huh? Okay, now it makes sense."

Brock had leaned against the dryer and crossed his arms.

"What makes sense?"

"My father said he had someone he was going to send over who was highly recommended. He has ties to Guardian."

"Wait, your father?"

"Yup."

"Who is your father, and why would he have input into my placement?"

"My father is Chauncey King."

She blinked at him and waited but he just stared at her. "And what does that mean to me?"

"He's the Hope City Police Commissioner."

She dropped her hip against the counter. "Well, fuck."

"Yep."

"That's…" Well, that was fucking scary if she was honest, but she said, "interesting."

"Look, I work for Davidson. My old man is a stickler for following rules and protocol, so I don't get any benefit from him being my dad… at work at least." A smile spread across his face. "He's one hell of a guy, and I respect the fuck out of my old man."

"I can see that. So, that accounts for the fishing

about nepotism. I wondered." Well, okay. All in all, the revelation changed nothing.

"Yeah, damn bottom-feeders. What happened to your husband?"

"Sorry, what?" Did she miss some portion of the conversation?

"Your husband, what happened to him after you testified?"

"Oh. He was sentenced to fifteen. Served five. Got out two days ago and has already called to threaten me."

"Threatened you, how? The texts you keep getting?"

"That and a phone call. You know, the usual shit." She channeled Liam Neilson and said in her best *Taken* voice, "*I will hunt you down, and I will find you.* You're working with me. You deserve to know the baggage that comes with me. What about you? Any baggage?"

He drew a breath and stared at the ceiling before he said, "My father is the police commissioner. He's put his career in my hands by leaving this case with me. What else? I grew up here in Hope City. One brother works J-DET, one is a fireman. I have two sisters, both too good to be related to me, a mother who could guilt trip a corpse, and I have a caffeine addiction."

"Wow. Not sure I can handle all that. Might have to request a new partner. What about a wife?"

He shook his head.

"Girlfriend?"

He let his head drop back again and stared at the ceiling. "I've been looking."

"No finding?"

"Nibbles, but sometimes women look at who they are dating."

Kallie made a point of closing one eye to examine him. "Kinda fucking hard to miss you." There wasn't a single woman on the planet who wouldn't want a chance with the detective.

"Yeah, all this is hard to miss, huh? But…" He chuckled and dropped his eyes before he shrugged.

"But what? You really need to finish that statement." He picked up the cat. The orange hairball patted his face with his paw, and the giant of the man in front of her smiled down at the feline. He pet the cat, and it rubbed its head against Brock's cheek. Her heart melted just a little bit. Okay, more than a little bit.

"I'm not a monk by any stretch of the imagination, but the women I've dated lately wanted to be on the arm of the big, bad cop. They got off on my badge, you know, the image and the thrill of dating a cop. Not that I didn't take what they're giving away, which kinda makes me a fucking dog, doesn't it? But I want more than a random piece of ass or a chick with a badge fetish." He lowered the cat and carefully tucked him into the cat carrier.

"Yeah? And what do you want, Mr. King?" She grabbed the bag of kitty kibble. He grabbed the bag of litter.

"What everyone else wants. I want the family thing, and I'm definitely looking for someone who isn't chasing a badge."

Kallie let him exit the utility room first and turned off the light before she followed him. "I get that. God knows I get that, but it's kinda hard to meet that type of person doing the job. Unless you're going to start dating witnesses or another cop."

"Yeah, and wouldn't that be a fucking mess? No, I want what my folks have. I want somebody who is willing to put up with the shit the job dishes out."

She took that comment on the chin. Hell yeah, her relationship turned into a disaster. Dating a cop should be taboo. Should be. "You want a fucking unicorn."

He laughed; the low rumble filled the small apartment. "Yeah, I guess I do."

"They're out there, man. They're real, a leprechaun told me." She wanted to believe it, but it was easier to joke about it.

"Yeah, did you find the pot of gold?" Brock set the cat carrier down as he opened the front door for her and grabbed the keys from the ceramic bowl.

"Nah. I think I'd have better luck looking for that unicorn."

"Let me know when you find one, until then I'll roll with the punches and keep hoping there is a woman for me. BTW, I'm taking you home and picking you up. You didn't ask about parking, and I saw the keys you slid into your pocket. No car key on them." He locked the door behind them.

"Damn detectives," Kallie grumbled behind him as they walked down the stairs they'd just climbed not five minutes ago.

He grunted in response; fuck, he'd spewed more personal information to the woman behind him in five minutes than he had to Jordan over the course of their entire partnership. Yeah, from here on out, he was keeping it caveman. Grunts and single word responses. Why the fuck had he word-vomited that drivel? Probably because he hadn't slept more than a couple hours in the last year or so. Maybe someone could just give him a lobotomy and then he wouldn't have to worry about his new partner thinking he was fucking mental. Or God, worse, that he was *emotional*. Fuck, paint his nails black, because whatever had just gushed from his mouth in Jordan's apartment reeked of Emo-itis. *Keep your fucking mouth shut, King.*

He'd never admit it to anyone, but part of the reason he worked so damn much was that he didn't want to go back to his empty apartment. Making meals for one sucked. The walls didn't ask him how his day went, and the drapes sure as fuck wouldn't talk to him when the gore of murder scenes was all he could see. Pathetic, but true.

They settled Fester in the back seat and plopped the food and litter down on the floorboard. "Where do you live?"

"I have an apartment on South Martingale."

"Well, welcome to the neighborhood. I live over on Hemmingway." The two roads ran parallel to each other two blocks apart. "You found everything you need?" *So much for caveman.*

She turned and put her elbow up on the back of the seat. "I've been here for a couple of months. I've gotten the lay of the land. I use the supermarket over on Halverson, and I found a gym."

He chuckled. "Please don't tell me you use the Golden Ticket."

She slapped his arm. "Hell no! I found this little place around the corner–"

"Vito's?"

"Yes! I don't need fancy equipment. Give me a jump rope, a heavy bag and a sparring partner, and I'm good to go."

He could see her excitement in flashes as they drove under streetlights. Fuck. He focused his attention on the road ahead of him. He needed to snip his budding attraction *to his partner* right now. Thou shall not ogle the woman who has your six. He was pretty sure that was a commandment. If it wasn't before, it was now. Fuck him. The idea of this woman sparing with him sent all kinds of unpartner like thoughts to his now completely overactive imagination. Somehow, he had to shove Kallie onto that 'do not mack' list. Still, he couldn't leave it alone. He cleared his throat. "Spar?"

"Huh? Oh, yeah, my bosses at Guardian gave a demo when I first got there. The woman, Jade DeMarco, man, she literally kicked ass. I mean, I had self-defense in the academy, and I can take down a perp, but she picked four of the biggest, baddest mothers in the group and told them to take her to the mat. The woman destroyed them. Since then, everyone in the division had mandatory training. She's trained in a blend of martial arts, which we were taught. I fucking love taking down someone bigger and stronger than me."

And that was probably one of the hottest things he'd ever heard. Change of topic. Change it right now. "Ahhh... I've always thought Jade was kinda crazy. I haven't seen her in, damn, it's been years."

She narrowed her eyes at him. "Say what now?"

He glanced over at her. Clearing his throat again, he asked, "Did you like working at Guardian?"

"Yes. The organization is phenomenal. Integrity is really their hallmark. I've never experienced a total buy-in like that before, but stop diverting. How do you know Jade DeMarco?"

"Her maiden name is King."

"Fuck me. Your sister?"

"Hell no. First cousin. Her dad and my dad were brothers."

"Were?"

"Yeah, her dad died a long time ago. So, you left Guardian and the best of everything because you missed working twenty-three hours a day, bad food, worse coffee, and grumpy partners."

"You're not grumpy."

He laughed and hit the turn indicator as he slowed for a red light. "I'm not talking about me. Grant is your official full-time partner. He's a cranky motherfucker." He wasn't, but hey it was fun to poke at her.

"Yeah? Well, I've dealt with those types before." She smiled at him. "Tell me, Detective, are you hungry?"

"Fuck yeah." He glanced at the neighborhood. "Not much open right now, though."

"Ummm…"

"Ummm?" He taunted her with her own unfinished statement.

"Okay, I don't want to get any shit about this, so if you say anything to anyone about it, I'll cut your balls off, but I'm a damn good cook. In the past month I've loaded my freezer. How does a bowl of chili and some homemade cornbread sound?"

He turned his eyes toward her and stared at the woman. Fuck him. God was testing him. Yep, or there was a hidden camera somewhere in the car. Someone had set him up. No woman was this perfect. Nope, she was a plant. Had to be. The vehicle behind them blasted its horn, startling them both. Her full-on laugh rolled through the car. She laughed with abandon, a full body release that was… enchanting.

"I didn't ask for your first born, detective. Do you want some food or not?"

He kept his eyes on the road and nodded. "I would. Thank you."

"Awesome. You can bring Fester up; we don't want him to turn into a block of ice while we eat. I'm three blocks up on the left."

He changed lanes and parked in front of a nice-looking building. It wasn't new, but it had been kept up, and it had locks on the lobby. He followed her up the stairs and into a decent-sized apartment decorated with pictures, pillows and plants. The three 'P's' that his mother insisted made a house a home.

"Take your coat off. It will take just a moment

to warm everything up. You can let the cat out. He can't hurt anything."

Brock shouldered out of his coat and opened the cat cage. A streak of orange darted from the carrier and bolted toward the back of the apartment. "I think you might have an overnight guest." Brock shoved his hands into his pockets and leaned against the kitchen door.

"Why's that?" She turned to him as she scooped cold chili into a saucepan.

"Fester is loose and hiding."

"Oh, that's not a problem. If we can't get him to come out from wherever he's camping, we can set up his box here. I like animals." She handed him a wooden spoon. "Stir this. I'll be right back."

Brock blinked at the spoon and watched her leave the kitchen. He stuck the damn thing in the pot and gave it a stir. The smell of chili and beef made his stomach growl. Hell, he hadn't eaten since that damn cinnamon bun.

The chili was bubbling nicely when she returned. Brock did a double take. She'd changed into an old pair of blue jeans and a long t-shirt. Her hair was down, and holy hell, did she have a lot of hair. It fell to the small of her back, and flirted with her slim waist. He'd bet next month's paycheck that his hands would fit perfectly on her hips. Fuck him. He even noticed the way she smelled. Vanilla and cinnamon with a deeper note of something he couldn't describe. He filled his lungs hoping to catch another waft of scent. Hell, he even noticed the little bumps that ran through her hair caused by the braid she'd wound up in a bun at the back of her head.

"Thanks. The corn bread is in the fridge, bottom shelf. Could you put it in the microwave for a minute?"

"Sure." He did as she asked, then unbuttoned his shirt sleeves and rolled them up his forearms.

She had the chili on the table along with a dish of soft butter by the time the microwave chimed. "So, tomorrow we work the phone and take a look at whatever else Samuel's left us."

"Right. But we also need to drop by Treyson Enterprises and talk to the people on the Board."

She nodded. "What time do you think those executive types get to work?"

He took a bite of chili. A glorious combination of spices, meat, and sauce exploded in his mouth. He closed his eyes and moaned. The low guttural sound filled the kitchen. He opened his eyes and looked straight at the woman he'd known for less than twelve hours. "Woman, you're going to marry me."

She threw back her head and laughed. "The chili is that good, huh?"

"Marriage proposal good." Fuck him, the taste was damn near orgasmic.

"Name the place and time, big boy, but be warned, I'm high maintenance. I demand a lot from the men I ensnare with my cooking."

He pointed a finger at her. "You accepted. It's a done deal. Set the date." He was laughing, but the idea wasn't all that fucking funny.

"Shut up and eat." She sectioned the loaf of cornbread and gave him a thick warm slice before she took one. He slathered it in butter and ate. He downed three bowls, and between them, they finished the loaf of cornbread. Conversation centered on the safe topic of the neighborhood and prevented him from acting like a fucking moron—again. Ask a woman you barely know to marry you… yeah, that fell straight into the you-don't-have-a-fucking-brain-left-in-your-head column.

"Shit, I'm stuffed." She groaned and picked up her bowl.

Brock picked up his bowl and took hers from

her hands, before he snagged the now empty cornbread plate. "You cooked; I'll clean." That was his mother's voice in his head.

"You don't have to do that. It's late. I'll rinse them and throw them in the dishwasher. It'll take me two minutes."

Brock put his dirty dishes in the sink and turned, leaning against the counter. He knew he should get going so she could get some sleep, but he didn't want to leave. He caught sight of the empty cat carrier. "Fester is still MIA."

"He's fine. You'll have to bring up the litter and the food. I'll make a temporary box until he comes out."

He shoved his hands into his pockets. God, he felt like a teenager. "Thanks for dinner. It's been a long time since I've had a home cooked meal."

She gave him a look that said 'bullshit' better than any verbal response.

"What?"

"You said your family was in Hope City."

"Yeah, well, I don't get to the house as often as I should. I made it home about three months ago, but I was called back to work about a half hour after I got there." He glanced at his watch. "And I have a command performance this Sunday. My old man wants me there because my mom is probably pushing his buttons. Don't let me forget, yeah?"

She tipped her electronic watch toward her mouth. "Set a reminder." The watch asked for the specifics. He provided them and she echoed them. "I'd lose my ever-loving mind if I didn't have this thing. It tells me what to do and when to do it."

He smiled and found himself staring at Kallie. Tall and athletic, she was strikingly beautiful. Her full lips and high cheekbones were accentuated by her soulful chocolate brown eyes. Top that off with the fact she was a cop who understood what being a cop meant. She was the perfect woman for someone like him. Hell, for any cop. That thought sent a shot of possessiveness through him. He was so screwed.

The cat wandered into the kitchen and meowed, breaking their connection. "Right, well I better go. I'll be back here at 8:00 a.m." He scooped up Fester and got him into his crate. He grabbed his jacket and shoved his arms into it. Getting gone before he did something stupid was an absolute priority.

She opened the door for him. "I'll be ready for you."

He blinked at her choice of words. A blush

bloomed over her cheeks. He nodded and left, heading down her hall. As he reached the end of the hall, he glanced over his shoulder and damned if he didn't catch her watching him. She waved and popped back into the apartment. He raised the crate and looked at Fester. "You know, dude, this case might not royally suck after all."

CHAPTER 8

Kallie shut the door and dropped her forehead against the thick wood. "Don't. Just. Don't. You know better." Her rueful burst of laughter echoed around her and confirmed that she did know better, but damned if she wasn't smack dab in the middle of a conundrum. Brock wasn't her permanent partner. *Good thing.* Going by the way the man was acting, the attraction between them was mutual. *Damn good thing.* The case wouldn't be affected by whatever was building between them. *Fucking perfect thing.* But... she'd been down this road before. *Bad, bad thing.* Her piece of shit, murdering ex-husband was released from prison and looking for her, which would put anyone spending time with her in danger. *Fucking worst thing.* Then again... Brock was a cop and a damn good one. *Yep, very good thing.*

She straightened away from the door and made quick work of rinsing the dishes and arranging them in the dishwasher. Not a bad first shift. She'd met her temporary partner, submerged elbows deep in a case, and determined her partner was a complex mix of contradictions and sex appeal, *aaannnddd* the Commissioner's son, no less. As she turned off the light and checked the locks one more time, she tried to recall what his father looked like. Lord, she hadn't even thought to connect those dots. Of course, she'd seen pictures of the Commissioner on the Hope City Police Department's website. She vaguely remembered a page full of shoulder-mounted stars, blue uniforms, and bios that were impressive as hell.

Peeling off her clothes, she folded them and placed them on her dresser before she slipped between her silk sheets. The cool fabric was a splurge and an impulse buy when she left Atlanta. The soft, pale blue material warmed quickly against her skin. She propped her head up with a second pillow and stared at the darkened ceiling. Images of her new partner streamed across her thoughts. The jeans he'd worn hugged his thighs and that incredible tight, muscled ass. His long sleeve Henley had stretched over his shoulders and biceps, but had hung loose over the badge he'd carried on his belt. He'd hiked the hem up behind his service weapon. And those eyes. God, those eyes were intense blue with a darker ring edging the iris. His dark brown hair was long enough to curl at his neck. All in all, he was everything she'd used to look for in a man and then some.

Kallie groaned, flopped over onto her stomach and punched her pillow. Finding someone like Brock should make her giddy, hopeful, excited… except she'd let all those wonderful feelings in once and look how that turned out. *Damn you, Rich.* Damn him for stripping away her hopes and dreams with a single pull of a trigger. Damn him for letting the scum he lived with while he was undercover change him from the man she married to a cold-blooded killer.

A shiver skimmed over her. Had he changed or had the real Rich emerged? He'd been reprimanded before for his overzealous handing of suspects and… She brushed a tear away. He'd hit her. She'd never reported it because he was so damn sorry. Any report of domestic abuse would have finished his career. He knew it, and so did she. He swore he'd never do it again and that he hadn't meant to hit her. She'd been so desperate to believe him. So. Damn. Desperate.

She'd been faithful to him while he was undercover. Cheating never entered her mind. The trial had proven he'd cheated, with the woman he killed and others. He'd lived with the woman for ten months. According to one of the men who testified, they were one of three couples who swapped partners routinely. He was impressed by Rich's ability to make his woman scream. She threw the pillow she was holding across the room.

Frustrated, she drew a deep, cleansing breath and released it slowly. No good could come of dragging up the trash of her past.

She was starting a new chapter in her life. A new location, a new job and a new, albeit temporary, partner who she liked. Liked? She snorted and rolled onto her back. No, not liked. *Wanted*. She could imagine that big body over hers. The muscles that flexed under his shirt bared to her hands. Would he have hair on his chest? The five o'clock shadow that had started about noon yesterday suggested he might.

She trailed her nails over her breast and teased

her nipple. In her imagination, he'd be an aggressive lover, but one who made sure she was satisfied. She pinched her nipple and rolled it between her fingers. He'd make sure he teased her and excited her. Her other hand crept lower and stroked the side of her clit, enough pressure to make her arch into the touch. Brock would make her crazy with desire. She could almost feel his lips and that scratchy scruff against her heated skin. Her fingers stroked faster and applied more pressure. She moved from one breast to the other and rolled the nipple. The muscles in her legs tightened, and she longed for his body to fill the space between them.

Her fingers shuffled faster as need tightened inside her. She gasped, reaching for release. Her hand flew against her skin until she peaked, orgasming against her own touch. She undulated through the release, but the end result was, as always, a desolate consolation. The silence of the room was punctuated by one set of lungs. There were no soft touches. No warmth of a body holding her, or a tender kiss with whispered words of love. The aftermath of solitary pleasure was so damn lonely.

Brock slowly registered the vibration of Fester's purr on his chest. He opened one eye and pushed his head into the pillow as his eye focused on the tip of the cat's nose about two inches from his face. "Fuck, man, don't you have boundaries?"

Fester stretched his paws forward and patted his cheek as his purr ratcheted up to motorboat level. He carefully grabbed the paws and held them so he could turn his sleepy gaze to the clock on his nightstand. Well, son of a bitch. He'd slept six hours. That was a record. He eyed the cat. "It's not you. Great food and near exhaustion put me in a coma. It has nothing to do with you in my bed."

The cat meowed and moved his front paws from Brock's light grasp. The mangy animal stood and strutted regally to the other pillow where he promptly lay down and recommenced the kneading. Brock blinked and yawned. Damn, he needed the rest, but with all the shit rolling through his brain, he was amazed the damn thing turned off long enough for him to latch onto some REM cycles. He grabbed his phone and checked his emails. Miriam Treyson's attorney sent one last night that he'd read just before he closed his eyes.

The board of directors were convening an emergency meeting this morning, at nine. He scrolled through the bullshit emails and opened one from a detective in Vice he knew. Samuel Treyson's Bentley had been found. That left the McLaren as Treyson's means of transportation to the warehouse. A cursory glance of the ride share apps on Samuel's phone hadn't shown him hiring a car in over a week. He thumbed through the emails again and dismissed the rest. Tossing the covers off, he headed into the small bathroom.

He cranked the shower before he took care of business, shaved, and brushed his teeth. By the time he stepped under the showerhead, steam had fogged his small bathroom into a near-sauna-esque state. Just the way he liked it. He got busy with the soap as he ticked off the laundry list of things he and Kallie needed to get through today. God, what they needed was a break in this case. He swiped his hand over his cock and under his balls. The suds and friction jolted him awake more than hot water and coffee ever could and that was saying something. Kallie's image filled his mind as he stroked his length. Was it wrong? Probably. Did he care? Not really. He'd made a damn fool of himself last night. All that emo crap he'd spewed was sitting there between them, but there was also an attraction. He felt it, and gauging her reactions in the kitchen last night, she did too.

He leaned against the tile and gently tugged at his balls with one hand while the other slid up and twisted over the head of his cock. His gut curled low and tight. The last time he'd found such an immediate attraction with someone had been during his hitch in the Marine Corps. The attraction hadn't lasted through divergent assignments and far too much time apart.

He stroked harder. Bringing himself off lately had been as exciting as sanding a plank of wood, methodical and bland. Only this morning, instead of his normal slide and glide, he pictured those beautiful fucking lips around his cock. Kallie's big brown eyes looking up at him. Yes, God her eyes and that mouth. Lightning seared through him, igniting his fantasy with a million joules of sexed-up satisfaction. He groaned, the sound echoing around him in the small shower. His release thundered up his shaft following the strike of fantasy-laced electricity, and he erupted over his fist as he stroked himself through the orgasm.

He dropped his head into the water and closed his eyes. He needed the case to be over. He needed justice for Treyson's family, to take his old man away from those fucking bullseyes, and the opportunity to explore something more with Kallie. Three damn good reasons to take down whoever killed Treyson. He turned off the water and grabbed his towel. There was no such thing as a perfect murder. There was something connecting Treyson to his killer. They just needed to find it.

A shiver ran through Brock as he huddled in his car and waited for the defroster to gather enough heat to melt the sheet of ice that had formed under the inch of snow on his windshield. When winter decided to show her face, she did it in grand style. He glanced at his watch before he punched his brother Brody's picture on his phone. The screen went black for a couple seconds before it rolled into the call. Damn, even the cell phone hated the cold. Winter was no longer coming, the fucker was here, no white-walkers required.

"'lo?" The sleepy rumble of his brother Brody's voice floated over the connection. Obviously, he'd woken his ass up.

"Hey, man. Got a favor to ask you."

"Fuuuck… dude, do you know what time it is?"

"7:30."

"In the fucking morning!"

The shock in Brody's voice was worth the shit he'd get for the call. His brother had been permanently assigned as sergeant to a joint agency drug enforcement task force operating in Hope City and the J-DET crew worked some crazy fucking hours.

"It is the time normal people go to work."

"No. No, it isn't. Normal people go to work at 9:00. They are sleeping for another thirty minutes, minimum."

"Depends on your definition of normal."

"You are not normal, bro, you've never been normal," Brody grumped into the phone.

"Right, you don't want me to drag up *your* past, now do you?"

"Shut up. What do you want? Tell me so I can say no and go back to sleep."

The playfulness left as Brock drew a deep breath. "I picked up a murder."

"Yeah, Treyson. Heard about it."

"Fucking cops are nothing but gossips." Brock shook his head.

"You know it. This favor has something to do with that?"

"Yeah. I know your crew has feelers on the street. Treyson was in an abandoned warehouse. No vehicle found although everyone said he had a platinum ride. If I text you the make and model, can you make some inquiries? Knowing what happened to that car could give me a vector to shoot an azimuth."

"Yeah, I can do that. How is the investigation going?"

"Big money equals big problems." *Four lovers and a partridge in a pear tree.* Brock flicked the windshield wipers and watched as slush slid away from the bottom of the windshield. At this rate, he had another five minutes before he'd be able to head to Kallie's. She'd be waiting for him, and that put a smile on his face.

"Pop is taking some huge pressure on this one." He could hear Brody moving in the background.

His good mood disintegrated. "Yeah, I've been apprised." He fucking hated that his dad had a target on his chest.

"The Governor held a press conference last night. Did you catch that? He had Dad standing up there like a chastised schoolboy as the fucker said he was going to make sure Samuel Treyson's killer was brought to justice. The son of a bitch said he was going to give HCPD one week to solve the murder before he sent in the fucktards from the State to oversee the investigation. One fucking week. The bastard is castrating Dad on a state-wide stage. Hell, he relegated Dad to a fucking back-drop." Brody's anger gained speed as he woke up.

"I didn't see it live, but a couple of the guys at work told me about it. We caught it on the internet before we left last night. I'm working this fucking case as hard as I can."

"I know it. You got any leads?"

"Too fucking many this time. Kallie and I are going to focus on working his last twenty-four. We got a warrant for his phone apps and need to go through that info dump."

"Text and call log?"

"Tech is running the calls and printing up text messages. We should have who said what to whom by the time we reach the office."

"Wait... hold on..." Brody yawned into the phone. "Go back."

"Go back to what?"

"Who the fuck is Kallie? Where's Jordan?" The

sound of a one-cup coffee maker brewing in the background made him smile. He and his brother lived on coffee, unlike Blay, the health nut of the family.

"Jordan got called up by the Bureau to assist in the Grappelli debacle. Kallie Redman is my temporary partner."

"Fuck, sorry about Jordan, that sounds like a cluster-fuck of epic proportions." His brother took a sip of coffee and the sigh that came next was predictable.

"Yeah, I figure I'll be whored out until he gets back, or until Davidson gets tired of the rotating door and assigns me someone permanently."

"Fuck that would suck."

"It would. You making an appearance at the homestead on Sunday?"

Brody grunted. "Have to. I've been MIA for almost two months and, unfortunately, I don't have an active case going. We're standing down while the DA preps us for the Serenity case."

Brock nodded to himself. The J-DET team had intel about a freighter, The Serenity, stuffed full with cocaine. Brody's team also ended up hauling in half the dock workers in Hope City as a huge drug smuggling ring unraveled. "Is that finally coming up for trial?" He hit the wiper again and watched another chunk of ice slide to the side and fall off.

"Yeah. The ADA wants to prosecute all the defendants together under the Rico Statute, and the union lawyers have been fighting it, but the judges know the ADA is on solid ground. Our witnesses just need to stay alive long enough to testify."

"Worried?"

"Always. So, about this Kallie woman. She good people?"

"Seems to be. She's smart. She worked for Jade before she came here."

"Jade? As in our cousin, Jade? Wait, that doesn't compute. How does a personal security officer turn into a homicide detective?"

"She was homicide in Houston. Had a fuck-ton of shit happen. Worked for Jade for a while and then transitioned here."

"Huh."

"Yeah."

"She hot?"

"God. You are such a dog."

"That means yes." Brody laughed; the rich

sound filled the car. "She's a temporary partner, right?"

"Yes, yes she is."

"Oh, God... you do like her."

"Shut up." Stellar comeback. He rolled his eyes.

"Brock, seriously, if you like this woman, go for it. Life's too fucking short, you know what I mean?"

He flicked the wipers again and watched as the final piece of ice slid down the windshield and was pushed to the side. Unfortunately, his brother Brody had a shit track record with women, too. He glanced at the rear windshield. The heated coils running through the rear window had cleared it sufficiently to see behind him. He put the car into drive and inched the vehicle from his parking space. "I do know what you mean. Hey, you heard from Blay or the girls?"

"I saw Blay over at the Celtic Cock. The new rooster on the sign is hilarious, the fucker is wearing a kilt. Blay was hanging with the usual crowd of spark-heads. The girls? Brianna fed me yesterday when I stopped into the restaurant. Her new chef is amazing. Justin sent this one her way."

"How many restaurants does that guy have now?"

"No fucking clue, but I'm happy for him. Jared called about a week ago asking me to put feelers out for anyone looking to go Federal. Guardian is hiring… again."

"You tempted?" He stopped at a stoplight and flicked his blinker to the right heading to Kallie's.

"Fuck no. I love what I do, no matter how much it fucks with my sleep schedule. What about you?"

"Nope. Never had the desire to do anything but this. Hear anything from Bekki?"

"No, but that isn't unusual. I'll hear from her when she needs something for a story she's working."

Brock snorted. "She's a spoiled brat."

"True, but she's also the baby, so the princess act isn't surprising."

"No shit. All right, look, I gotta go. Thanks for asking your contacts about this, I'll text you the description."

"Roger that. Stay safe."

"You too." He pushed the end button as he drove up to Kallie's apartment building. She bounded down the steps, and he smiled. The woman had adapted to the Southern District already. The precinct they worked couldn't sustain suits. They had trouble enough trying to bridge the gap between cops and the people who lived in the poorest regions of the city. The fact she keyed in on it without asking was another mark in her favor. She wore jeans, combat boots, a sweater, and a brown canvas parka that snapped for quick access to her weapon, cuffs and badge. Her long hair was back again, braided and coiled tight against the back of her head. She opened the door and dropped into the car. "Did you order the snow?"

"Hell no. Cold weather only increases our workload."

"Just like the hot weather." She nodded. "Summer heat brings out tempers and escalates fights into murders, but the winter cold just silently kills."

"The cold is a motherfucker, that's a fact," he agreed and handed her his phone. "Do me a favor and text Treyson's vehicle information to the last number I called."

She reached into her coat and produced her notebook. "The Bentley or the McLaren?"

"The Bentley was found this morning in a downtown parking garage Treyson used. Send the details on the McLaren."

She tapped at the phone and pushed send. "There were no tracks at the crime scene?"

"Nothing that helped. The fire department obliterated any tracks at the front of the building when they responded to the fire. The back of the building only had patrol car and coroner's van tracks."

"So, you're thinking someone took the... 2019 720S McLaren Spider and is trying to what... sell it?"

"It is a four-hundred-thousand-dollar car. That's plenty of motive. Chop shops make bank on the parts, or the black market for resale is an option. If that car is in Hope City, Brody will find it."

"Brody?"

"My brother. He is the sergeant for the J-DET team here in Hope City."

"You are the only two in the police department, right?"

"Right. Blay is a fireman. Brianna owns a restaurant, and Bekki is an investigative reporter for the Hope City Journal."

"Does your family have a thing for 'B' names?" She placed his phone back on the seat next to him.

"Yeah, well, it's a family tradition on my Dad's side. All his brothers' and sisters' first names start with C; my cousins, in each branch of the family start with the same letter. We are B. Although it was rumored Dad wanted to name Brianna, Wolfgang."

She cocked her head, eyes wide in expectation, so he dropped the old family joke. "Before she was born, my dad used to tease my mom that he was naming the next child Wolfgang."

"I think Brianna is a better name."

"Yeah, she defo isn't a Wolfie. However, Brody was next in line after her, and he would have loved to have been a Wolfgang." He laughed at her expression. "What? Wolfgang is an awesome name."

She blinked at him like he had five heads and twenty eyes. "First, never say 'defo' again, and no, it really isn't."

"What, you don't like my 'hip' language?"

An inelegant snort shot from her. "Hip? Hello, Boomer."

"Oh, hell no, you did not just make me fifty something and millennial snark my ass."

"If it speaks like it's fifty…" She let the sentence trail off before muttering, "Walks like a duck, quacks like a duck…"

He glanced at her. Whoa... That teasing smile and those sparkling eyes lassoed a rope around his chest and drew it tight. She was beautiful. He forced his attention from her and tried to breathe again. "Watch it, Detective, or I'll be dumping all the bullshit leads on you."

"As if I'd allow that." She flipped through her notebook as she spoke. "Where do we start today?"

"We're heading across town. Treyson Enterprises has a special meeting of the board of directors at 9:00 this morning. I want to catch them as they come into the meeting, sequester them, and then interview each of them separately."

"How did you find that out?" She turned and narrowed her eyes at him.

"Miriam Treyson's attorney sent an email last night, or should I say this morning. By the time stamp it was intentionally sent when he didn't think I'd be awake to get it."

"Damn, that bastard has a passive-aggressive streak, doesn't he?"

"He does." He slowed down, driving through a bank of slush on the road.

"Makes me wonder if that bastard worked for Samuel, too," Kallie tossed out.

"Why's that?"

"Just suspicious of everyone at this point. I mean, do we know for a fact the person Samuel wanted to bring into the fold was actually a woman?"

Good point. Damn good point.

CHAPTER 9

Kallie followed him when they exited the private elevator. "Well, that was a complete and utter waste of time."

He agreed. The Board of Directors for Treyson Enterprises were nothing but pompous, positioning, megalomaniacs. The world revolved around them. Of course, none of them knew of anyone who would want to hurt Samuel Treyson. He hadn't expected anything less.

"Detectives, my name is Latoya. I'm here to take you to see Mr. Treyson." The soft silky voice behind them spun each of them on their heel.

The woman was strikingly beautiful. Glancing at her clothes, he'd hazard a guess that she shopped at the Black Crane or other stores of that ilk. He shoved his hands into his parka. "I'm sorry, I was unaware we had an appointment with Mr. Treyson." So, Daddy wanted to talk to them. The elder Treyson was on their list, but they were told he was still out of the country.

"He just arrived from Switzerland. If you would please accommodate us." The woman's disdain dripped from her words.

Obviously, they'd been measured and found lacking. That was okay. He enjoyed being underestimated. He exchanged glances with Kallie and subtly nodded his head. She arched an eyebrow in acknowledgement. They wanted to get a good measure of Sebastian Treyson. Now was the time.

As they followed the woman down the richly decorated hallway, he centered himself, adjusting to the curveball in their schedule and the pending conversation. The woman waved a hand directing them toward a closed door. Kallie did the classy thing. She stopped and knocked. There is no way he would've.

They heard a muffled command from behind the door. Kallie turned the handle and opened the wooden panel into a luxurious corner office. The floor-to-ceiling windows showcased Hope City's skyline. The drab cold gray of the winter's day couldn't take away from the splendor of the cityscape. This far up, everything looked beautiful. Well, except for the man sitting on the ornate Victorian couch in the corner of the room. That man looked like hell.

"Mr. Treyson?" Kallie walked across the room and extended her hand to the gentleman who struggled to get off the couch. He finally stood, and Kallie continued, "My name is Detective Redman, this is Detective King, we've been assigned to your son's case."

The elderly gentleman sagged back onto the couch. He dropped his head into his shaking hands. "Have you found the bastard who killed my boy?"

He and Kallie exchanged glances. This wasn't the overbearing son of a bitch he thought they'd meet. When Kallie took a seat across from Sebastian Treyson, he sat down in a chair further away to observe the interaction between his partner and the old man. As Kallie spoke, Mr. Treyson trembled. There were tears in his eyes. He listened and asked specific, direct questions. The pain of losing his son was obvious, and the man's grief didn't register as a pretense.

"Do you know of anyone who would want to hurt your son?" Kallie asked quietly.

Treyson slowly shook his head back and forth. "My son wasn't like me. He was a good man. People who did business with him respected him. Not because he ruled with fear, or maliciousness. They respected him because he was a good businessman who is… was ethical and loyal. Everything I'm not, Samuel was. He was the best parts of me. And now he's gone." The man stared toward the window and shook his head. He spoke to the skyline, not them. "Would someone come after me? Absolutely. I'm a bastard. Go after the business? Understandable. But this?"

He leaned forward. "Mr. Treyson, could it be somebody was trying to get to you by killing your son?"

Kallie gave him a quick glance and a slight nod. They were on the same page.

Watery, aged blue eyes swung his direction. "Oh… God. You don't think… is there reason to believe that?"

"We are examining all possibilities, sir."

"I have enemies. There are people who would love to see me fall to my knees." He leaned forward and dropped his head in his hands. "You'll be investigating two murders if I find who did this before you do."

"Threats of that nature aren't taken lightly, sir." Treyson had power and the ability to make the threat a reality.

"He'll never know how I felt about him." Treyson's murmured words reached him.

He could only imagine what the guy was feeling. During his tours in the Marine Corps, he'd seen people like Sebastian Treyson. The ones who developed a clear zone around them, and could block emotions. It was a preservation tactic forged from necessity, so he understood the guy in front of him. He'd seen people's regret for not telling those who were closest what they meant to them. He'd witnessed the scenario played out numerous times, both overseas and here working homicide.

The man lifted his head and stared directly at him. "Find who did this before I do, Detective, or that threat will become a reality."

"Sir, we'll need a list of who you believe would have a grudge or a reason to retaliate against you."

Kallie took over the conversation, directing it away from the volatile ground they currently trod.

"I will have Latoya send that over to you. Give her your card on the way out." It was a dismissal. The man leaned back and closed his eyes. They both stood and started to the door.

"You know... I'm a bastard. Hell, I fucked his wife just because I could, and now... How do you take it back? I did it on purpose. I treated him like shit, used my money to make him crawl, all because he was everything I couldn't be. I was envious, and now he's gone." Tears rolled down the man's face. "How do I make amends?" The question was tossed to the universe, and not at them.

He wasn't sure why, but he responded, "Honor his memory, sir. Something good should come from this." It would be a start. Not that the relationship could be repaired, but perhaps the man in front of them could put himself back together as a better man.

Kallie followed him as they left and was the one to pass Latoya their contact information. They were silent until they got into the car. "Where to next?"

"We head back across town. Treyson had some receipts in his wallet."

"Yeah, I saw that." Kallie flipped open her notebook and thumbed through the pages. "Coffee shop and a dry cleaner."

"The coffee shop was where we got the lead to find Ava."

"Which led to the others. So, let's hit up the dry cleaners. The receipts were to be ready for pick up the morning after he was killed."

"And again, I ask myself why a billionaire would drop off his dirty laundry?" He drove a McLaren and was made of money. Why would he lower himself to mundane chores? Of course, nothing about Samuel Treyson was as expected. The man went for coffee with his girlfriend, took vacations with all his lovers, and by all accounts was everyone's best friend. This was probably just one more idiosyncrasy to add to the list of things that didn't make sense.

"He didn't trust anyone with his clothes?" Kallie chuckled, "Or he liked doing something for himself? Hell, maybe he was a control freak."

"Didn't get that from any of the interviews."

"No, you're right. The picture I'm getting of Treyson was he liked order but was willing to let others lead. Ava arranged multiples. Chloe protected him from the world by turning off the internet and keeping their relationship about peace and quiet, and Garrett took the lead in their relationship. Treyson had built himself a well-rounded life."

"But it wasn't perfect because he wanted to bring someone else in." For some reason that fact stuck in his mind.

"True. So, we keep digging." Kallie pointed to the side of the street. "Coffee shop with a drive through. I don't know about you, but I'm dying over here."

"There is a better shop about a mile up. Can you survive?" He'd been going to The Perk for years. They knew his order.

"Don't mess with my caffeine levels, Detective, or you'll see a very ugly side of me." Kallie thumbed through her notebook as she talked. "Do you know when the ME's report is going to come in? We should have leap-frogged the other cases down at the morgue, right?"

"Yeah. The medical examiner's policy is they bag and tag and then bring them in, but schedule the autopsies for the following day, so they should be doing it now. We'll get the preliminary info by tonight. The pathology and toxicology reports won't be back for weeks even with the pressure that is coming down on this case."

"What is the standard here?"

"The backlog is ridiculous, so for normal situations, you're looking at a month for the final pathologist reports."

"Wow, there are going to be some seriously pissed off detectives and families when Treyson jumps to the front of the line."

"Exactly. Why is his murder any more important than someone else's family member? This is actually the first time I've seen a case bumped to the front of the line, but then again, I work in The Desert. Our victims aren't affluent nor are they usually high profile."

Kallie turned in her seat. "They matter, though."

"They damn sure do."

"Why is it called The Desert?"

"When the gangland wars started back in the late eighties, the detectives started calling the streets deserted. Nobody walked the streets. The place was a deadly ghost town. A desert. It stuck. Hell, Channel Five did an exposé on the area about a year ago. The gentrification of the dock area is pushing a lot of new money right up against The Desert's boundaries. There have been issues."

He pulled into the coffee shop drive-through and ordered them both an extra-large caffeine injection. Kallie handed him a fiver. "Nah, you keep that. You fed me last night. This is the least I could do."

"Detective King, are you trying to get on my good side?"

"Would it get me invited for dinner again?"

"There is a very real possibility that could happen."

"Then my answer is hell, yes." He laughed and took a long draw off his coffee. "What is the address of the dry cleaner's?"

"Um... hold on. 5725 East Halstead Avenue. That's near Richland, right?" She glanced at him as she took a sip of her coffee.

"Yep. Been studying our fair city?"

Kallie snorted and deadpanned, "That's me, a student at heart."

"Nothing wrong with wanting to know where the hell you're at. I grew up here, and I still need a fucking GPS sometimes."

"I'd wager you don't for your precinct."

"That would be correct." There wasn't a nook or cranny in The Desert he didn't know about.

"Who owned the warehouse that was torched the night Samuel died?"

"As far as I could tell, some kind of small holding company. Smartsmith, LLC. I have the tech team running down who is behind the organization, but right now, there are no ties to Treyson."

"Do you always get tech support?" She flipped to the first open page in her notebook. "What is the name of the company, again?"

"It is in my notebook, after the list of apps on the phone, about seven or eight pages in. I don't usually get tech support. I'm thrilled to have it with this one, though."

She grabbed his notebook and opened it. His phone vibrated in his coat pocket. He palmed it and activated the speaker. "King."

"I need an update." Lt. Davidson's voice whipped over the connection.

"We've interviewed all the people he was in a relationship with, the man's wife and his father, plus the board of directors. We're on our way to check one of his last stops before we head over to see if Dr. Carpenter has finished preliminaries."

"Anyone looking good for this?"

"Not a damn one."

"Sir, this is Redman. Sebastian Treyson is sending over a compilation of people who he believes may have it in for him."

"Fuck me, this couldn't be a simple open and shut case, could it? All right. What do you need from me?"

"We'll need another team to run down those leads when they come in." He glanced at Kallie who nodded in agreement. "I asked Brody to put feelers out for the McLaren and once we are done talking to Dr. Carpenter, we're heading back to work through the phone dump tech should be bringing over."

"It's here. Tech delivered it about a half hour ago. Pops called up to let me know he was done logging it in."

"Roger that." He hung up the phone and turned onto Halstead.

"You requested the info from the phone in paper form?"

"Yes, yes I did." He glanced at her and winked.

"Okay, Boomer, may I ask why you didn't just have them send it to you electronically?"

"No, not a Boomer, I'm definitely a Millennial, but one with experience. Electronic evidence can be deleted."

Kallie turned to him, her coffee cup halfway to her lips. "You think someone would tamper with evidence?"

He cleared his throat and admitted, "My old man took over from a long legacy of good ole boys. The stink of their corruption ran deep. This is a high-profile case. I'm not taking any chances."

Kallie pointed to a building as they passed. "Four thousand block."

He nodded and maneuvered into the right-hand lane of the four lanes heading East.

"Dirty cops..." She shook her head.

"Police officers are human. Sure, we screen, and we test, but at the end of the day, we are a microcosm of society, and quite frankly, sometimes our society sucks. The only thing *we* can do is be the best fucking cops we can be."

"There are thousands of us."

"And the few that fuck up, who are aggressive, biased, abusive, they make us all look bad."

"So why do we do it?" Kallie pointed to an empty parking slot just beyond the dry cleaner's storefront.

"I don't know what your reason is, but I protect and serve because I believe people should be able to live without fear, and someone needs to speak for the victims." He put the car into park after a quick parallel park.

"Exactly. Yeah, I missed it. This. When I was working for Guardian. I missed making a difference for a community. Guardian is exceptional at what they do, don't get me wrong, but they are so many levels removed from this." Her eyes scanned the street.

"Well, we are in the thick of it." He glanced down the busy city street. "Why would Treyson come all the way over here to drop off laundry?"

"Is it close to where one of the lovers lives?" Kallie thumbed back through her notebook looking for addresses.

"It's nearer Garrett's and Chloe's. Not as close to Ava's." He turned off the car. "Ready?"

"Yep."

They made their way into the Plaid Iron and stood at the back of the lobby. A line several people deep waited at the counter. A pretty redhead, an arm and one ankle in a cast, knee propped up on a scooter, rolled to counter. "Here you go, Mr. Robinson. I'm sorry about the wait." She fished the hanger off a small bar someone had installed on the side of the scooter. It looked flimsy, but seemed to do the trick.

"No worries, Cynthia. Can't you take some time off? You're looking tired." The older gentleman took the jacket she handed him.

"Oh, no. I'm fine. Just really clumsy."

The older man shook his head. "Honey, no one is *that* clumsy."

Warning bells clamored in Brock's brain. He stared harder at the woman–black slashes under her eyes, fat lip, bruised cheek. Looked like someone had used the small woman as a punching bag.

"Yeah, you'd think that wouldn't you? But, then there is me!" The woman smiled brightly. Unfortunately, it didn't reach her eyes. They waited as she processed the line, pushing her little scooter for items she couldn't access by using the conveyor belt of clothes.

"Ticket?" The woman's hand shook as she extended it.

He displayed his badge at the same time as Kallie. "Detectives King and Redman. We have several tickets issued to a Samuel Treyson." What color was left in the woman's already sallow complexion drained.

"Mr. Treyson?" She looked from one of them to the other, her brown eyes wide. Her mouth dropped open, and she wrapped her good arm around herself protectively. She seemed to shrink into herself.

"Yes. When was the last time he was in here?" Kallie opened her notebook and stared at the woman, her pen ready to take notes.

"Um... I don't remember? I'd have to look at the ticket. Is he in trouble?" Her fingers traced the edge of her half cast.

"Were you in an accident?" Kallie nodded at the cast.

"Uh, no... I fell. Fell down the stairs at my apartment building. Tried to stop my fall with my arm and that didn't go well." The woman shook her head and winced slightly.

"When did you fall?"

"When? Oh, um... a couple days ago." She glanced behind her. "Is there something I can help you with? I can't release the clothes without the ticket."

Brock leaned forward, crowding the counter on purpose. The woman moved back, her eyes narrowed, and she looked away. *Fell down, his ass.* More like pushed down or worse, beaten. "How well did you know Mr. Treyson?"

"He had a couple of places on my route. I'd see him from time to time."

"Your route?" Kallie asked for clarification.

"Yeah, I work the pick up laundry service."

Brock stood up giving the woman room before he prompted, "You met him then?"

She nodded. "He's really nice. "

"So, you met the people he lived with?"

Her brows furrowed and she echoed, "People he lived with?"

"Yes, at the places you picked up his laundry."

"No. I mean, yes. I delivered the clean clothes in the afternoon. I didn't have the delivery route long. But to answer your questions, other people answered the door and took the clothes, but I never really 'met' them, you know?"

"Got it. You no longer do laundry delivery service?"

"No, not for a while now."

"Why's that?"

"She works the front and runs just about everything." Cynthia's head whipped around. A big, barrel-chested man strode from the back of the facility. He wore a wifebeater and low-slung jeans. He pushed his too long hair from his face. He had two full sleeves of tats and from the looks of his shoulders, a lot more ink under the wifebeater. The man loomed over Cynthia. "The woman who used to run the counter service found a job closer to home. Cynthia filled in on the route for me when I wasn't feeling well. Since then, I've been moved to the back, and she's taken over the front." He extended his hand. There were bruises all over his arm along with scratches, and was that a bite mark on his bicep? "Dawson Jenkins. This is Cynthia White."

"Dawson and I are engaged." Cynthia added.

Brock's eyes darted to the woman's hand. No ring. He cocked his head at the announcement.

"My hand swelled up after I fell. Had to take it off or risk the possibility of losing a finger." She glanced over at Dawson's outstretched hand and then darted a quick look at the man.

The guy dropped his hand. "I'm sorry. I didn't catch your names."

"Detectives King and Redman. How well did you know Mr. Treyson?"

The man's brow furrowed.

"Samuel Treyson." Kallie repeated the name when he didn't speak.

"Is this about his murder?" Dawson snapped his attention to Kallie.

"Murder?" Cynthia's eyes widened, and her hand covered her mouth. She sank back on the leg still propped up on the scooter.

Dawson didn't look at Cynthia. "He was killed--at the warehouse district. It's all over the news."

"You didn't answer the question." Kallie stood straight and looked the guy in the eyes. Direct, authoritative, and completely composed.

Dawson gave her a look of disdain and then looked back at Brock. "I knew him."

"How well?"

The man crossed his arms over his chest. He sent a quick glance at Cynthia. "As well as I know the rest of my customers. Do I need to get a lawyer?"

"Do you think you need a lawyer?" Kallie returned.

"Nah, I don't, 'cause I didn't do anything wrong." He tried, but failed, to hold Kallie's stare.

"Maybe not to Treyson." Brock leaned away from the counter and looked directly at Cynthia. "If you need anything, anything at all, you come find me at the Southern precinct." He pulled one of his business cards and handed it to her as he stared at the motherfucker next to her.

"I'm not sure what you mean." The woman looked up at Dawson and smiled, although once again her eyes weren't mirroring the expression, they were... vacant.

Kallie asked for and received both Cynthia and Dawson's information. They lived in separate apartments of the same building. She also jotted down their cell phone numbers.

"We'll be back in a couple days. Follow up questions." Kallie closed her notebook and pocketed it. The same motion moved her coat behind the weapon she wore on her waist, not in a shoulder holster, like he did. She arched an eyebrow and then winked at Dawson. "Be seeing you around."

"Oh, I'm really looking forward to that, Detective," Dawson said with a smile, with almost a hopeful look on his face, which was... weird and tripped bells, although he had no fucking clue why.

They made it two steps past the window before Kallie lost it. "That motherfucker is abusing her."

"Yeah, he could be." He hated there was nothing they could do about it.

"Could be?"

"Unless she comes forward, it is hard to prove."

"I'm going to be coming back."

"She's got to make a complaint, or you have to

catch him in the act." There were no handprint bruises on her that he could see, and he'd looked. He'd wanted a reason to put cuffs on that bastard.

Kallie stopped on the sidewalk and palmed her phone. Glancing at the screen, she growled in irritation before shoving the phone back in her pocket. "He's going to end up killing her," she snapped. She wrenched the car door open and dropped inside the car.

"She knows to come looking for us at the precinct. Next time you stop by, I'll give you a couple business cards for local shelters and social workers." Brock turned on the vehicle and waited for traffic to clear before he merged into the lanes of traffic. "Was that the ex again?"

She waved a dismissive hand. "She's so freaking tiny. He was what… six-two or three and at least a hundred pounds heavier than her? I hate abusive pricks." She ground out the words and flopped her head against the headrest. "Okay, sorry. I'm picking up my soapbox and heading home now, and yes, I know she needs to make the complaint. It is just frustrating."

"That fire in your gut? That's the reason you do this job. You, my dear detective, are a warrior for the underdog and you can preach to me from your soapbox anytime."

"Yeah, well, we all need someone, don't we?"

"Always." He wondered if she realized she'd included herself in that comment. His admiration for this woman just reached a new level. She was a survivor. He depressed his turn indicator and headed toward the morgue.

CHAPTER 10

Kallie hated morgues. Hated them with a passion, but as far as morgues went, Hope City's wasn't the worst she'd ever seen. As a matter of fact, the building was new, and it appeared to be more of a business office than a morgue.

"Over this way." Brock led her to a reception area. "Hey Dori, how you been?"

A brunette gave Brock a long thirsty look—like he was a glass of water and she was dying from thirst. "Hey Brock. I'm fine." She leaned forward and gave Kallie a once over. "New partner? What happened to Jordan, and why haven't you called me? We should hang out."

"Jordan is being loaned to the Feds. This is Kallie Redman, my new partner. Kallie, this is Dori

Chamberlain. She went to school with my baby sister, Bekki. I've known Dori since she was in diapers."

The amusement in Brock's eyes when the woman nearly had an aneurysm was not funny. Okay, it was hilarious, but all the sexy eyes and want on the woman's face was placed quickly and firmly in the 'you're too young for me and this shit is never going to happen' category. He'd obviously had to set the woman straight on other occasions because he was damn good and succinct with the shoot down.

Dori finally jacked her jaw off the floor and huffed, "What do you need?"

"Dr. Carpenter?"

"She's in Autopsy Four. You can sign in and go through to the observation loft." Brock made quick work of signing in and grabbing a badge for each of them. They headed down a long corridor, but Kallie waited until they turned the corner before she started laughing. "Please tell me you've let her down gently in the past, because that was not nice."

"That girl." Brock groaned and pointed to the right. "She was out of control in school. I joined the Marines and came back, and she's grown up and more determined than ever. Seems she thinks we have chemistry."

"Do you? Have chemistry?" The woman was all smoldering beauty and tight clothes.

"Hell no. The only thing we have in common is my baby sister. I'm sure she thinks those faces and looks are sexy, but all I see is the dirty little tomboy who used to climb trees with Bekki. Through here." He pointed to the door to the right.

Kallie went through the door he held open and did a double take. *Well, damn.* "Nice."

"Yeah, and no smell." He moved down the small incline to the front row of a small theatre separated from the autopsy room by windows of glass and took a seat. The dead body on the slab was Treyson. From the looks of things, Dr. Carpenter was just about done. Her personal protective equipment was still in place, but the Y incision was sewn up, so she'd already finished the autopsy. Brock reached over and flipped the intercom. A gentle chime stopped Dr. Carpenter in her tracks. She looked up at the window above her. "Hello, Detective. I heard you caught this case."

"Hi Doc, yep. This is my new partner, Kallie Redman."

Kallie waved.

"Nice to meet you, Detective. What happened to Jordan? Did the feds finally pull their heads out of their asses?"

Brock laughed and nodded. "They did."

"Speaking from a strictly medical point of view, the position has to be uncomfortable. So, what questions can I answer? Pending histology, trace, and toxicology, of course."

"Of course. Let's start with the basics."

"All right. Male, thirty-seven-years old, identified as one Samuel Treyson by the next of kin. I conducted a forensic autopsy as required by state law due to unexplained, suspicious death. My examination revealed he died of exsanguination."

"That probably had something to do with the ear to ear throat slit." Brock chuckled when the doctor flipped him off.

"Smart ass. Based on the angle of the wounds, I would feel comfortable concluding the person was taller than Samuel or in a position behind the victim with the victim on his knees."

"From what I saw at the death scene, I agree, although I hadn't considered him kneeling." He glanced at Kallie. "We need to re-examine his clothing. I didn't look for anything on his slacks, but there was ash everywhere."

Dr. Carpenter continued, "I already sent his clothing to the lab. Here is something you probably didn't know. In addition to what appeared to be ash covering his skin, over the mouth, cheek and chin area we found something that *almost* resembled adipocere."

Kallie leaned forward. "Isn't that when the fat of the body turns into soap due to wet environments?"

"Oh, Detective, you need to keep this woman. She's sharp. Yes, Detective, it is, but as this victim was transported within hours of his death and was not exposed to the elements, the appearance of this material makes no sense. Upon further examination, there was irritation, almost like a burn, which would explain the resemblance of the spot to adipocere. I took samples and sent them to the lab for analysis along with his clothes for examination for trace evidence."

"Did he inhale anything?" Kallie stood to look over the table.

"Ah, that is the most frustrating part of this job. Visually, I couldn't see anything, but we won't know for sure until we get the reports back."

Brock stood up. "Doc, this case needs to be jumped to the front of the line."

"Indeed. I've been called no less than seven times, each person stressing the importance of prompt resolution. The only person I haven't heard from is your father."

"He won't call."

"And that is why he is the best man for the job. Now if you'll excuse me, detectives, I need to finish up and start my report."

"Do you have any idea when we can expect the lab results?"

They could hear a long exhale of breath even though they couldn't see the woman's mouth because of the PPE she wore. "Normally, I'd say six to eight weeks, to account for redundancy testing. We're jumping the backlog, so that will eliminate maybe three weeks. That leaves secondary confirmation, the written report and the QC process. Hell, you'll be lucky to see the tox and histology reports in three to four weeks. The trace? That's inhouse up at Briar Hill, so you'll have that answer within a day, maybe two depending on their mass spectrometer backlog."

"Thanks, Doc." Brock reached for the intercom, but the doctor's voice stopped him.

"Sorry I couldn't give you more. This guy had a long life ahead of him. It's a shame someone decided to take that from him. Get that son of a bitch, will you?"

"Yes, ma'am." Brock flipped the intercom switch, and they left the viewing area. As they entered the hall, he stopped to glance at his phone. "Perfect. We now have access to Treyson's schedule." He tapped the screen and smiled. "Look at that. Three meetings we didn't know about before.

Kallie nodded. Her mind swirled with a thousand details, but a few were like grains of sand. They stuck against something in her brain and irritated her. She'd learned to pay attention to those small things. Brock waved at Dori as they hustled to the car, and she waited until the engine started to turn to her partner. "Brock, in my mind there are things that don't add up."

Brock nodded. "Why did Treyson stop the laundry pick up at the apartments and start taking his clothes to the storefront?"

Kallie nodded. "That's one. Two is why was Treyson at that warehouse? Who was he meeting?"

"Three, where is that damn car or barring that, how did he get there?" Brock drove away from the parking slot.

"Four, who was he looking to add to the group? Could it have been Cynthia?"

Brock nodded. "It could explain why he was going to the storefront instead of using the home service, but we have nothing to back that up."

"Then we need to dig." She clicked her seatbelt into place.

"Let's mark off the taxi companies on the way to the office. We're looking for any fares to the warehouse district the night of the murder and reconfirm with the car service he used that he, in fact, didn't use them that night."

"On it." Kallie pulled up her search engine and started making phone calls. As much as she hated the why of her job, she lived for this. Tracking the bastards that killed. Her phone lit up as she searched. An unknown number. She accepted the call but didn't put it on speaker. "Hello." She wasn't going to answer with her name because Rich's threats, while on the back burner of her mind, were still an issue.

"Kallie. How have you been?" She recognized the voice, it was Lance, Rich's brother.

"What do you want?" She hadn't heard from the man since Rich went to jail. He'd been to the trial. He'd seen the shit show.

"I deserve the hostility. I'm sorry I haven't contacted you before this."

"It was kind of you to give Rich my number." She glanced at Brock who was pretending not to listen. She sighed loudly and hit the icon to put the call on speaker phone.

"I fell for his line of bullshit. Never again. He's obsessed with finding you, Kallie. He's called me at least fifty times in the last two days. I finally blocked him, but you needed to be warned. He isn't the man I used to know." Lance cleared his throat, the words catching as he spoke.

"I've done everything I can. I changed my name. Moved. I'll be ready for him if he finds me." She glanced over at Brock again. The man's hands gripped the steering wheel tightly and his jaw was clenched tight. Yeah, she wanted to strangle something, too. *Damn, would Rich ever stop haunting her?*

"He won't get a thing from me, but look, in full disclosure, I'm all the family he has left."

"Okay... and?"

"And I live in Hope City. He may show up here."

"I'm not going to ask how you know I'm in Hope City. I wasn't aware the NSA had a satellite office here."

"I moved here about two years ago. I have my own business. Government pay sucks."

"Right. Okay. Thanks for the warning."

"Kallie, be careful. He's... not right."

The crazed texts on her phone flashed through her mind. God, Rich's brother was a certified genius, and he'd *just* realized that? "I'll watch my six. Thanks for the heads up."

"I guess this is goodbye, then."

"I would imagine it is."

"Have a good life, Kallie. You deserve it."

"Goodbye, Lance. The same to you."

She hung up the phone as Brock asked, "Is there something I need to know?"

The huff of air she expelled was supposed to be a laugh, but she missed the target by a mile. "Rich, my ex, has gone over the edge. His brother, who used to work for the NSA, is now living in Hope City. Lance is Rich's only living relative so the likelihood of him showing up here is good."

"How did Lance know you lived in Hope City? You changed your name?"

"Lance is an... uber hacker? He tried to explain it once, but he claims he hasn't found a system he can't access. If he wants to know something, he can find it. Anyway, he said that Rich had called fifty times in the last two days. And yes, my married name was Clarkson, my maiden name was Booth and I changed it to Redman."

"Why Redman?"

"It was on the advertisement I saw when I was completing the paperwork. I think it was a pest control ad."

"No shit?"

"No shit. Pest control. I needed to control Rich. It made sense at the time."

Brock chuckled. "Well damn, love that rationale. Okay, so Rich was pumping his brother for information on you?"

"Probably, I didn't ask, but that is a logical conclusion."

"Do we need to get a restraining order?"

"Nah. If he shows up, he's not going to be stalking me. He'll try to kill me. But I'm not a defenseless prostitute with a drug problem. I'll take him out or make him wish he were dead before he kills me."

"If there is an imminent threat, you need to let Davidson know."

"I can do that."

"What can I do for you?"

"This is good. Just... this."

"You got it." He glanced over and winked. "Now about those taxi companies?"

She chuckled and woke her phone. "On it."

God, he was the perfect partner. No drama. No posturing, he-man shit. Find the facts, decide a course of action, and move forward. She hit the hyperlinked number on the web page and put the phone to her ear. Yet another reason she was attracted to this man.

CHAPTER 11

His jaw was clenched so damn tight, his teeth were breaking. That bastard had better not show up in Hope City or he'd wish he was still in jail. He had a name now, Rich Clarkson, and Brock had connections—connections within Guardian which meant he had global reach. If he needed to do it, he'd use them to find this asshole. Kallie didn't need to worry about this son of a bitch, but he wasn't going to overstep and take away her control of the situation either. It killed him to be still, not to act. The fucker had already killed in cold blood.

He listened as Kallie ran through the taxis companies and then called the car service Treyson used. "That was a strike out. One had no fares to the area. The other one refuses to go to the warehouse areas due to an incident last year. One of their drivers was killed."

"Yeah, a strung-out kid killed the driver and injured the passenger. He was looking for money. Found a fuck-ton more than that. He shot one of the local gang lord's old lady. She had a flat tire and had hired a taxi to take her to meet her man. We arrested the kid. He was tried, convicted, and remanded. He didn't make it three weeks in the pen."

"What happened?"

He parked at the precinct and killed the engine. "Killed by one of Peña's crew. The man, Sanchez, who took the kid out, is Peña's enforcer behind bars. Sanchez is doing life, times seven."

"All because the punk was doped up and in search of money for drugs."

"Yeah. I don't know how my brother works the J-DET team. You stop one hemorrhage, and another starts."

"You know he'd say the same thing about what you do." Kallie shouldered the car door, opening it against the wind.

He followed her rushed hustle into the building. "Probably." They climbed the stairs and both diverted to the break room for coffee.

"I'll go talk to Davidson now and let him know about my dick-wad ex." She didn't wait for an answer, but turned on her heel, coffee in hand, and headed to the Lieutenant's office.

His phone vibrated in his coat as he crossed the bullpen. He grabbed it from his pocket and answered, "King."

"Found your McLaren... kinda." Brody's voice fought against the sound of the wind through the mic on his phone.

"Where are you?"

"West of town by the Cascade River. Your car was found totaled."

"How?"

"Probably when it launched from Skyline Ridge and hit the river. It lodged hard. Airbags deployed. The tow truck just brought it up. The interior is filled with sediment. If there was any evidence in that vehicle, it's buried deep, but I'm having it sent to the lab using a priority tag on it based on the case. If there is anything in it, it is going to be under about five hundred pounds of muck."

"Shit."

"A succinct summation."

He looked up and watched Kallie stride across the open area. "So, either the killer took the car for a joyride and dumped it, or someone stole it, didn't know how to handle all that horsepower, and it ended up in the river."

"Sounds about right. I've got my guys going over the bank up above, but with the recent snow, there isn't much chance of finding anything."

"Appreciate it."

"No problem, I'll add it to the number of favors you owe me."

"Without a doubt. See you Sunday." He disconnected the call and dropped into his chair.

"They found the McLaren?"

"Lodged in a riverbank, buried in sediment."

She sat down. "Damn. Okay, so traffic cameras?"

"It's a possibility. We can call tech and see if they have any cameras, but if I were a criminal, I wouldn't drive that flashy ass car through the city."

"Yeah, back roads. It never hurts to ask, though."

"Concur. Tech's number is on the directory.

Give them a call while I run down Treyson's appointments on Wednesday."

"Roger that." She grabbed the laminated piece of paper from the top of the desk and picked up the desk phone.

Brock sat straight, popping his back and stretching his arms. Whoever said a cop's life was full of action and adventure had no fucking concept of what they actually did. Hours upon hours of following threads to find dead ends. Days of tracking minute details only to realize the information was irrelevant or overcome by events. A detective's life was ninety-nine percent Blood Hound and one percent Rottweiler.

He glanced at his watch. Fuck, they'd worked through lunch and past dinner. "How far have you gotten?"

Kallie glanced up at him and blinked. "I've worked through the last meeting of the day. You?"

Brock opened his mouth to answer but snapped it shut when he looked up. One of the beat cops escorted a bicycle courier across the bullpen toward them.

"This dude said he can't release this shit to anyone but Detective Brock King."

Brock stood.

"You'll need to sign for it... after I see identification, please."

The man looked absolutely ridiculous with his helmet perched over his knit skull cap. How anyone rode a bike in this weather was beyond him. He reached for his creds and flipped them for the guy.

"Cool. Sign?" He handed Brock a tablet.

He scribbled his name and watched as the man produced envelope after envelope from his leather tote. The man turned and left with the patrolman right on his ass.

"What the fuck?" Brock opened one of the manila envelopes stacked neatly on Jordan's desk. Kallie moved over to look at the paper. Brock scanned the document. "These are the guys who Sebastian Treyson thinks hate him enough to come after his son."

The briefs were concise. The conflict between Sebastian and the person named. The date it happened, the consequences, which, going by the file in his hand, was financial ruin for the other party, and then... Transcribed voice messages and texts, each threatening to ruin Treyson.

"How many are there?"

Kallie did a quick count. "Twenty-seven."

Holy hell. Twenty-fucking-seven more suspects. This insanity had to stop. They needed to work the man's last twenty-four hours. These other distractions... fuck him... He raked his hand through his hair and drew a deep breath, thinking out loud more than directing. "Okay. We need to ask Davidson to release those extra bodies now. We can have them run these to ground and look for ties to Samuel—recency, proximity, opportunity. We'll absorb any that pan out, but if we start chasing this, we'll never get through what we already have." He glanced at his watch. "Let's talk to Davidson."

Kallie motioned to the document envelopes. "What do you want to do with this?"

"Bring them with us." They loaded up and made their way to Davidson's office.

"Damn it, I see you two more than I see my wife," Davidson snarked as they walked in.

"Yeah, well I won't tell her if you don't." Kallie returned fire without missing a beat.

The woman fit this precinct. A perfect fit.

"What is this?"

"Twenty-seven additional suspects."

Davidson cocked his head at them and narrowed his eyes. "The fuck did you just say?"

"Treyson's old man. These are the people he believes would be willing to cross lines to get back at him. We need someone to clear these or let us know they are a legit avenue to investigate."

"All right. Hansen and Bettis just cleared their last case. I'll give this to them. You'll need to bring them up to speed. Where are you at with the investigation?"

"We're working our way through his last day. The meetings..." He glanced at Kallie.

"I'm working that now. The first meeting in the morning was a meeting to review the forecast for the next fiscal year. It lasted three hours and Samuel was in good spirits. One meeting was at the offices of Burroughs & James, Attorneys at Law, in regard to some ritzy apartment building Treyson was purchasing. The last meeting of the day wasn't a meeting, exactly. Treyson had a standing date for dinner and drinks with some of his college buds. The attendees varied from month to month depending on who was available. I'm trying to piece together everyone who made an appearance on Wednesday. The gentleman I spoke to indicated he popped in late, and Treyson wasn't there."

Brock was hearing this for the first time, but that was only because he'd been buried going through emails. "What time was that?"

"7:45 p.m."

"What time did the get together start?"

"6:00 p.m."

"Which was before Treyson called Chloe."

"He called her at 6:30."

"Right, so sometime between his closing on the building and before or during his get together with friends, he calls Chloe to cancel and heads to the warehouse."

"Right." Kallie nodded.

"Where was this get together?" Brock crossed his arms over his chest and ignored his lieutenant as he spoke.

"The Waterfall. You're thinking of their surveillance system?"

"That, and if they are regulars, what with this being a standing arrangement, the staff will know who they are. It will speed up the discovery portion as to who was there." He nodded, working off her enthusiasm, even though it had already been a long-ass day.

"Are we going to need a warrant?"

"Not if we use the right words."

Kallie narrowed her eyes at him. "Words like... media attention?"

He nodded. "That's right."

"Damn, if Jordan wasn't coming back, I'd partner you two permanently." Davidson snarked before he pointed to the door. "Go, I'll give Hansen and Bettis an overview and get them started. Find me that killer."

Brock gave his lieutenant a two-finger salute and followed Kallie out of the office. At last, something to work.

The trip to the Waterfall, an exclusive bar and restaurant in Briar Hill took about an hour longer than it should have due to an overturned semi, construction and detours. Fucking progress was anything but progressive. He slammed the car door and shivered as the night wind cut through his clothes and attacked his skin. They hurried to the front door where they were promptly stopped.

"I'm sorry, but there is a dress code. Tie and jacket for the gentlemen, cocktail dresses or business attire for the ladies." A dour faced man blocked their way into the main area of the establishment.

Brock presented his badge. "This is my tie and coat."

"Here's my little black dress." Kallie flipped her creds open at almost the same time.

"With all due respect officers, could I please ask you to go around the back? I'll inform management you're waiting."

"Ah, no Jeeves, that doesn't work for me. Call your manager up here for me."

"Sir, I must insist."

Kallie swiveled and looked up at him. "Can I arrest him for obstruction? I haven't arrested anyone today."

"Obstruction?" The man's jowls wiggled.

"Yeah, of a murder investigation."

"Murder?" That one sent his jowls into flight.

"Or we can just tell the press that the management of the Waterfall refused to cooperate with police." Kallie was having fun.

Brock crossed his arms and added, "Sebastian Treyson will be extremely upset."

"Please, there is no need for any of that. I'll call my manager right away." The man opened the inner doors.

Three minutes later they were shown into a state-of-the-art surveillance room by a harried, middle-aged man with a pot belly. He seemed intent on keeping them away from his establishment and clientele and almost shoved them into the security room. A skinny man-child with a mop of brown hair and black plastic-framed glasses too large for his face stood to greet them. He pushed his glasses up and pointed to the monitor on the far left. "That is from Wednesday night. I queued up the recording starting at 6:00 p.m."

He flashed his badge and gave his full attention to the man at the console. "Detective King, this is Detective Redman. How did you know we were looking for that information?"

"I'm Cory Sullivan. I hear and see everything in this place. You're investigating a murder, although you didn't say whose. You told management you wanted to see the tapes for last Wednesday night."

Kallie chuckled. "You hear everything?"

"Hear *and* see. Some shit these rich people do... bleach couldn't wipe it from my brain." Cory chuckled and handed him a remote. "Hit play with this." He indicated the button. "Stop is here and the date and time stamps are in the lower right-hand corner. Do you need me to leave?"

"No, actually stay, if you would." Brock handed the remote to Kallie. "Have you been working here long?"

"My old man owns the place. I handle all the security feeds. Most of the time it's quiet. I study and get paid. Every now and then the bar starts hopping. The back rooms are...interesting."

"Back rooms?" Kallie paused the feed.

"Yep. The more affluent clientele pay for private rooms in the back. There have been some raunchy parties back there. Consensual, and usually with professional ladies who come in through the back, but yeah, the rich are just as fucked up as the rest of us."

"Is this feed going to show us the back rooms?"

"Nope. It would help if I knew who you were looking for." The kid pushed his glasses up his nose again.

"Samuel Treyson."

"Ah, that would be the Ivory Room." The kid sat down and started typing on a keyboard. "They meet once a month. Nothing wild there. Just a bunch of friends getting together and swapping war stories. Well, financial conquests would be more their style." He pointed to another screen. "There you go."

He stared at the kid. "Does your clientele know you monitor them?"

The young man shrugged. "We post the proper surveillance notifications. We aren't breaking any laws." Cory crossed his arms over his chest. "We don't record the sound, just the video. I have audio wired into this office so I can have people respond quickly if necessary."

Kallie pushed play on the feed. "You can fast forward if you want." The guy leaned over and pointed to the correct button. Kallie hit it and the men in the room scurried around like ants. She hit play again as soon as Samuel Treyson walked into the room. "Sucks that he got himself killed. That guy was a class act." Cory watched the video with them. It seemed as if Treyson was well liked.

"Freeze that for a minute, would you? Who are the rest of the men in the room?" Brock motioned to the screen.

"Well, that is Richard Emerson, that guy with the grey scarf, he's Skip Chastain. I think the one there is Pierce Willington, but it might be his twin brother Preston. I don't know who that man is… wait, that one over there that's Clive Hollingsworth." Kallie started the feed again and the man continued to list off names as men entered and exited the room.

"Wait." Brock snapped his fingers and pointed to Treyson. He had his phone to his ear and had moved to a corner away from the long table in the middle of the room and the men who were laughing and drinking. Samuel glanced at his watch and then over at the people he was with. A frown stretched across his face and he shook his head.

"He does not look happy. Oh, there. He made another call. Time stamp on the calls?"

"6:24 p.m. and 6:27 p.m." Kallie glanced down at her book

He pointed to the monitor. "Can I get a copy of this?"

"Sure, hang on. I can send it to your email or float it to your cloud if you can give me the correct address to route it."

Like he'd know that? "Ah... I'd prefer a thumb drive."

"Damn, old school, okay. Hold on." Cory opened several drawers before he found a small silver tube. "Eureka."

"Walks like a duck and talks like a duck...." Kallie bumped into him and let her body linger against his as she looked up at him and mouthed, "Boomer".

He leaned into her, intending on giving her shit, but... damn. Wisps of her hair had loosened from that tight braid and softly fell across her cheek. The glow of the monitors illuminated her eyes. They stared at each other, and he knew she was right there with him. The chemistry between them was off the charts. Fuck him, she looked edible, and he was suddenly starving. Ravenous.

Brock tore his eyes away when Cory removed the flash drive from the computer with a flourish. "Here you go. From 6:00 p.m. until the waiter turned off the light at 9:30." Cory handed him the drive.

He reached to his inside coat pocket and produced a small evidence bag. He opened it and had Cory drop it in. It took the work of seconds to seal and initial the bag. He had Kallie initial as witness and gave Cory a receipt for the property. "You realize I don't need or want that back, right?"

"Don't stress it. We have to follow the rules. Keeps our ass away from the flame if you know what I mean." Kallie extended her hand. "Thank you."

"No worries, that I can understand. Have a good night."

Brock held the door open for her and followed her past the main dining area and back into the parking lot. He glanced at his watch as they slid into the Crown Vic. He shoved the key in the ignition and cranked the beast up, flipping the heater to high. He turned in his seat. "I think whoever killed Samuel called him at the restaurant."

Kallie thumbed through her notebook. The damn thing looked frayed already. "The timestamp was for 6:24 p.m. Yeah, here. I didn't write down the specifics about the call, but according to the information tech sent over, he received a phone call at 6:23 p.m. It lasted for just under a minute... and here is the outgoing call. The security camera and the phone times are off by a couple minutes."

"I remember looking at that call list. The call in was the last one he received. I did look at the specifics, but there were none noted, and I asked tech to trace that call."

"When will they have that information?"

"Should have it already. Give them a call, and I bet you dinner it comes back to a burner phone."

"Well since I was making dinner anyway, I'll

take your bet, but yeah. The odds are not in our favor." She punched in the numbers to tech and waited and waited. She removed the phone from her face and squinted at the time. "Well, no wonder they aren't answering."

"Late?"

"Almost 8:00 p.m."

"Damn, I'd love to have regular office hours."

"Would you really?" She hung up the phone and leaned back into the seat.

"Meh, for maybe a week out of the year. Sometimes it seems like all I do is work." His stomach rumbled loudly. "Did you say you were making dinner?"

She laughed and fastened her seatbelt. "Caught that did you? You should be a detective. Do you need to feed Fester?"

"Yeah. I'll drop you off and then come back?"

"That works." Kallie sat silently as they drove through the city. When he double parked in front of her apartment building, she grabbed the door handle but hesitated. Finally, she blurted, "Bring a change of clothes with you, Detective King, and give the cat double water and food. You won't be going home tonight."

She was out of the door and up the stairs before

he could pick his jaw up off the floorboard of the car or form a coherent response. A horn honked behind him forcing him to move. A slow, smug smile spread across his face. No bullshit, no games. And he thought he was attracted to her *before* that invitation, or was it a command performance? Whatever, he'd follow any orders that woman gave him.

CHAPTER 12

Kallie bounded up the stairs and laughed as she hit the landing on her floor. She felt like a teenager going on her first date. Only she had much bigger plans than just hoping for a kiss. The attraction she felt for Brock was dangerously strong. Dangerous because she could imagine falling for this guy, and that was something she'd avoided while she was with Guardian.

The door was open a heartbeat later. It took thirty seconds to set the oven temp and slide the casserole she'd left defrosting in the refrigerator this morning into the oven. She then all but levitated down the hall.

She turned down the duvet on her bed as she passed through the bedroom on the way to the bathroom. Showered, hair down and brushed, and staring at the dresser drawer, she shook her head at her lingerie selection. Anemic at best, but she hadn't been expecting to find someone like Brock.

Settling on a jade green thong and bra, she slid into them and then her favorite pair of yoga pants and chunky sweater because they gave her confidence. Not the lingerie, the clothes. They hugged her curves in all the right places, and she needed to feel a little sexy because tonight was a milestone, and she really fucking hoped it worked out. She left her hair down; she'd seen the way Brock regarded her last night when she'd let it down from the coil at the back of her head. Any advantage she could get, she'd take. She wanted Brock. She wanted Brock to want her, and just maybe, it would work for more than a roll in the sheets.

She stumbled; her mind and feet lost synchronization at the thought. This was more than sex for her, wasn't it? *Crap. Yeah.* Her stomach had butterflies flapping around in crazy flight patterns. Her skin prickled in anticipation of his arrival. She rubbed her arms as she headed into the kitchen.

Oh, fuzzy duck balls. Liking him presented a problem, then, didn't it? Well, at least for her. She opened a cupboard and took down a bottle of bourbon and two low-ball glasses. Sizzling chemistry aside, she really liked Brock and wanted to nurture that... friendship, but her invite for a romp between the sheets put them on the precarious lip of a slippery slope. Fuck, they needed to talk, didn't they? *Crap, crap, crap.* Why couldn't she just throw him into the bed, use him, and call it a day?

Because he wasn't that type of a guy, and she wasn't that kind of woman. Kallie dropped her arms to her sides and stared up at the ceiling. Shit. Did she just put him in the boyfriend zone? She did, didn't she. Holy crap. Next she'd be writing his name and making scrolly hearts all around it. *Two days. Two days! Seriously, woman, you need to shake yourself out of this romance novel you're writing in your brain and jump back into reality.* She'd invited Brock over for food and sex. Her flights of fancy, aside, those were the cold hard facts.

She nodded her head to punctuate her self-scolding and slammed open the silverware drawer. "You don't even know if he's interested in anything more than a roll in the hay." She collected the silverware as she grumbled. Her internal argument didn't abate while she put the place settings on the table, or while she did a quick inspection of the front room. It certainly didn't end when she padded back into her bathroom and ran a brush through her hair again, nor did it subside when she turned on the lamp beside her bed.

The knock at her apartment door, did however, shut down the argument. It also threw her into a quick panic. Straightening her shoulders, she drew a deep breath and headed to the front door. She could do this. She could.

Brock smiled when she opened the door and that simple act calmed her.

"I fed Fester enough for tonight and tomorrow. He has fresh water and litter, and I spent some quality time petting him before I came back." He hefted a small duffle bag. "As directed."

She opened the door and motioned him in. "Should I apologize for that? The directive?"

He sauntered in the door and stopped in front of her. "Regretting it already?"

"No. I have no regrets about asking you to spend the night." She shut the door and stepped toward him. "Do you?"

"Regret you asking me? Abso-fucking-lutely not. I was trying to plan a way to get to us to this point. But we can't let this—" he motioned between them, "— interfere with the case." He placed his duffle beside the table in the small entryway and slipped off his winter jacket, dropping it over the bag.

She walked past him as she said, "I'd like to believe we are both more professional than that, and I agree, the case comes first. As much as I don't want to say this, maybe we should talk before we jump off the cliff?" She poured a shot of bourbon into each glass and handed him one.

"Talk?" He ran his eyes up and down her and leaned on the counter. He lifted his glass in a silent salute and took a sip.

She dropped her eyes. Oh, hell. Words were going to be difficult because she really wanted to see what was hiding in that bulge of denim. "Ye–yeah." She cleared her throat and took a drink. "Ground rules."

"Like?"

"No inappropriate actions at work. Strictly business."

"We will need to let HR know we are seeing each other." He took another sip and set the glass on the counter.

"I have no problem doing that. Do you?"

He shook his head. "What else? You said rules, as in plural."

"This may be stupid, but I enjoy the way we work together, and I don't want to lose that, because of this." She used the hand that held her bourbon to motion between them. God, that sounded... so freaking emotional. She rolled her eyes. Damn it, heat roared to her cheeks. She spun and grabbed at a potholder, though she didn't need to pull the casserole for another thirty minutes.

She felt his warmth behind her. Big, tall, and hard, he stepped up behind her and placed his hands on her hips. He bent down and whispered, "You captivate me, Kallie. I know you've had a hard time in the past. I'm not him. I'm never going to hurt you like that. We have chemistry, both sexual and personal. I'm on board with us working on both of those levels."

She turned around. His arms encircled her. She shifted her gaze up and saw the honesty in his eyes. "I'd like that. Both levels."

Her breath caught in her throat when he lowered to kiss her. He hesitated millimeters from her lips. The needy sound that came from her was embarrassing and one hundred percent honest. When his lips swept hers, she shivered. One of his hands traveled up her back and cupped her head. He angled her and dropped his lips again, this time asking for, and being granted, access.

Her arms circled his neck out of necessity. Her bones turned into goo, and she would have slid to the floor without his strong arms around her. His tongue explored her and danced with hers. His strong arms supported her, and he bent her back and drew her into his body. Oh hell, feeling the hard ridge pressed into her abdomen drew another whimper from somewhere deep inside her. She pushed against his shaft and rotated her hips, drawing a growled response from him.

He kissed his way from her lips, to her ear. "Turn off the oven."

She blinked, bringing the ceiling into focus. His lips traveled down her neck, and she shivered when he nipped the junction of her shoulder. She dropped an arm from around his neck and patted to the left. She moved just enough to see what she was doing and hit the button to shut off the oven.

He glanced up at the range before he reached down with both hands, palmed her ass and lifted her up to him. She shrieked, wrapped her legs around him, and latched her arms back over his neck. "Put me down; I'm too heavy!"

"No, you're perfect against me. Bedroom?"

She nodded in the direction of the hall before she leaned into him closer and ran her tongue up his neck. He squeezed her and stopped in the middle of the hall. She shifted so she could see his face. "What's wrong?"

"Nothing. I'm trying not to come in my jeans like a horny teenager."

She laughed and leaned back in, swiping the same path as she had earlier.

His hand popped her on the ass. "Minx. So that's the way you want to play it, huh?" He strode into her bedroom, and they both tumbled onto her bed. It wasn't a gentle descent, more like a crash landing, but it got them on the bed, and that was perfect.

She pushed at the hem of his sweater. He tugged it up and whipped the bulky sweater off, taking the t-shirt under it also. He was magnificent. His thick pecs, bulging biceps and tight, flat stomach on full display, she allowed her fingers to reach up and play with the light dusting of hair on his chest. The muscles under his skin jumped under her touch. She trailed her fingers over long jagged scars and down farther to his belt. He leaned down and took her mouth, possessing her with a heat and need that matched her own. She flicked open the buckle and unbuttoned his jeans. She found his shaft under a layer of cotton and ran her palm down the length of it. He was thick and long, hot and ready for her.

"Clothes have got to go," he grumbled and pushed away from her to stand at the side of the bed. She watched as he toed off his boots and pushed his jeans and boxers down in one swoop. Lord, she'd never seen an Adonis belt as pronounced. The bulky winter clothes and coats he wore totally obliterated his exquisite body. "Now you."

He reached down and grabbed the waistband of her yoga pants.

She shook her head and rolled off the bed. "Lie down."

He stretched lazily on her queen-sized bed and dwarfed it with his size. His hand drifted down his stomach, following the ridges until he palmed his cock and stroked it slowly.

She leisurely worked her sweater off and removed it.

"Fuck, look at you." Brock's words of praise emboldened her.

She turned around and peeked at him over her shoulder. Smiling, she shimmied her yoga pants down to reveal the top of her thong. Brock growled, literally growled, when she slid them down over the swell of her ass.

She heard him move, standing up behind her as she bent over, pushing the clingy material down her thighs. His hands grabbed her hips, his hot cock pressing against the top of her ass. He lifted her, one arm tucking her close to him and the other traveling up her neck. He tilted her head and kissed her from behind. The kiss was messy, filled with passion, desire and need. The hand around her waist traveled north, and he caressed her breast through the green lace. She closed her legs tightly. The need that pooled there demanded friction. She rolled her hips into his cock.

"I want you like this," Brock husked as he broke the kiss.

"Then take me." She needed him. Needed release. Needed to be… desired.

He spun them and pushed her toward the bed, bending her so her forearms rested on the mattress. "Just like that." His hand trailed down her spine and gooseflesh rose in the wake of his touch. He knelt behind her and his hands ran over her ass and down her thighs before they retraced their path. This time, he carefully escorted the waistband of her thong over her ass and down her legs. She moved her leg when he tapped it. "Spread your legs out. She did and then gasped. He spun so his back was to the bed and pushed in between her legs, moving them to wedge his shoulders between her and the bed. His arms circled her legs, and he kissed the V of her leg.

Oh God, what he was going to do... Her legs trembled when his fingers split her folds. She jerked when his hot breath blew across her exposed skin, and she damn near jumped out of her skin when he put his mouth on her. The sensations confused and excited her. Her hips undulated against his face of their own accord. She dropped onto the mattress, her arms useless. Words fell from her lips, begging, pleading for more. His tongue assaulted her clit with a relentlessness that left her gasping, but then he added his fingers. She bucked against his face as he penetrated her. He curled them and added his thumb below her clit while his tongue continued its assault.

A wave of sensation tightened into a single point low inside her and then exploded. She gasped, probably screamed, and lost control of her legs. Brock grabbed her hips and dragged her down onto his lap. She lay against his chest, her head resting on his shoulder as he rested against the bed. She could feel his cock under her and groaned as it flexed against her sensitive skin. "I think you melted me."

"Did I?"

She nodded. "Yes, I'm going to allow you to do that again, and again, and again."

"Glad to hear it."

She pushed away from him and used her thumb to clean her release from his chin. "Time for you."

He smiled. "Oh, believe me that was for me as much as it was for you."

She ground down onto his cock. "And yet, I have evidence to the contrary."

"Well, Detective, what are you going to do with that piece of evidence?" Brock palmed her neck and drew her in for a kiss.

She could taste herself on him, and she was glad, glad that he tasted of her because that meant this was real, that she'd overcome her past, and she was moving forward. So many little victories culminated in that kiss. When they drew apart, she leaned away. "I think, Detective, I'm going to have to examine the evidence closely." She scooted back on her knees until she was over his thighs. His cock, red and hard, lay on his stomach. His balls were tight against his body, and she could tell he wasn't far from reaching his end. God, she loved that she could get him that excited.

"How close an examination do you plan?" His voice—damn, the deep baritone of his voice—had taken an elevator ride straight down to sexy as fuck, with a very noticeable orgasmic accent. The man radiated sex, and right now she wanted to give him a measure of what he'd given her.

She bent down, keeping her eyes fixed on his. "A very detailed examination. Evidence has a way of... making things hard... to understand." She dropped her eyes momentarily as she cupped his shaft with her palm and moved it away from his body. She lined his cock up and wrapped her tongue around the cap like a lollipop.

His hands grabbed her hair, fisting it. He didn't pull or demand, simply held her as she worked his cock like it had a chocolate center, and she wanted that sweet candy treat. She was good at this. Her ex always wanted her to go down on him. *No. He wasn't welcome here.* Kallie looked up. Brock was here with her. Once she'd slicked his cock, she opened her mouth and drew his hot shaft inside her mouth. He was big, deep throating wasn't going to be an option, not with her gag reflex, but she would make sure he felt good. Her hand circled his cock and stroked from the bottom of his shaft to her lips. She sucked the head hard and then teased the slit with her tongue before she lollipopped his crown and started all over again. His low words of encouragement and praise fueled her hunger, and she devoured him.

His hands tightened in her hair. "Close. So close."

Good. She swallowed his crown and sucked hard, letting her hand fly up and down his cock. He tugged at her hair again.

"Kallie, fuck… yes." A guttural sound accompanied his orgasm.

She drank everything he gave her, and when he moved away, sensitive and sated, she focused on him and licked her lips. He looked as melted as she'd felt earlier. His hand cupped the back of her head and brought her to his lips. She settled on top of him, and the kiss they shared was nothing like the previous ones. It was slow, sensual and sated. A kiss between two people who felt right in each other's arms.

His hand slowly caressed her back. As the kiss slowly ended, she sagged onto his chest and closed her eyes. He was using the bed as a backrest. He kissed her hair and continued with that slow circular motion of his hand. "Thank you." His words rumbled under her ear.

"Right back at you, Detective." His stomach rumbled beneath her and she smiled against his skin. "Dinner was sidetracked."

"I enjoyed the detour."

"So did I." She ran her fingers through the hair on his chest, debating on whether or not she should delve into the specifics of what the detour meant for them. Probably not. Men had different wiring than women. If she brought up a possibility of seeing where this went with them, Brock could freak. She didn't want that. She'd keep her questions and concerns to herself. They'd already set the ground rules. Professional at work and outside of work? Friends-with-benefits. A casual relationship. She could do that.

His stomach rumbled again, long and low. She laughed and sat up. "I'm going to go get dinner going again. Meet me in the kitchen?"

"Deal." She liked the way his eyes lingered on her as she pulled on her yoga pants and sweater. It had been a long time since she'd wanted a man to look at her that way. A lifetime ago. She leaned over and kissed him before she made her way to the kitchen. It was time to let go of the past, of Rich, the deceit, the lies and the disappointment. Brock might not be 'the one' but she wasn't going to let the past disrupt her future any longer.

Brock watched Kallie as she swayed seductively from the bedroom. He drew his hand through his hair and scrubbed his face. His new partner was fucking amazing. The attraction between them was off the charts, at least on his end. He could see himself with her long-term. She understood what being a cop meant, knew the dangers, the mind fuck of a death scene, and the anguish of not being able to find closure for some of the victims.

He got up off the carpet and padded into her bathroom to clean up. He snatched up his jeans on the way. The smell of something wonderful drew him down the hall. Kallie was ladling huge bowls full of stew. There was bread and butter on the table. "Sit down. The stew was warmed through by the residual heat in the oven. I heated up the bread in the microwave."

"God, it smells fantastic." He slid a chair away

from the table and waited for her to come over. "You sit, I'll grab the other bowl."

She did a double take at him before a shy smile spread across her face. She placed the bowl in front of his seat before she sat down. "That's yours. Larger portion."

Well shit, wasn't that interesting. His little detective wasn't used to common kindnesses. What kind of bastard had her ex been? He waited until she sat and helped scoot her chair in. He grabbed her bowl from the counter and placed it in front of her. He'd watched his father treat his mother like a queen his entire life. Hell, Colm McBride was the exact same way with Sean's mom. They treated their wives like precious gifts.

He sat down and glanced at the blush that spread over Kallie's cheeks. She was fascinating. A ball-breaker, tough-as-nails homicide detective with a laser sharp mind. When she laughed it was with her entire body, her amusement complete and compelling. She wasn't beautiful in the classic sense, but she was striking and to him, mesmerizing.

"So…" Her face blushed darker as she stirred her stew.

"Regrets?" He leaned back in the kitchen chair,

the cold, painted wood against his spine a sharp reminder that he'd come to the table half dressed.

Her head popped up. "What? No. You?"

"None." A smile spread across his face. "You were saying?"

"Right... yeah, good. That's good. No, what I was going to say is, I don't really have the right to ask you, but while we're decoding what is going on between us, could we just keep it between us?" She slathered a piece of bread with butter, studiously avoiding his gaze.

Okay, there were a couple ways to take that comment. "Just between us as in, tell no one that we've been together, or just between us, as in we only see each other?"

Her eyes jerked up. "Would you be embarrassed to tell people that we've..." She motioned between them with her knife.

"No, but I'm a stickler for details. Goes with the job description. Tell me what you meant, Kallie. I'm not going to jump up and run for the door." He had a feeling that was what she anticipated. This uncertainty had to be the work of her bastard ex.

"I'd like to be exclusive," she whispered to her plate. She put her bread down and squared her shoulders. She met his eyes and with a stronger voice, she continued, "Tonight when I invited you up here... I thought I could do casual sex. Hell, even lying on top of you ten minutes ago, I told myself I could, that asking you to be exclusive now would make you run for the hills, and I get that this is way fast. But see, I've experienced the disaster of a year-long adulterous relationship, one which was dissected in detail in a courtroom full of my peers. When you live through something like that, sliding into casual relationships becomes difficult. I'm sorry if that is too much for you, and I get it if you want to leave–"

He reached over and placed his hand over hers, stopping her rambling. "We'll get a handle on what is between us, and while we are doing that, it will be just you and me."

Tension left her shoulders, and one of those shy smiles spread across her face. "That works for me."

He leaned back in his chair and pointed to her bread with half a pound of butter mounded on top of it. "Are you going to eat it like that, or are you willing to share some of that butter."

Laughter filled the small kitchen and the awkward silence disappeared. They ate and talked about nothing and everything until he started doing the dishes. She picked up a towel and bumped him with her hip. "Thanks for not freaking out on me earlier."

He rinsed the soap suds off one of their bowls and handed it to her to dry, gauging his response carefully before he spoke. "How bad was it?"

Kallie's fluid movements stuttered at his question. She drew a deep breath and wiped the bowl carefully.

"You know, looking back, I could see signs about him. He was abusive, mentally more than physically, and there were nights when he said he was at work that didn't compute, you know? No open case, but he claimed he was stuck with surveillance. I didn't want to see it. I looked the other way. I hoped the man I married would suddenly reappear." She took another bowl as he finished rinsing it. "Not all marriages will last. I get that, but marriage counseling is off the table when you hear from several people how hard your husband could make his girlfriend and several others scream during sex." She gave a rueful laugh. "The thing is, I rarely orgasmed when we had sex, and usually those times I did climax was because I stimulated myself while he was going through the motions. And you know what? I was okay with that. I was okay with my life. I was willing to bob along on the water and move with the tide. How pathetic is that?"

He turned off the water and used the towel in her hands to dry his. "It isn't pathetic. It is hindsight. Our vision is always perfect looking back. The future is uncertain, and I think it is human nature to want to cling to the status quo."

"Better the evil you know than the one you don't."

"Exactly."

"I really loved Houston. I mean, minus the traffic, it is a great city. I would have liked to have stayed."

"Why didn't you?"

"His attorney branded me as a liar and alleged I was having an affair with one of my superiors. He theorized I lied about what I saw because I wanted to send my husband away so I could continue my illicit affair. Rich had friends, and that rumor spread like a California wildfire. It took on a life of its own and morphed into me setting up and framing my husband for murder. Made him the wronged party. After his conviction, I thought things would return to semi-normal. I was so wrong. I rolled up on an armed robbery in progress, called in for back up and the response was tanked, on purpose. I sustained a GSW to the arm, and almost died. I figured it was time for a change."

Motherfucking sons of bitches. He wrapped her in his arms and dropped his chin on the top of her head. "People suck."

She huffed a rueful laugh. "Yeah, they do. But then I accepted a job with Guardian. That was like a breath of fresh air. Guardian is all about integrity, but I missed doing the job, you know?"

"I do. Even though we see the bowels of humanity, what we do... matters."

"Exactly." She leaned away from him and cocked her head. "But I don't want to talk about my ex or my baggage." Mischief danced in her eyes.

"No? What do you want to talk about?"

"How about I show you instead?" She pressed her palm into his semi and the sensation moved more blood into his cock, forging a steel bar under her hand.

He cupped her neck in his hand and brought her closer for a kiss as her hands undid his jeans. She was pushing the denim down his hips when his brain engaged and decided she had far too many clothes on. While he stepped out of his jeans, he was pulling off her sweater. Damn, she still had that green bra on. Sexy. As. Fuck. With a flick of his fingers that green material loosened, and she shrugged it off. Fuck. Just as he pictured her. So damn sexy. He swooped in for another kiss as he pushed down her pants. Sex this time was going to be hot, fast and from the way things were progressing, up against the kitchen counter.

Her skin was so damn warm under his hands. The softness over firm muscles was an instant turn on. Kallie kept herself fit, but her softness hidden by clothes and a cop's hard veneer was all his right now. Didn't that make him feel like he'd won the lottery. She was just as excited as he was. Her hands grabbed his biceps and those fingernails bit into his arms. Fuck, that little slice of pain brought his lust to a laser-like focus. He consumed her lips. Any thought of slow, sensuous sex flew out the window when she broke the kiss and spun around, leaning down onto the counter and wiggling that gorgeous, ripe ass at him. She looked over her shoulder and said, her voice low and heated, "I want to feel you in me."

Fuck. Yes. Literally. He drew his hand down her spine, moving her long brown hair to expose her skin. "Stay right here. I need to grab some protection."

"Hurry."

Fuck yes, he'd hurry. It took five steps to get to his duffle that he'd dropped in the hallway. Five steps back and he had the package of the condom open. He sheathed his cock and dropped over her back, kissing her shoulder, needing a minute to calm down. He didn't want to come the second he entered her. She wiggled her ass and ground into him. He groaned against her skin, "You are going to make me come."

"That's the idea." She laughed and wiggled her hips again.

"Minx." He found her center. The slide in was excruciatingly wonderful. Tight, slick heat gripped his cock. He braced his hands on her hips, stilling them both.

"Oh, God. So damn big. So good." Kallie's words were exhaled in the sudden silence.

Yep, she was going to kill him. Death by orgasm. It was a thing. Had to be. He closed his eyes tightly and slowly moved away only to thrust back in until he couldn't go any farther.

"Yes, fuck… harder, Brock. Please."

Harder? God, yes, he could do harder. He

leaned over her, drawing his hands up her back. He kissed her neck before he wrapped his arms under her, crossing his arms and grasping her shoulders. Fuck, they fit perfectly. He withdrew and used his grip on her to brace her as he slid home again. He set a fierce, almost brutal pace, but fuck him, the whispered words of encouragement from her kept him going when he would have slowed.

She bowed under him and pushed back to meet each thrust. Sweat dripped from his brow onto her back. He lost his grip on her sweat soaked skin and leaned away from her back. He regripped her hips and leveraged forward.

"Yes! God, yes!" Kallie shouted, and her body spasmed around him. She pushed against the counter as he thrust again.

White hot lightning bolts of one hundred percent pure octane pleasure pumped through him. White spots exploded behind his eyelids and morphed into red when he came. He ground his teeth together, but the feral sound he made couldn't be stopped.

Breathe. Fuck. Air in. Air out. The concept was simple. He braced his arms on the counter next to Kallie, for her comfort and his safety. At the current moment there was a real debate as to whether or not he had legs. He'd face plant if he had to move.

"Holy shit." Kallie panted, dropping her forehead on his hand. "Detective King, you are under arrest."

He chuckled, kinda. "For what?"

"Murdering my idea of what constitutes good sex because that... that was ah-mazing."

She moved, and he managed to stand without getting dizzy. Good. His blood supply must have rearranged a bit. He slipped from her, but held her with her back to his chest, wrapping his arms around her. "Just wait until I actually get you into bed, Detective Redman. Your charges may increase."

She turned in his arms. Her sex-tossed hair fell wild around her face and tumbled in waves over her shoulders, dropping over her breasts. Her rose colored nipples peeked through the drape of thick locks. Her face was flush and her lips full and dark red. She glanced up at him with her big brown eyes, and the emotion he saw there wasn't humor. He saw vulnerability. Wrapping his arms around her, he drew her closer, his protective instincts roaring like a lion announcing his claim on his territory.

She reached up and caressed his cheek. "I just had the best sex of my life." Wonder filled her voice.

He could have easily turned the moment into a joke, played the comment off, but her honesty deserved the same from him. He cupped her neck with his hand and brushed his finger over her cheek. "I agree. The sex was amazing, but what made it special for me, was that it was with you." He leaned down and kissed her. A soft gentle sweep of his lips against hers. A thank you.

"You better watch it, Detective King, or I'm going to end up liking you. A lot." She smiled up at him, leaned into his chest, and shivered.

He reached down and scooped her up. She squealed and then threw her head back and laughed, a full body, completely happy, laugh that filled the apartment. As he took them back to her bedroom, he decided that sound should be bottled. It would stop any bitter argument and could quite possibly heal the wounds of the world.

CHAPTER 13

Brock slapped at his alarm.

"Ouch, damn it. Chill the fuck out, I got it."

His eyes popped open. His hand fell off Kallie's back as she rolled and silenced his phone. "Shit. Sorry." He sat up and squinted at Kallie and then around the room. He'd slept so damn hard he'd forgotten where he was.

"You shower first, I'll get breakfast." Kallie made a move to get up.

He snaked an arm around her and tugged her back into him. "Or we could both take a shower and then grab a bite on the way to work."

She wrapped her arms around him, and he pushed her hair away from her face. "That would be an amazing idea, but my shower is barely big enough for one. Two people in that space and we would flood the apartment downstairs."

Brock frowned and dropped his head to her shoulder. He flicked his tongue across her skin and smiled at the shiver that ran through her. "Or... an alternate possibility. We take a moment for ourselves, then shower." He hoped she'd agree.

"Drive through food?" Her nose scrunched. "I have a confession. I abhor fast food."

He laughed and dropped his head to his hand, propped up on his elbow. "What? Are you telling me you're a food snob?"

"Guilty. I'm a foodie from way back." She shrugged and ran her hand up his chest nearly freezing any chance of cognizant thought.

He rolled over on top of her. "Or we could go to Casey's Diner. He does a damn good breakfast. We can stop by the office, grab the trace reports, and go over them while we eat."

"I like *that* plan."

She wrapped her arms around his neck, and he slipped between her legs. The kiss they shared was slow, searching, and hot as fuck. He rolled them and reached to the correct nightstand to find the strip of condoms that had migrated into the bedroom when they'd relocated. Shifting her so she was on top of him, he reached up and tangled his hands in her hair. "Ride me."

She pushed up on his chest and smiled down at him. "Lazy first thing in the morning, are we, Detective King?"

"No, but when I'm working through all the shit the day is going to throw at us, I want to have the vision of you on my cock." He handed her the foil packet.

She took the condom from him and opened it, sliding back so she could suit him up. She stroked his cock several times, taking him from 'hell yeah, I'm interested' to 'completely invested' in zero point two seconds.

Her teeth raked her bottom lip as she slid onto him. She took her time sheathing his cock in glorious tight heat. He lifted his hands and held her breasts as she moved up and down. Her hips started a back and forth motion when she brought their bodies together. He rolled her nipples between his fingers each time she did it, and fuck him, if she didn't put her hands over his and without words asked him to roll those tight nubs a little harder. Not with words, but with touch. He squeezed a bit, and she moaned, throwing back her head. Oh, fuck, she picked up the pace. His cock pushed into her again and again. The sensation building in his balls sent an urgent signal to his lust-filled mind. Her movements became erratic, less coordinated, and more needy. He stopped her on a downward effort. "There, stop there."

Her eyes popped open, confused. He rocked his hips and thrust into her at a rapid pace. She fell forward. The change of angle lit up the nerve endings of his shaft. He squeezed tight and drove home. Her fingernails dug into his shoulders, and he opened his eyes. The sight above him was one he prayed he'd never forget. Her body dancing and swaying over him, her eyes closed, her mouth open, a blush falling over her face and chest. Her hair fell over her shoulders, brushing his chest as his body filled her. Her eyes opened, and she stared down at him. His breath caught in his throat. She was absolutely beautiful. This woman was vital to his future, he just wasn't sure how what lay ahead for them would play out. She gasped and her eyes rounded seconds before her body convulsed. The gripping heat took him over the edge, too. She dropped down on top of him, and he wrapped her in his arms.

The six flights up to the office weren't as steep as they usually were. That could be due to the fact he'd actually slept, or the woman striding up the steps with him. Okay, it definitely was Kallie.

On the stairwell landing, she touched his shoulder. "I'm dropping into HR. You get us both coffee and I'll be up as soon as I'm done doing the paperwork."

"You got it." He winked at her and continued up the stairs when she opened the fourth-floor fire door and headed to HR to complete the paperwork required when officers were in a relationship. Of course, the office rumor mill would spin out of control for a day or so until the next bit of gossip flitted through the offices. You'd think with as much crime as they were working, cops would have more to do than gossip like a yard full of old clucking chickens, but… no. Brock left the stairway at the sixth floor and headed straight for the break room. He waited in line and watched as the last cup was poured and the next pot was made. He nabbed his tankard, his spare for Kallie, and doctored his java while he waited for the brew to finish. Finally, he emptied half the pot into his cup and half into Kallie's and prepped a new pot before he capped them and headed to his desk.

He'd just accessed the police department's intranet to check on the forensic trace report as Kallie worked her way across the bull pen, and he didn't hide the way he watched her. There was a bit of territorial claim staking on his part, although no one knew… yet.

"Done?" He slid her tankard toward her.

"Yep. Clara says, 'hi.'" She arched her eyebrow at him and took a sip of her coffee.

"One date. Nothing happened," he whispered, so only she could hear.

"But she wanted it to, didn't she?" her words were just as low as his.

"No clue. But there was no chemistry on my side." Would he have fucked her if the opportunity arose? Yeah, but he didn't invest time in people who were fake, and that woman was as fake as a three-dollar bill.

She smiled behind her thermal mug. "Good. Is our trace report in the system?"

"Yeah."

"Cool. Print it out, and we'll go over it at Casey's. I could eat a horse, I'm so hungry." He watched as she pulled out her cell and scanned the face of the device. She pocketed it again.

"The ex?"

She grunted an acknowledgment. "Going to do something about that?"

"Doing what I can."

He clicked his mouse several times, sending the report to the printer. "Do they do that a lot in Houston?"

Her head popped up and she frowned. "Do what?"

"Eat horses? Here in Hope City, we prefer other sources of protein." He dodged a playful slug launched in his direction.

"Don't be a dick." She grabbed her coffee cup and stood waiting for him.

He leaned over pretending to pick up a pen, whispering, "I thought you liked my dick."

She narrowed her eyes at him. "Boundaries, Detective King. Not. At. Work."

He crossed his arms and stared at her before retorting, "Okay, Clara."

She cocked her head and then sighed. "Point taken. We'll both need to get better at that."

"Indeed."

They swung by the communal printer and

made sure they took only their report before they made the quick trip to the diner, which was packed. He scanned the tables and stopped when Lieutenant Davidson waved them over to the booth he occupied. He nodded to the paperwork in Kallie's hands. "Trace?"

"Yep. We brought it with us."

A waiter flew by and Brock ordered for both of them as Kallie started to read the report. "God, you'd think all the mumbo jumbo could be simplified," she muttered before she took a drink of her coffee.

"That would make too much sense," Davidson said between bites of his breakfast omelet.

"Huh." Kallie's forehead scrunched. "Looks like Dr. Carpenter is on to something. There were trace amounts of dirt and cement along the front of Samuel's slacks. Slight wear at the knees, consistent with the minor abrasions to one of his knees. Small scratches to the top of his shoes in the toe area."

"She thinks he could have been put to his knees before he died? Execution style? Fuck."

"One possibility. He could have gone to his knees when he was killed, too. If the murderer didn't hold him up, or couldn't because of his size and weight, he'd pitch forward. Then the guy moves away and Samuel falls back to the wall. That scenario would fit, too," Brock said as he thought.

"Okay. What else does it say?" Two breakfast specials dropped in front of them with the hallmark efficiency of the diner, and Brock started to eat while Kallie continued to read.

She turned the page. "That stuff on his face? The stuff the doc said mimicked the look of adipocere? It was identified as a chemical... um... perchloroethylene."

"What the fuck is that?"

"Don't know. We'll have to do research." Kallie reached for a piece of her toast and continued to read the report.

"Call the forensic investigator. They will be able to tell you." Davidson leaned back in the booth and took a sip of his coffee.

"The forensic what?" Kallie's head snapped up, and she swung her eyes from him to Davidson.

"Forensic investigator. We have six assigned to the coroner's office. Mainly they are for the high-profile, unexplained deaths not classified as suspicious. They've been brought in on the drug front due to the workload. They work in conjunction with our office and are great with the technical jargon. Most have advanced degrees and hundreds of hours at death scenes. Who responded to your scene?"

"Didn't get one, or at least we cleared the scene before one showed up." Brock shoveled his scrambled eggs onto a fork.

"With the Mexican and Dominican gangs waging a turf war, I imagine they were all out. I think I read on the hot sheets there were seven murders the night you got the call on the Treyson case." Davidson freed his wallet from his suit jacket, produced a twenty, and laid it beside his plate. "Google that shit. It will get you started. I'll go put in an official request for a forensics investigator to go through the case since no one appears to have been assigned."

"Will do."

"You got anything solid yet?"

Brock shook his head. "We're still plodding through what we have, trying to sort through the noise to reach the facts."

Davidson squared up and leveled his steel grey eyes at him. "Your old man talked to me last night. Asked if we needed additional resources. I told him no."

Kallie slid her plate in front of her. "As long as you have Hansen and Bettis going through the elder Treyson's list of disgruntled associates, we can handle this."

"That's what I thought. Call me if you need anything." He slid from the booth and dragged his wool coat with him. Brock watch him leave. The man was built like a linebacker and was respected by damn near everyone in the precinct. He was fair and above board. He'd walked more than a mile in detective shoes. He knew the frustrations, the need for high cover, and when to pull a case because there were no more leads to follow.

He finished his toast in two bites and wiped his hands before he grabbed his phone from his pocket and slid the trace report toward him. He thumbed through the pages until he found the word he needed to type into the search engine. He keyed it in and took a long drink of his coffee, taking the top off, signaling the waiter he needed a refill.

The waiter shot by, filled his cup and waited for him to open Kallie's cup, filling that one, too. Brock added his cream and sugar as Kallie watched and shook her head. "You should be five hundred pounds."

"Nah, I work out. Sometimes at really weird hours, but I work out."

"Yeah, that's why I like Vito's gym. Open twenty-four/seven."

"Well, imagine seeing you here." Sean McBride slid into Davidson's empty seat.

"Dude, what brings you to The Desert?"

"Leg work, man. The cases never end." Sean turned his attention to Kallie. "Hi, I'm Sean McBride. I've had the unfortunate destiny of being this guy's best friend since birth, and you are?"

Brock apologized quickly, "Shit, sorry. Detective Kallie Redman, meet Detective Sean McBride, HCPD."

Kallie wiped her hand on her napkin and extended it across the table. "So, you've put up with this guy your entire life? How did you do it?"

"Man, pure intestinal fortitude, let me tell you."

"Hey, I'm right here, you know." Brock tried for mock outrage. It ended up as a laughing snort, which started Sean laughing. God, he missed spending time with his friend.

"He's a jerk and a dick at times, but I wouldn't have anyone else on my six when I need backup."

"Awww... love you too, you dork." Brock

dodged a wadded-up napkin that Sean pitched at him.

"You two work together or..."

Sean left the question open and fuck it, he barged through it. "Kallie is my partner on the Treyson case."

"Where's Jordan?"

"Fibbies called him up to work the Grappelli case."

"Damn, sorry to hear that. He was gone for almost what... three years before?"

"Yeah." Brock nodded.

"So, you'll be his partner for the foreseeable future?"

"No. My partner is coming back from an overseas assignment. We've only got this case together."

"The case notwithstanding, we have other things we are working on together." Brock stretched his arm over the back of the banquette. A casual move, but one his friend would understand.

Sean blinked at him and then swung his attention to Kallie before he leveled Brock with a stare. "Holy fuck, your mom is going to be over the moon."

Brock chuckled. "Yeah, I have dinner at the 'rents tomorrow. What about you? How's things?"

Sean sighed and rubbed his face. "Chasing my tail and trying to keep an insurance investigator from killing me or herself."

"Say what now?" Kallie stopped with a fork full of eggs to her mouth.

"Nothing. Suffice to say I'm happy for the two of you and wish you luck. Call me and we'll set up something." He slid from the booth.

"No time for breakfast?"

"Nah, I needed to get some information and then get back to my office. I ran into Lieutenant Davidson as he was entering the precinct. He told me you were here. Call me, shit-head, I mean it. Kallie, it was nice to meet you."

"Nice to meet you, too, and any advice you can give me dealing with this guy would be appreciated." She laughed at Brock's groan, and Sean clasped her extended hand.

"We'll talk. I have so many stories to tell you. He was crazy as a teenager."

"Don't you start, McBride. I have just as much on you."

"Yeah, but it isn't *my* woman asking for intel." He waggled his eyebrows a couple times, and Brock groaned, because, yeah, that was true.

"Whatever. Take care of yourself." Brock would never admit to the heat he felt in his cheeks.

Sean winked at him and headed out. "You, too. Both of you."

He watched Sean leave before he glanced down at Kallie. He decided to leave his arm where it was.

"He's nice. What precinct does he work for?"

"Special Investigations up at Briar Hill. He's an Arson Investigator."

"Arson, huh?"

"Yeah, he was already on scene when I arrived for Treyson's call out."

"Speaking of which—" she put her last forkful of eggs in her mouth before she nodded at the phone "—wazzit say about the chemical?"

Brock removed his arm from the back of the booth and recapped both of their tankards before he picked up his phone, waking it up. "It says the chemical compound is a metal degreaser... and it is used in making other chemicals." He scrolled up and jolted forward. "Holy fuck. Check this shit out. It is also a common solvent used by dry cleaners." They stared at each other. His mind ran through the implications. "Dawson killed Samuel for hitting on his woman."

"Son of a bitch." Kallie dropped two twenties

next to Davidson's and exited the booth before he could snatch their mugs. They had that motherfucker. He grabbed both mugs by their handles and palmed his phone to call Davidson.

"Sir, we are heading downtown. We have a suspect. Dawson Jenkins. Cynthia White's fiancée."

"Explain the sudden realization." Davidson got right down to business.

"We believe Treyson may have wanted to bring Cynthia into his polyamorous relationship."

"How did you reach that conclusion?"

"Treyson was picking up his own laundry even though there was a delivery service."

"I'm not following."

"She was doing the delivery service for a short time, and we believe that is where Treyson met her. Treyson's lovers confirmed he wanted to bring someone new into the relationship, but the person's partner was an issue." They jogged to the Crown Vic and Kallie grabbed the mugs so he could drive. He started the car, Kallie hit the laser strobes, and they tore from the parking lot heading to the dry cleaners.

"So, you're thinking Treyson hits on laundry girl and wants to bring her into the love fest and fiancé takes issue with the proposition and kills him?"

"Makes sense, and we have trace evidence that points to him. The chemical on Treyson's face is one used in dry cleaning solution."

Davidson grunted, "I'm sending a patrol as backup."

"We make first contact. Have them hold for us if they arrive first."

"Got it. Get that bastard." Davidson hung up, and he dropped his phone in his coat pocket.

"Dawson works in the back, around the chemicals." Kallie held onto the dash as he powered around a corner.

"Yeah." He slammed on the brakes and switched lanes. "We need to bring them both in and separate them. If she knows anything, she's not going to talk if he's around."

"We'll have the patrol bring Dawson in, and we'll take Cynthia," she agreed.

Brock double parked in front of the dry cleaners and motioned the patrol car that followed them to watch the rear. The car barreled off and hit the corner on two wheels. He opened his coat to give him access to his weapon and noticed that Kallie had done the same. The windows to the laundry were steamed from the heat inside. He doubted they'd been seen. When they entered there were only four people in the lobby. They herded the people outside with a flash of their badges and their hands on their weapons. Brock jumped the counter with a quick lunge and a palm to the top of the faux marble counter. He turned just in time to watch Kallie vault the obstacle the same way.

They made their way to where voices were raised in the back.

"What do you mean it isn't ready? The tag says it will be ready today."

"It would have been ready if Dawson was here. That's on you."

"You're fucking incompetent, Eric. Get that suit and get it into the queue. I'll process it. I'm going to lose money on this because you can't read and work simple tags."

"You're a money hungry bitch, Cynthia. There are more important things, you know."

"Yeah, name one." Cynthia's retort zinged back at the other man.

Brock motioned for Kallie to approach from the other direction. They split up and silently approached the back.

"What happened to Dawson? He should be here doing this, Cynthia, not me. I'm only supposed to be doing pick-ups until you can hire someone else, and I'm pissed enough about that."

"Whine later, will yah? Get your ass going with this suit. Besides, it's about time you earned some of that money your old man gives you. Fucking silver spoon in your mouth and all you can do is bitch. You can do the pick-ups after you get today's slips loaded. Dawson will be in tomorrow, and believe me if he knows what's good for him, he'll…" Cynthia turned and saw him. Her angry sneer fell immediately. "Detective? You're not supposed to be back here. Insurance and all that." The woman visibly jumped when she noticed Kallie coming from the other direction. "What's going on?"

"Cynthia, do you know where Dawson is?"

"Home? He called in sick this morning." Her attention swung from one to the other. "What's happening?"

"We need you to come down to the precinct." He stopped and nodded at the patrol officers who stood just inside the back door. He caught Kallie's eyes as he spoke. He was changing course in mid-stream, and he wanted to ensure his partner was with him. "The officers will give you a ride."

"I can't leave! I have a business to run."

That was a new wrinkle. "You own this business?"

"No, my uncle does, but I'm in charge of this store."

"So that move from pick-up driver to the front of the house was guaranteed, then?" Kallie kept her eyes on the other man.

"Hell, Cynthia works wherever she wants, whenever she wants. If she works more positions, she gets a better cut of the profits."

Brock turned to the man. "Who are you?"

"Eric White. My dad owns this shit hole and five others just like it. I'm only here because Dawson called out again."

"Does he do that often?"

"No more than any other fucking slug she hires." Eric drew his hands up on his hips.

Cynthia was a different person today, and he had a feeling the woman they'd first met wasn't as placid as they had thought. Granted, she was still getting around on that little scooter, her limbs still in plaster, but her attitude, that *had* changed. She was caustic, and her cousin wasn't much better.

He tipped his head. "That so?"

"Yeah." The guy looked pissed.

Brock didn't care. He gave a big fat, fake smile and some not so subtle directives. "Well, Eric, you need to call your old man down here. Cynthia is going to come with us."

Kallie motioned toward the back door. "That's right. Do you need a coat, Cynthia?" Brock caught the way Kallie ushered her toward the back without giving her any choice.

He moved toward Eric and caught his arm. "You will not call anyone to tell them we were here. Do you understand me?"

"Like I'd call that jerk?"

He narrowed his eyes. "Are you talking about Dawson?"

"No, I'm talking about the boogie man. Of course I'm talking about Dawson." Eric yanked his arm from Brock's grip and shoved his phone to his ear. "Yoh, old man. You got some serious shit going down at Cynthia's store. Yeah, the cops are pulling her in and looking for that loser she's hooked up with." The man headed to the front of the store at a rapid clip.

"Are you arresting me?"

Brock's head whipped around at Cynthia's

question. "We just need to get some answers and our information is down at the station. You've been so helpful so far. We do appreciate you taking time away from your business to answer our questions again. We just have to dot some I's and cross a few T's."

The woman pushed herself on her scooter, her casted ankle dangling off the back. "Well anything I can do, but I don't understand why I need to go down to your office."

"We need you to write an official statement. The same thing you told us, but official. No worries."

"Okay. Yeah, I can do that."

"Perfect. If you go with this officer, we'll meet you downtown." Kallie handed her over to a young officer who courteously assisted her into her coat that was on a peg by the back door. Brock motioned for the other officer.

When he got close enough, he whispered. "Don't know where she falls in this case. We'll sort that when we get to the precinct. You or your partner stay on that woman. She needs to be isolated and kept at the precinct. Do not let her leave."

"Roger that."

The older patrolman headed to the door, and he joined Kallie. "My bullshit meter is chiming." He sent her a quick look as they walked back to the front of the store where Eric was apologizing to a line of customers who had formed. They hopped the counter again and headed to the Crown Vic.

"What was the address on Dawson's apartment building?"

Kallie rifled through her notebook after fastening her seatbelt. "989 East Lancaster Avenue, Apartment 5C. Cynthia's apartment is 1A."

"She said she fell down the stairs at her apartment. Maybe he pushed her when she left his apartment?" Kallie's brow drew together. She was thinking out loud, but he wasn't buying that premise anymore.

He glanced at her. "Tell me I'm not the only one catching the Jekyll and Hyde routine that woman had going on."

Kallie nodded. "I keep falling back on the fact that abused women act differently around their abusers. But yeah, I'm getting an uneasy feeling. Like I missed something."

"*We* missed something. This isn't a single person investigation." He glanced over at her before he put the car into gear and headed to Lancaster Avenue. It was a fifteen-minute drive when traffic didn't suck. Unfortunately, the suckage was extreme on this particular morning.

"What the literal fuck? Why is there so much traffic?"

"What's today?" His brain did a mental rolodex of city activities.

"Saturday."

"Shit. The Mustangs. Damn it." He glanced over at her and laughed at her raised eyebrows. "They are the Division One college team in town. Damn it, today is the big rivalry game. Fuck, no wonder we have traffic. People are trying to avoid traffic around the college and stadium which dropped them into fringes of The Desert." He flipped his lights on and pushed his way across three lanes of traffic before cutting through East Central on his way to Lancaster. Once they were away from the main flow of traffic, he was able to make decent time. They drove up to the front of the building, and he jammed the nose of the Vic into a vacant area near a fire hydrant.

"We go in the same fashion. Get him to come

down voluntarily if we can, and discover what the actual fuck is going on." Brock took her hand. "Watch your six. I don't like the vibe I'm getting."

"I'll take care of my ass. You make sure you don't get yours shot off. I haven't had enough time to admire it." He did a double take in her direction, and she winked at him. They stood silently, staring at each other in the elevator. The door opened, breaking the connection. They strode down the hallway to Dawson's apartment. Brock knocked on the door. "Dawson Jenkins, Detectives King and Redman. We need to speak to you."

There was a muffled bump in the apartment and then a slow shuffle toward the door. From behind the door, Dawson spoke. "I'm not feeling well, Detective. Can we do this another time?"

"I'm afraid not. We need to talk. Now." Brock stared at Kallie as he spoke. It took several seconds, but the deadbolt turned, and the door cracked open. Kallie pushed the door open. What greeted them stopped them both in their tracks.

"What happened to you?" Contusions littered Dawson's face; his left eye swollen to the point he couldn't open his eye. His lip was split, and his arms were a dazzling display of black, blue and red.

"Nothing." The man turned slowly; his hands wrapped around his midsection. He took two steps before he swayed and leaned against the wall. "Look, I don't feel so hot, man. Can we please do this another time? I got nothing to say to anyone." Dawson coughed, his arms still held tight against his body, and swayed radically. Brock's eyes widened and he reacted the same time Kallie did, moving to help keep the man upright. This close he could hear the rattle of the man's breathing. "Call it in, get an ambulance rolling." He put his hand around Dawson and held his hip.

Dawson hissed, "No, I'll refuse treatment. I don't have insurance, man. I didn't do anything. I didn't. I swear. I didn't..." Dawson's weight fell against him. The man whispered the words over and over.

"Who did this to you? Tell me who beat the fuck out of you?" He helped the man to the tiny living room. It had been trashed. A baseball bat had been jammed through a small aquarium and broken glass covered the soaking wet area rug.

Dawson closed his eyes and shook his head. A tear dropped. "I didn't do anything."

"All right, I hear you."

Kallie came into the room and he nodded to

the bat, mouthing the word 'fingerprints'. She nodded and plucked a pair of latex gloves from her coat pocket. "The lock wasn't broken or pried that I could see. Crime scene techs are on their way."

He nodded and turned his attention back to the beaten-to-fuck man beside him. "Dawson, who did this to you? You let them in, didn't you?"

The man opened the one eye he could. He coughed again, and Brock waited until the man could breathe again before he asked, "You can tell me, man. I'll make sure this is handled the right way."

"I got nothing to say to anyone. Why are you here?" Dawson looked across the room, but he really didn't think the man was seeing anything.

"We want to talk to you about Samuel Treyson." The man looked at Brock and shook his head. "I'm so damn tired. Life's too fucking hard, man."

Kallie sat down on the small recliner across from the couch. "It just seems like it. You can't give up. It gets better."

"You believe that?" The hollow disbelief in the man's voice rang through his words.

She nodded. "I know it. Where you're at right now? I've been there. My story is an abusive ex-husband who killed someone. Thankfully, it wasn't me."

Dawson closed his eyes. "I can't help you."

"Can't or won't?" Brock watched the man swallow hard and shake his head. Not an answer, but not a denial either.

"I'd like to take you by County, let them check you over." He was worried about the way the man was breathing.

"I got no insurance. I've been beat worse. Ribs are broken. Nothing anyone can do about that."

"You could have a punctured lung."

"I ain't spitting blood. Besides, I couldn't be that lucky." Dawson pushed forward and stood on shaky legs. "I'll need my wallet."

The crime scene techs showed up before they left. Brock also called in a favor. Bettis, one of the detectives Davidson had assigned to go through the elder Treyson's grudge list, showed up to take over the crime scene. If the assault was connected to Samuel's murder, he wasn't going to allow sloppy handling of the scene to affect the outcome of the case. The trip downtown was slow and torturous, not only for Dawson, but also for Brock and, by the tightness of her expression, Kallie, too. Nothing was adding up. He'd broken his golden rule of assume nothing and verify everything. They'd assumed Dawson was the abuser in the relationship, but it could very well be that Cynthia was the aggressor. It was something they hadn't considered. Still, there were too many questions, and they needed to get to the bottom of it. Now.

The looks they got when they walked into the precinct with Dawson shuffling between them were expected, as was Davidson's sudden appearance outside the interview room. He waited quietly until they got Dawson settled and shut the door behind them.

"Why the fuck isn't he at a hospital right now?" Davidson was never one to beat around the bush.

"Refused all of our requests to take him for medical attention." Kallie crossed her arms over her chest and turned to look at him.

"How the fuck could Cynthia use a bat? She has a cast on her hand."

"I'm wondering now how those injuries she's sporting actually happened." Brock scratched his beard. "Sir, we need a warrant for her medical records. I'm not sure where she was seen, but if we can access the centralized medical information database, we can track that."

"What are we going to use for probable cause?

We got nothing but speculation." Davidson shoved his hands in pockets and rocked back on the heels of his highly glossed shoes.

"Let me see if I can get her to talk to me." Kallie glanced between the men. "I treat her like the victim, get anything she'll divulge; see if she slips up. Now that they are both potential suspects, I want her to give me her alibi. Dawson, too."

"We'll talk to Dawson after we talk to her. Sir, can we get one of the patrols with medical training to come up and look at him? I know it isn't standard procedure, but..."

"Good idea. I'll call the squad room and talk to the duty sergeant. Kallie goes in without you to interview the woman. If she can work the solidarity angle, maybe we can get more from her."

"I agree." Brock nodded his head at the observation room. "I'll be watching and taking notes. We'll have the tapes as backup, but don't worry about getting information down on paper, Kallie, I want you to be fully engaged in what this woman is saying."

"Got it. Do me a favor, sir, give me like ten to fifteen minutes and then bring in a file folder. I don't care what's in it. Put it down on the table and say, something like 'the information has been confirmed.'"

"You got it." Davidson spun on his heel and marched down the hallway.

"You've got a plan?" Brock stepped closer than necessary. He discreetly ran a finger down her shirt sleeve.

"She's got an aggressive, mean streak. We saw that earlier. I'm going to get her started on her original statement. I'd like to see if I can get her to contradict herself or give us more than she has. That file will give me leverage. Or at least she'll think I have leverage." Kallie winked at him. "It's been a while since I've played hardball, but I think I still got what it takes."

Brock chuckled. "Why does that turn me on?"

"Because you're dating a cop, and you think I'm sexy?"

He chuckled and stepped away before he did something stupid—like kiss her. "Oh, yeah, there is that. Go get 'em, tiger."

Kallie took a deep breath and leaned around him, looking down the hall. A patrolman with a medical kit trotted toward them. "Lieutenant Davidson said I needed to look over a witness?"

"Interview two. If you need me, I'll be in observation." Brock pointed to the observation room joined to Cynthia's interview room.

"Got it." The uniform knocked politely once, opened the door, and disappeared inside.

"Right, well, let's get this shit sorted." Kallie spun and grabbed the handle of the door. Brock winked at her and headed into observation.

Kallie opened the door and gave an exasperated sigh. "Cynthia, I am so damn sorry it took so long. You wouldn't believe the stuff that has been going on. But I'm here now. Do you need anything?" She sat down across from the woman. She had a bottle of water and her foot was propped up on her scooter, her ass planted in the solid metal chair bolted to the floor on the other side of the table.

Cynthia sneered. "This is borderline abusive."

"Abusive?" Kallie blinked and smiled. "Oh, no. Sitting in a nice warm interview room is not abuse. I think we both know what constitutes abuse." She watched Cynthia's eyes narrow. "But let's get to the business at hand." She retrieved her notebook and thumbed through it to the page where she'd talked to Cynthia and Dawson. "Now when we first spoke to you, you stated that you met Samuel Treyson when you..." She let the question trail off and looked at Cynthia expectantly.

"I met him when I did the pick-ups for a time."

"Was that before or after Dawson did the pick-ups?"

"Why does that matter?" Cynthia crossed her arms over her chest and stared at Kallie.

"Timeline. We need to make sure we can put people in place correctly. This is a very high-profile case, and of course, we need to ensure we are exact."

"I don't know, after, I guess."

"You guess or you know?"

"I know." Cynthia huffed in exaggerated irritation.

"How long did Dawson do pick-ups?"

"Why?"

Kallie tapped her notebook. "Timeline."

Cynthia shrugged and looked up and to the right. The mannerism indicating a lie didn't go unnoticed. Whatever came from Cynthia's mouth next would need to be double and triple checked.

"He mainly works in the back."

"Why?"

"Why does he work in the back?" Cynthia blinked at her.

"Yes. Is he trained to work with the chemicals?"

Cynthia's brows crunched together. "You don't have to be classroom trained. Only the managers do. The machines need to be inspected and you have to post the proper warnings, but there isn't like a class you have to go through to work back there."

"Oh, so anyone can work the back. It's pretty easy?"

"No, that's not what I said. I said you didn't have to be classroom trained. It isn't easy to do it right. It takes a lot of time to get it right."

"And Dawson does it right?"

"Eh... he's quick. I get complaints that he doesn't get all the stains out, but I take those returns from his check and do them myself, so I know they're right."

"Do you work in the back a lot?"

"Some, why?"

"Just wondering. The chemicals you use are pretty strong then, huh? To get all the stains out?"

"Well, yeah. It isn't like you can get the stuff over the counter, you know? Perc is some serious stuff. But what does any of this have to do with my statement?"

"Oh, nothing at all to do with your previous statement. What's Perc? You work with it?"

"Perchloroethylene, and yeah, all the time. It's what most dry cleaners use."

"Oh, okay. Sorry for that detour. Let's go back and fill in my timeline, okay?" Kallie flipped her book back. "Where were you on Wednesday?"

Cynthia cocked her head, "Why?"

"Oh, I'm sorry, I thought I told you. I'm recreating everyone's day so we can show in court why some people are not suspects and some people are. It is a precaution for when we go to court."

"Oh, so you found the person who killed him?" The woman leaned closer and stared at Kallie, waiting for an answer.

"You know, I'm waiting for just a bit more information, but my partner and I are pretty sure we know who is involved."

"Well, that's good. I'm glad you caught them."

"We're working on it, but while I wait for my boss to bring me that information, I'm filling the schedules of people we've already talked to."

"Okay. You're going to talk to Dawson, too? He's sick, so you might want to wait a couple days."

"Sick?"

"Yeah, horrible. Flu. You don't wanna catch that stuff."

"No doubt." Kallie cocked her head. "Aren't you afraid you'll catch it? You're his fiancée after all."

Cynthia blinked at her and shrugged, glancing right. "I got my flu shot, but I ain't seen him today."

"You got your flu shot at the same hospital where you were seen for your accident?"

"Huh?"

"Where were you seen for your fall?" Kallie didn't look at the woman. She wrote nonsense in her book.

"County."

"And when was that?"

"A… early Thursday morning."

"Thursday morning like 6:00 or 7:00?"

"No earlier. Midnight-ish. A little after maybe."

"Wow, okay. Sorry, our definitions of morning are different." She chuckled and wrote a few notes. "How did that happen again?"

"I fell down the stairs."

"You live on the first floor." Kallie continued to write in her book. Her scribbles were nonsense as she listened to the woman in front of her.

"I was coming home from Dawson's."

"Oh. Okay. Did you stay with Dawson on Wednesday night?"

"Uh… yeah."

"Cool. What did you do? I can fill in two timelines with one question."

"Ah, we ate dinner and watched a movie. I went home after."

"What movie?"

"What?"

"What movie did you watch?" Kallie glanced up for a second.

"I don't know. Something on television."

"Okay. So when you went home is when you fell down the stairs and broke your wrist?"

"Yeah. That's when."

"Dawson took you to the hospital?"

"No."

Kallie looked up at that. "No? Your fiancé didn't take you to the hospital?"

Cynthia squirmed in her chair and shook her head. "He fell asleep, and I didn't want to bother him."

Kallie dropped her pen and leaned back in her chair. "Can you explain that?"

"Explain what?" The woman snipped. "What does that have to do with my statement?"

"Again, we are trying to establish where everyone was and when they were in those locations so we can deliver a complete picture to the District Attorney."

"I didn't want him to take me. Okay?"

"Why?"

"Listen, Dawson's not the smartest guy, yah know."

"Oh-kay?" Kallie extended the word and made it a question.

"Look, I'm not going to press charges or nothing, but he pushed me, and I fell down the stairs. I wasn't going to let him take me to the hospital and make things worse."

"So, Dawson pushed you down the stairs?"

"Yeah. He did."

"What time was that?"

"I don't know. Eight or so."

"And you didn't go to the hospital until midnight?" Kallie swung back to Cynthia's previous answer. The woman was digging herself deeper and deeper.

"Yeah, I thought I could shake it off."

"You thought you could shake off a broken wrist and a broken ankle?"

"I'm tougher than I look."

"Obviously..." Kallie stopped talking when the door opened. Davidson walked in and slapped the folder on the table. "We confirmed everything." He stabbed the folder with his finger and an evil smile spread across his face before he swung his eyes to Cynthia. Holy fuck, one day she wanted to sit in the observation room when the Lieutenant did an interview. It would be epic.

He turned on his heel and left the interview room. "Perfect." Kallie slid the folder to her and opened it.

"What did you confirm? Do you know who killed that guy?"

Kallie looked up and cocked her head. "I believe I do."

"Who? Who killed him?"

Kallie moved to the door. "You might want to have a seat. This is going to take a hot minute." She was gone before Cynthia could sputter a response. Brock exited the observation room.

"Dawson is up next." She nodded to the interview room.

"I'll take him." Brock slid his notebook from his coat pocket and flipped the page open. "Ready?"

"Go get 'em tiger." Kallie winked when she threw Brock's words back at him. The man gave her a lusty smile and waggled his eyebrows before he headed to the interview room door.

Brock winced internally at the sight of the beaten man. He listed to the left. Several butterfly bandages held together the cut over his right eye, and he could see an ace bandage wrapped around the man's ribs through the thin cotton of Dawson's t-shirt. "How are you doing?"

"Been better. Can we get this done with? I gotta..." The man stopped. "Hell, I don't know what I'm going to do."

"Yeah, sure. Dawson, can you tell me where you were this past Wednesday night?"

The man nodded. "Fire and Ice, over on West Hampton. I had dinner with my friends and spent the evening drinking and dancing." Brock held his surprise behind his professional demeanor. Fire and Ice was a gay club.

"All evening?"

"From 9:00 p.m. to about 2:00 a.m."

"Who were you with?"

Dawson rattled off some names, and when Brock asked, he gave their cell numbers, too.

Brock leaned back in his chair. "You and Cynthia didn't have dinner on Wednesday? You sure?"

"God, yeah, I'm sure. She threw her car keys at me and told me to get lost. She gets that way sometimes. Why?"

"Nothing, just checking. Are you gay or bi?"

"Bi." Dawson closed his eyes.

"When did you meet Samuel Treyson?"

"About four months ago? Cynthia got pissed at the old delivery guy and fired him, so I'd go in, get the machines ready for processing and then go do the collections. Thought it was weird that Treyson had more than one apartment." He chuckled, but the sound turned into a pained moan.

"He tell you why he stayed at more than one place?"

"Yeah. Pretty amazing set up, huh?"

"If you're into that type of thing, then yeah, it would be sweet." Brock leaned forward. "Tell me what happened between you and Samuel." Dawson opened his eye and stared at Brock. "I need to know, man, so I can get justice for him and now for you, too."

"Justice? Man, people like me don't get justice. We get pushed to the side or shoved down."

Dawson's jaw worked, and he swallowed hard. "Life don't give people like me easy times."

"This time, life is staring you in the face and telling you to speak up. Believe me, I can protect you from whoever did this to you."

"It wasn't Cynthia."

"Didn't think it was. She couldn't swing a baseball bat that hard. Not with the cast." Dawson grunted in acknowledgement. "She said you pushed her down the stairs."

Dawson bolted forward and gasped in pain. "Fuuuck... I never. I wouldn't hurt her. Never. She hits me, bites me and treats me like shit, man, but I wouldn't lift a hand against her. I wouldn't."

"How did she break her wrist?"

Dawson shrugged. "She told me she was in a car accident."

"Wednesday night?"

"Yeah. She showed up at work the next afternoon with the casts. I went to the medical supply store to buy her the scooter."

"What happened between you and Treyson?"

Dawson stared at the tabletop for several minutes. "He was so nice to me. He treated me good, you know. Like I was someone. He..." Dawson cleared his throat. "He asked me out. I really liked the way he treated me. I met him for dinner. He told me he wanted to take care of me. Can you believe it? Me? He wanted me..." Dawson sucked in some air and continued, "Cynthia found out. She was so pissed. She beat the fuck out of me, but I never hit her. I swear." His eye popped up.

Brock saw the truth in the man's stare. "I believe you. How did Cynthia find out?"

"She saw Sam bring me home one night. We'd had dinner and then went to his place up in Briar Hill. A big house. We went in through the back. The kitchen was the size of the dry cleaners. Sam, he was a gentle lover. I really thought maybe something was finally going right in my life, you know?" He leaned forward and winced. "Anyway, after she found out, that's when she stopped me from doing pick-ups. She took my phone and... it was bad. I guess she went to visit Sam. Like I said, she took my phone. I didn't memorize his number, so I had no way of contacting him. I tried to go to one of his places, but..." Dawson closed his eye and a tear escaped down his swollen, bruised cheek. "I got nothing, man. Nothing. That job she gave me keeps me from living on the streets. I've been on the streets. I'll do anything to keep a roof over my head." He shrugged his shoulder a fraction of an inch. "Then he showed up at the cleaners. I was working both the back and front that day. He said he was worried about me and came to see me. He brought his clothes in regularly after that. I tried to work up front. Cynthia doesn't like dealing with customers, so she let me. The last time he came in was last Tuesday. I thought he was going to ask me to come with him when he saw what she'd done to me. The bite marks and bruises. I would have left with him if he'd asked, but Cynthia, she came up from the back. She told Sam I was her fiancé and that I wasn't interested. She told him to leave and never come back or he'd regret it. She threatened to fire me, to put me on the street, and she threatened to out Sam. What could I do?"

"Were there any witnesses?"

"No. We were the only ones in the store."

"Is there a camera system at the front of the store?"

"Yeah, I think. I don't know if it works. I don't get to go into the office. It's locked."

"Okay, let's go back, can we? You said you tried to go to one of his places. What happened when you went, Dawson?" Every instinct told him all the pieces to the puzzle were going to come into play during these interviews. He needed to keep the man talking.

"The guy he lived with got all up in my face."

"Can you describe him, the guy?"

"Sure, but I know who he is. Sam talked about him, and I'd seen him before. His name is Garrett."

"You saw him at one of Samuel's apartments?"

"Yeah."

"Who beat you, Dawson?"

"I dunno."

"You had to have let them into your apartment, or did Cynthia let them in?"

Dawson shrugged his shoulders. "Did you let him into your apartment?" Brock pushed the question again.

"No. He was there when I came home."

"Did he say anything? Do you know why someone would beat you?"

"To keep me from talking to you. He told me to keep my mouth shut, or he'd shut it permanently."

"Why didn't you call us? Report it?"

"What good would it do, man? He should have just used that bat on my head. If he killed me at least it would all stop."

"Dawson, do you know who killed Sam?"

The man shook his head. "I can only guess."

"Who would you guess?"

"Cynthia."

"Not Garrett?"

"No, he loved Sam."

"Why do you think it was Cynthia?"

"She's... She's threatened to slit my throat while I slept. One night I figure she'll do it. She's not right, Detective."

"Why do you stay with her?"

He shrugged again, a mere fraction of an inch. "Where the hell would I go, dude? Tell me. Where would I go?"

Brock hands rose trying to calm Dawson down. "Okay. Can I get you something to drink? I need to run through a few things, but I'll be back."

"Am I under arrest?"

"No. You are not a suspect at this time."

"I would never hurt anyone, Detective."

"I believe you, man."

"Detective?"

Brock turned at the door. "Yes?"

"She really said I hurt her?"

"Yes."

Dawson nodded and closed his eye. "I wish he would have killed me."

CHAPTER 14

Kallie waited with Lieutenant Davidson in the observation room. Watching Dawson's interview had been enlightening. The man was broken. Absolutely broken, but broken they could work with. Brock stepped into the room with his cell phone pushed to his ear. He held up a finger quickly, "I'm calling the impound lot. If Cynthia was driving the car, we should be able to tell."

"How?" Kallie moved away from the table where she'd been leaning.

"Seat position for starters. Samuel Treyson was over six feet tall. She's what? Maybe five feet tall?" Davidson said quietly from the other side of the room.

"We need to ascertain if there was anything of

Cynthia's left in the car. Phone, purse, coat, whatever. If she drove it over the bank and hurt herself, she was trying to save herself, not her shit."

Kallie pointed at Brock. "You said it was filled with mud."

"Yeah, that is what Brody said. He was going to have the techs go through it. Hopefully they've had time to shovel all that shit out." Brock held up a finger stalling their conversation and spoke for several minutes before he ended the call. "They are about halfway through mucking it out. They are documenting everything, bucket by bucket, so there are no questions as to how they found anything or what they found. So far, they can tell me that the seat was forward, but until they get it cleared out, they don't know what size human would fit comfortably behind the wheel."

"Good. So, based on what Kallie has told me and what I just witnessed, what are your combined guts telling you?" Davidson assumed what Kallie was beginning to realize was his thinking stance. Feet shoulder width apart, hands in his pockets, and weight back on his heels.

Kallie sat on the table and sighed. "We need to validate Dawson was at Fire and Ice like he said he was."

"Agreed. The people he was with need to be interviewed, and we need the security feed at the club."

"Give me that information. I'll have Bettis and Hansen run that down. We can get that video and confirm his alibi. In the meantime, you hold both of them." Brock scribbled the information on a sheet of legal paper left on the table Kallie was sitting on. "Run with the assumption Dawson is telling the truth. The next time you talk to Ms. White or him, it is under rights advisement. We don't want anything to slip through the cracks."

"Roger that." Kallie acknowledged his directive. It wasn't needed. She wasn't going to say a word to Cynthia without Mirandizing her, but hey, he was the boss, and he was covering their asses.

Brock shook his head while staring at the toe of his boot. "I don't know how she'd slit his throat, though. Like you said, she's small. What could she possibly say that would put him to his knees–voluntarily?"

Davidson nodded. "The wound on Treyson mimics the threat Dawson alleges Cynthia made to him. That detail wasn't given to the media, so Dawson wouldn't know about it. Those threats are oddly specific to the crime." Davidson grabbed the handle of the door. "Work this hard. I'm going to give you high cover and keep this shit contained, but if the press gets wind you have two people in custody, they are going to start circling looking for a carcass."

"Roger that, sir," Kallie and Brock acknowledged at the same time.

After the door shut, Kallie bounced all the information through her head again, looking for anything to use. "Physically could she do it?"

"If he went to his knees voluntarily." Brock nodded. "Yes. All she'd need is a sharp knife and the element of surprise."

Kallie stared at her partner. "Why would he go to his knees though?"

"I got nothing." Brock shrugged. "I mean, Samuel is a stand-up guy, right? He knows Dawson is in a shit relationship."

Kallie flipped through her notebook, looking for any fragment of information that would give them an indication as to why Samuel would have willingly gone to his knees. "He was known for doing the right thing. What would Cynthia have that would put him to his knees?"

"One of his lovers?" Brock speculated.

"Or Dawson." Kallie countered.

Brock nodded his eyes fixed on hers. "She could have used Dawson to draw Treyson to that warehouse, but why there?"

Kallie drew her bottom lip into her mouth with her teeth, trying to put puzzle pieces together. "Why would she bring him to the middle of nowhere?"

"Wait, the warehouse." Brock dropped to the chair and flipped through his notes. "Fuck, tell me you've got the name of the LLC that owned the damn warehouse." He continued to flip through the pages.

"Ah... wait, I've got it here somewhere. She licked her fingers and paged rapidly through her notes. "Yeah, here. Smartsmith, LLC." Kallie shifted her attention to Brock.

"We need to run down the ownership of that warehouse and see if we can connect the owner of the warehouse to one of Samuel's lovers or Cynthia and Dawson. We ran it originally and couldn't tie it to Samuel."

"We should run it against the names Sebastian Treyson sent us, too." Kallie added.

"Call Bettis and Hansen. If they need help, they can ask Davidson for more manpower."

"Roger that." She picked up the phone and

made the call while she watched Brock watching Dawson. His eyes narrowed, and he shook his head. After she hung up, she nudged him. Her phone vibrated. She picked it up and dismissed it quickly. Rich again. She leaned toward Brock. "What's eating you?"

"Why do people kill other people?" he asked, without taking his eyes from Dawson.

"The big three. Money, emotional ties, or power."

"With the exception of Dawson, we've alibied all of Treyson's lovers."

Kallie nodded. "So, Dawson stays on the list of suspects."

"Right. Then there is greed. Who stood to benefit from Samuel's death?"

"His lovers. Not Dawson, though. He wasn't in the fold, and as far as we know, not in the will. But again, we have nothing indicating the lovers were involved."

"Right. And power? Who gains from this guy's death?"

"His old man?"

"Nah, he already owns everything, but that guy is a royal bastard. It doesn't figure, Sebastian and Dawson, they are very unlikely bed partners, you know what I mean?" Brock rubbed his jaw and yes, she noticed the strong angle of his chin, but pushed that momentary lapse of professionalism to the curb.

"You need to talk to Dawson again."

Brock paused. "Why?"

Kallie flipped her notebook to the last page. "He said he was at Fire and Ice from 9:00 p.m. until 2:00 a.m. Where was he before that? If we go by the timeline established at The Waterfall, Samuel could have been at the warehouse by 7:30, even with fucked up traffic."

"Fuck. That's an excellent catch." He stood and turned, sitting on the table. "He could have killed Samuel for screwing with his only support system."

"Possible, or Cynthia could have killed him for messing with Dawson."

Brock shook his head. "I don't think she's that invested in Dawson. I don't get the sense she loves him enough to kill over him, you know. I don't get that passion from her. I think she likes to control his ass, but I don't see any passion. Do you? She doesn't seem entrenched, although she glares at him like she's afraid he's going to say something wrong."

Kallie leaned beside him. "That makes sense. I

can't help thinking we are missing the why of this situation. Why would Dawson kill his one ticket out of hell?"

"Yeah, Samuel was one hell of a gravy train for that man."

Kallie jumped and grabbed Brock. "Gravy train. We haven't looked into financials."

"You think Dawson or Cynthia were trying to blackmail Treyson? Squeeze him for money?"

"Yeah, maybe. Think about it. Dawson has nothing. According to her cousin's unsolicited comments today, Cynthia is money hungry. It's worth running it to the ground. They aren't going anywhere." Kallie motioned toward Dawson.

Brock nodded. "My gut is telling me Cynthia was driving Samuel's car and lost control of it around that corner." Brock thumped his notebook with his pen. "It's a hairpin curve. Hell, I can recall five or six cars being fished out of that damn river. Drivers going too fast and not paying attention to the warning signs. That guard rail has been replaced and fortified, but cars still go over."

"The techs are working that angle."

"But Cynthia doesn't know that." Brock looked at her.

"True. Neither does Dawson. He admitted

Cynthia threw her keys at him and told him to get lost."

"So, you think Dawson was at the warehouse?"

"Yep."

"Before or after the murder?"

"Don't know, but I think it's time to find out. Would you care to join me, Detective?"

Kallie turned and looked up at him. "Why does that turn me on, Detective?"

"Because you're dating a cop, and you think I'm hot."

"Nuclear, Detective. Nuclear. Your brain is sexy as fuck, too."

"Right back at yah, Tiger." Brock leaned down and kissed her cheek quickly.

"Boundaries, Detective King."

"Nobody was watching, Detective Redman." He wrapped his arms around her.

"Well in that case, kiss me like you mean it, and then let's go get us a murderer." She sighed into the warm embrace and delicious kiss. The quick intimacy was not enough, but with the way things were unfolding, it could be their only time alone, together, today. She leaned back when he moved away from her. "Are you ready?" She ran her hands up his arms.

"I am. You?"

Kallie chuckled. "Raring to go. But we can go question the suspect if you insist." She laughed at Brock's pained groan. She popped him on the arm with her notepad and headed to the door.

She waited for Brock outside the interview room and wiped the smile away, putting her game face on. They entered together. Dawson's gaze switched between them but he didn't ask any questions.

"We have a couple follow up questions, Dawson."

"Sure." The man nodded.

"Where were you between 6:00 and 9:00 on Wednesday evening?" Kallie leaned back as she asked and flipped open her notebook. She then stared at the man in front of her.

"I was with Cynthia."

"Where?"

"Ah... We worked that day."

"Until when? Oh, never mind. I can get the surveillance tape. What did you do after you left the store?" Kallie jotted a note down on the side of her clean sheet of paper and moved slightly as her phone vibrated in her pocket.

"I don't remember." The man looked down at his hands.

"Come on, Dawson. It's a simple question." Brock leaned forward and placed his forearms on the table, clasping his hands together.

"I think I need a lawyer." Dawson muttered.

"Are you telling me you want a lawyer or asking if you need one? See, there is a big difference in those two variations. If you want a lawyer, and dude, you've got every right to talk to a lawyer, as a matter of fact, let me advise you of your rights." Kallie recited the guy's Miranda Rights, pulling her card even though she knew the damn thing by heart. She asked him if he understood what she'd just told him. Her phone vibrated again.

"Yeah, I understand."

Brock took over. "Cool. So, the question is do you want to talk to a lawyer because let me tell you what is going to happen if you do that. We are going to get up and leave, and we are going to go in and talk to Cynthia. What do you think she's going to say, Dawson? Do you think she's going to hold back, or do you think she's going to paint us a picture with you as the bad guy, just like the allegations she made that you pushed her down the stairs Wednesday night?"

Dawson was adamant. "I didn't do that. I was at the club. I've never hurt anyone."

"And we are checking that out, because that's what we do. We find the truth. The real truth, not a convenient shade of the truth. Now, do you want a lawyer, or are you willing to answer questions?"

"It doesn't matter, man. I'm dead if I talk, and if I don't, they're going to say it was me, and I spend my life in jail."

"Where were you between 6:00 and 9:00 that night." Brock asked.

"We closed the store between 5:00 and 6:00. She was pissed, so damn mad. She told me to get into the car. We drove to the harbor. A big building. A warehouse." A tear slid down the guys face.

Kallie clarified, "To be exact, the 'she' you're mentioning is Cynthia White?"

"Yeah."

Brock snapped the next question, "What did you do there?"

"She met a guy. He told her to get Samuel to come out. She made me call him."

Kallie once again pushed for more details, "What time was that?"

"I don't know, it was after sunset, maybe 6:30, a little after."

Brock asked the next question. They were tag teaming the witness like they'd been doing it for years. "How did you call him?"

"She gave me a phone after she dialed the number."

"Was it her cell phone?" Kallie moved her attention from her notepad when she questioned Dawson.

"No, it wasn't it. It wasn't a smart phone, like she has. It looked like my pay-as-you-go phone." Dawson sniffed and wiped his nose on his sleeve.

"What did you say to Samuel?"

"What she told me to say."

"Which was?"

"She told me to say I slipped away, and could he meet me at the warehouse at the end of Livingston Avenue, down by the docks. I told him go to the back and come inside. I was afraid she'd track me down. I told him not to tell anyone where we were meeting."

"Then what happened?"

"Over in the corner of the place, she and some man argued. The words echoed around, and I couldn't tell what they were talking about, but she was pissed for a long time. Finally, she must have gotten her way because she laughed and said,

'Deal.' She threw her keys at me and told me to get fucking lost and stay lost until she found me."

"What did the man look like?"

"I don't know. I couldn't see him too good. He stayed in the shadows."

"Was he tall? Could you tell by the way he talked if he was from the local area? Did he have an accent?" Brock peppered the guy with questions.

Dawson shifted slightly and winced. "He was maybe five-ten, six foot. Cynthia had to look way up at him. He talked like a smart person. Proper speaking and shit."

"Did he sound young or old?" Kallie tried to get more information.

"I don't know, but I would recognize his voice if I heard it again."

"Okay, what happened then?"

"I left."

Brock cleared his throat and continued the interview, "What time was that?"

"I don't know, but I saw Sam's car when I got onto the freeway. He was going the other direction and taking the off ramp onto Livingston."

"What car was he driving?"

"The red one. The sports car. It's a..." Dawson shook his head. "I think he called it a McLaren. I don't know much about fancy cars. I'm not a gear head, but once you see that car, you know it."

Brock nodded. "What happened then?"

"I went to Fire and Ice and met up with some of my friends."

Kallie held up a finger, stopping Dawson. "What time was that?"

"9:00. They rang the late-night happy hour bell as I was walking in." Dawson sniffed and shook his head. "She killed him, didn't she?"

Neither she nor Brock responded to his question. Instead, she asked, "Did you see any vehicle besides the one you and Cynthia were driving?"

"No, but then again I didn't look around. She was really mad on the way out, you know? She kept muttering that the bastard couldn't do that to her. She kept saying he was cheating her. She was ranting about money. It makes me a fucking pussy, but I just didn't want her to start on me again. I shut up and kept my eyes on the floor. If she saw me looking anywhere else, she... I just didn't want to risk it."

Brock interjected, "And when you left?"

"I just got in the car and went, man. I didn't know why they wanted me to call Sam down to the warehouse, you know." He wiped his cheeks slowly, but deliberately. "Fuck, did I ever find out why they wanted me to do it. She said to keep my mouth shut if I wanted to live."

"Why were you beaten?" Kallie asked since he was talking and cooperative.

He shrugged. "I guess 'cause I told her I was going to call you. I took that card you gave her. She threw it in the garbage after you left. I should have known I was in a world of hurt."

"Why's that?" Brock looked up from his notebook.

"She wasn't mad. She was nice. She agreed we needed to tell you what we knew. She said that we'd see you, together. She told me to go home and wait for her but had me run the last drop off before I went home. He was there when I walked in."

"Did you see who it was?"

"No. I was hit as soon as I went in. All I saw was that bat."

"Did he say anything to you?"

"He said to keep my mouth shut. I thought he was going to kill me." Dawson sniffed again, not bothering to wipe the tears this time. "It would have been better if he'd finished the job."

She turned the interview back to questions and

not emotions. "Dawson, did you call in sick from work this morning?"

"No. I got no phone. How was I supposed to call?"

Brock shifted the conversation again. "When you drove to the Warehouse District, what route did you take?"

"Interstate to Livingston exit."

"And Cynthia White was driving her car. You were the passenger?"

"Yeah."

"The make and model of her car?"

Dawson gave them the make, model and color.

"Thank you. We're going to need a signed statement from you."

"Whatever you want, man. It doesn't matter anymore. Can you send someone to take me to the bathroom?"

"Sure, we can do that." Dawson closed his eyes and kept them closed as they left.

CHAPTER 15

They made their way to the observation room that overlooked Cynthia White's interview room after making a call to the front desk requesting an escort for Dawson. Kallie palmed her phone and looked at the texts. "Check it." She held her phone for Brock to read.

"Cynthia White's uncle owns part of that warehouse."

"Yep."

"Then she has access—"

"—to where Samuel Treyson was killed."

Brock glanced at his phone and grunted. "Bettis says he's got video of Dawson at Fire and Ice. First positive ID of the man is time-stamped at four minutes after 9:00."

"Let's get Davidson down here again, run this by him, and let him know what we're going to do. Plus, now we have probable cause, and we can use that to go for a warrant on financials. Davidson can run it by the District Attorney's office and ask them to get a warrant."

"I gotta ask. Keeping Davidson this close, it's not normal, right? I'm not criticizing, but we usually just briefed when we were arresting or if we had problems with external agencies."

"No, he's not usually this hands-on, but this isn't a normal case. My old man is taking a huge amount of heat. You saw the Governor's speech. If we don't get this fucker, my old man will be crowned with a dunce cap and pointed at by that megalomaniac. He'll lose the credibility he's worked so fucking hard to garner. I want him to get up to date briefings, and I trust Davidson to channel the information correctly." Brock rubbed the back of his neck. "I think Sebastian Treyson has put a full court press on the police department. He obviously has the Governor in his pocket. I'm waiting for the rest of the politicians to start toeing Treyson's line. Money isn't going to solve this case, but it will definitely ruin careers. Unfortunately, it's my dad who will pay the price if we don't get this bastard."

"Sebastian Treyson..." Kallie leaned against the wall and stared at Cynthia, who looked like she was asleep. Her good arm cradled her head, and her upper body sprawled across the top of the table.

The sound of Kallie's phone vibrating punctuated the silence. She didn't even look at the phone. He sighed. He'd lay odds it was the fucking ex again. He glanced through the window. "What's rolling around in that beautiful brain of yours?" Brock leaned back in his chair and put his feet onto the small table in the room.

"Who was the man with Cynthia, and what were they arguing about?"

"My bet is on money."

"But from whom?"

Brock closed his eyes. "Deepest pockets. Daddy."

"Do you think we can get a warrant to look at Sebastian Treyson's bank accounts?"

"Not with what we have now, and with his resources, who's to say any money that was exchanged came from this country."

"He could have brought it in with him."

"But he was out of the country."

"Was he?"

Kallie leaned forward. "We don't need a warrant to look at filed flight plans."

Brock opened his eyes. "No, no we don't. Assume nothing, validate everything."

"Knowing Daddy was actually across the pond and not blowing us off would allow us to eliminate him from the suspect pool."

"But what does he gain from Samuel's death?"

Kallie slid down the wall and ended up on her ass. She hugged her knees and stared over at him. She worried her bottom lip with her teeth. He'd noticed she did that when she was thinking. She glanced up at him. "Power?"

"Sebastian is the owner, he can't get much more powerful than that. What else could he gain?"

"Control."

"Yeah, but of what?" Brock batted her suggestion back at her.

"Well… how about control of Samuel?"

Brock dropped his feet and leaned forward. "What do you mean?"

"His son has an alternate lifestyle; one Samuel went to lengths to arrange and manage so Daddy *didn't* find out."

"Daddy had an affair with his wife. He knew Samuel wasn't going to rock the boat." Brock dropped his elbows to his legs.

"Yeah, but that doesn't mean he knew Samuel was getting any on the side. The old man was fucking his kid's wife. Power and control in the extreme. *He* was the one in charge. *He* was the one with the power. It got old, and Sebastian drops the wife when he gets bored, but he dropped her, she didn't drop him."

Brock followed the path Kallie was laying down. "So, Cynthia contacts Daddy and blackmails him?"

"She could, or she could contact someone at Samuel's company and threaten to go public unless she's paid off."

Brock followed her thought path. "And someone at the company contacts Daddy."

Kallie nodded. "Cynthia could've threatened to out Samuel's affairs."

"Dawson and Samuel, or hell, any of the others and Samuel. Sam's married. If he gets outed cheating on his wife, that's a stain on his public image. One that has been carefully crafted..."

"By Daddy." Kallie finished his thought.

"Fuck, its thin." Brock rubbed his face.

"But it makes sense."

"We'll need to be very careful."

"We do." Kallie chuckled when she folded her arms over her knees and stared up at him. "Damn, Detective King, you sure know how to show a woman a good time, don't you?"

He chuckled and grabbed his cell to throw Davidson a text. The man hit him right back. "He's tied up. He'll be here in twenty."

"Twenty whole minutes to ourselves. Whatever will we do with the time, Detective?" Kallie leaned back against the wall and watched him.

He dropped to his hands and knees from the chair he was sitting on. He crawled the three feet to where she was leaning back against the wall and flopped into position beside her. "If we didn't have boundaries in place, I could think of countless ways to pass the time."

"Countless?" Kallie dropped her hand, and he grabbed it, weaving his fingers through hers.

"I'm sure there is a limit to my imagination. That's when you can take over." He held her hand and kissed the back of it. It felt so damn natural.

"I'm afraid I'm going to wake up and all this will have been a dream." She leaned over and dropped her head on his shoulder.

"God, that would suck." Brock chuckled at her snort of agreement. "You know I'm probably going to fuck up. I've only had a couple relationships, and they ended because of the job."

Kallie shifted so she was leaning into him more, and he shifted, breaking their hand hold, to drop an arm behind her, pulling her into his side. "We both know the hours and commitment it takes to do this job. That's a plus."

"We both have this job, which means twice the shit to deal with." He kissed the top of her head and closed his eyes, leaning his cheek against her hair. This simple connection was everything. He'd arrived at the mirage he'd been chasing all his life. An oasis of peace and contentment.

"So what? It makes spending time together more important." She shrugged. He felt the lift of her shoulder against his ribs.

"It will. Do you have any regrets? Dating a cop again?"

Her fingers stopped the lazy trail up and down his thigh. "No. See, Rich and I met at the academy. We dated off and on for… eight years. When I made detective, he was pretty fucking jealous. So much so we broke up. Two years later, he gets his gold badge and all of a sudden he's back. I knew it was a mistake, but he was one of those guys who'd charm you. And yeah, I had all the warning bells and whistles going off. I ignored them because I didn't want to be alone. Our marriage was difficult. I wasn't happy, and neither was he. We probably wouldn't have survived him coming back from undercover. We'd both changed and grown."

She moved slightly and twisted to look at him. "With us? I don't have a single warning bell going off. There is nothing telling me I'm making a mistake here. You aren't him. I'm not the woman I was. Going through hell changes a person. I'll never let another person control me or my life, but I do want someone to walk through life with me. If that turns out to be you, then good. If we last for a short time, I'll have been glad to have been with you. No regrets."

Brock stared down at her big brown eyes. "You are so incredibly beautiful." He dropped his lips to hers, brushing over them softly. She chased his lips, and they connected. It was a kiss of promise, at least on his part.

"Davidson probably shouldn't catch us like this." He leaned down and gave her one more kiss, chaste and soft.

"No, might not go over well." She leaned up and

kissed him again. "But it was nice to have the time. A few minutes outside the madness swirling out there."

"An oasis." He verbalized his thoughts from a few moments ago.

"Yeah, exactly. A place to rest and revitalize." She turned to him. "That's exactly how I feel when I'm with you. Peaceful. It's really nice, isn't it?" She smiled and moved off the floor, reaching a hand down to him. "Come on, King. Up and at 'em."

He grabbed her hand and stood, not allowing her to take any of his weight. He stepped into her space and chucked her chin up so he could look into her eyes again. "It is more than nice." It was pretty fucking close to perfect, but it was too early to admit. He dropped another kiss on her lips and walked away, making it to the other side of the room before Davidson suddenly opened the door and walked in.

"What do you have?"

Brock and Kallie briefed their boss, and he listened carefully, asking questions when he needed clarification. They worked over the information and devised a plan forward. One that didn't rely on Cynthia's confession, but damned if they weren't going to push her for information.

"All right. I've got the information; I'll call Cliff over at the ADA's office and see if he can get us a warrant for financials. Samuel's won't be an issue. I need you to get me something from Dawson or Cynthia that implies this was a blackmail situation. Then I can run this up the flagpole and get a warrant for them and Sebastian Treyson's accounts. The good thing is the warrant goes straight to the banks and not through Treyson's army of lawyers." He motioned to Cynthia. "She asked for her phone call while you were in with Dawson. One of the uniforms escorted her to the phone. I extracted the recording. She called a number and left a message. Her message was, and let me quote, *It's me. The cops picked me up. You'd better get me out of here or you know what will happen.*"

"Let me guess, the number was a burner phone."

"As far as we can tell. The line went straight to voicemail, so I don't think the damn thing was on. We may have a short window of opportunity. Get to her before whoever she called shows up."

Brock looked at Kallie as Davidson paused at the door. "By the time you have her under rights advisement, I'll have Bettis down here. He'll work anything you need. I've got Hansen working the other issues. We'll work it. Bettis will have a direct line open to me." He yanked open the door. "You've got this. Let's wrap it up."

"That means we're up. Let's go play the Brock King variety of hardball."

Kallie glanced over her shoulder to make sure the door was shut before she turned back and waggled her eyebrows. "I love your hard balls, Detective King." She laughed and spun on her heel, leaving the small room.

Fuck, Brock reached down and rearranged himself in his jeans. He'd never interviewed a suspect with a hard-on before. Kallie would pay for that little taunt. A smile spread across his face, yeah, he could have some fun with this... he glanced into the interview room. Right after he got a confession.

Kallie was still chuckling when he stopped in front of the door. He rolled his shoulders and slid into interrogation mode. Kallie cleared her throat, and he watched as she slipped on a cloak of professionalism that they all wore.

"Game time." He said to her, and she nodded. He opened the door and walked in. Both he and Kallie sat across from Cynthia. The woman didn't move or acknowledge them. Brock slammed his hand down on the table.

The thunderous clap jolted Cynthia awake. "Fuck! What the hell?"

"Ms. White, you have the right to remain silent."

"What! Are you fucking kidding? You're arresting me?"

"No, ma'am, I'm reading you your rights."

She popped up on her one good foot. "Why do you need to read me my rights?"

Brock leaned forward. "Sit down and let me finish this."

Brock read the Miranda ending with, "With these rights in mind, do you wish to speak to a lawyer?"

"Why are you reading me my rights?"

And that was the opening he needed. "To start, you said Mr. Jenkins pushed you down the stairs. He has provided an alibi for that evening. Providing false statements to the police is illegal, Ms. White."

He watched her mind spin. The expressions that ran over her face were almost comical. "I didn't press charges, so you got nothing."

"But why would you lie to us?" Kallie performed the hurt cop act pretty damn well.

Cynthia shrugged. "It's none of your business what happened to me."

"Well, that's wrong, but it's also okay, because we know what happened." Brock leaned back in his chair and watched the woman. She narrowed her eyes and her gaze flipped from Kallie to him and then back again. "What is he talking about?"

Brock leaned forward, continuing to stare at her.

"Did you talk to Dawson? Is that what this is about? You had to, right, because he has an alibi? Well that's bullshit. The man lies. All the time he lies."

"And that flu he had? That was a lie?" Kallie asked quietly.

"He got into a fight." Cynthia leaned back into the chair.

"How do you know that? You said you didn't see him, that he called in."

"He told me."

"He said he didn't call you. He couldn't because you took his phone."

"I didn't take nobody's shit." Cynthia stared back at Kallie.

"Then when we search your apartment, we won't find anything?"

"Why you searching my apartment?" The woman leaned forward, but she wasn't scared. No,

Brock could tell there was nothing in the apartment, but they'd still search.

"Or the office?" Kallie followed up and that's when Brock caught the first look of terror flash through the woman's eyes.

"You need a warrant, and I ain't done nothing."

"We don't, actually. You see, your uncle has been very cooperative." Brock signaled Bettis to get the uncle to approve a search of the office, as in now.

"Whatever. That's like community property in there. Lots of people have keys."

"Yeah, but not Dawson."

"So?" Cynthia glanced at the door to the interview room.

"You can relax, Cynthia, I don't think whoever you called is going to show up. They are leaving you dangling here, all by yourself. You see, we know your uncle owns part of that warehouse. We know you went to the warehouse and sent Dawson away after you got him to call Samuel to the warehouse. We've spoken to everyone who was there that night and all fingers are pointing to you."

"That's bullshit." Cynthia's eyes darted to the door again.

"No, it isn't. You killed Samuel Treyson. You slit his throat."

"No! No, I didn't! I didn't kill no one! I got proof. I got video. Treyson begged, but that bastard killed him. I was supposed to be gone, but I waited. I wanted to see what he did. I can give you the video. I wanted money. That bastard told me he'd give me money. Then after, he laughed at me. He told me if I said a word to anyone, he'd kill me. Slowly. He has enough money; he can do it." Cynthia shook her head. "I didn't do nothing. Hell yeah, I'll tell you who did it."

The door to the interview room opened and Brock swung his attention from Cynthia to the man standing in the doorway. *Well, shit just got interesting.* The lawyer from Miriam Treyson's house looked out of place in his designer suit.

"Mr. Masters, are you lost?" Brock asked as he casually stood.

"No. I'm right where I need to be. I represent Ms. White. I'm going to ask you to cease all questions at this time until I have time to talk to my client."

"We have advised her of her rights. She hasn't requested counsel."

"It is in her best interest to stop talking, now."

Mr. Masters leveled a stare at the woman that would have singed the surface of the sun.

Brock swung his attention to Cynthia White. All the color had drained from her face. Her eyes were wide, and she was scared. Very scared. She shook her head from side to side. He wasn't sure if she knew she was doing it.

"It doesn't seem like she wants to talk to you."

"I've been retained to oversee her rights. You will cease questioning at this time." Masters slipped his hand in his jacket pocket in an awkward movement that set him on edge. Kallie stood and moved to his left, obviously alerted by the mannerisms, too.

Brock's eyes glanced over Masters' shoulder. Dawson had stopped in the hallway, a uniformed police officer held his arm, keeping him upright.

Dawson stared from Masters to Cynthia before he pointed to Masters. "That's him. That's the man she was talking to in the warehouse. I'd know that voice anywhere."

Masters turned toward Dawson. Brock saw it the second Masters registered what was happening. Brock dodged the briefcase that was chucked at him. Masters shoved the uniformed cop into Dawson, and tore down the hallway. Brock was on the man's tail in less than a heartbeat. "Stop! Police!" The shout was automatic and would bring half the building in response.

Masters twisted as he ran. A small handgun pointed directly at his chest. Brock dove forward, the echo of the weapon discharging ringing in his ears. He connected with Masters' legs, and they hit the floor in a tangle of arms and legs.

The gun came up. Brock covered the weapon and pushed it to the side just as Masters squeezed the trigger again. He ripped the damn thing from the lawyer's grasp and used the butt end in his fist to swing backward, knocking Masters into next week. The man went limp under him. The hallway was flooded in seconds, but all he could see were feet and legs.

Brock rolled off the guy and winced. He glanced down at his arm. "Son of a fucking, cocksucking, whore-mongering, motherfucking limp-dicked bitch! That damn pansy-ass lawyer shot me." He glanced up as Kallie slid on her knees to his side. "He shot me!"

"Well, yeah, he had a gun. Shit like that happens if you don't move fast enough." She ripped his shirt from the cuff to the wound on his bicep. "Damn, the bullet is still in there, too. You need to go to the doctor."

"Fuck that, we are this close to finishing this case." He moved his good arm and squeezed his fingers together. "I need something to stop the bleeding then we're going back in that fucking interview room and getting to the bottom of this motherfucking shit."

Kallie sat back on her heels. "You cuss this much each time you get shot?"

"No… Maybe." Brock frowned. He did, didn't he? Yes. Four times now, and yes, he swore like a wet rat each time. "Damn it. Motherfucking son of a bitch."

Kallie took off her hoodie and the long-sleeved shirt that was over her t-shirt. She wrapped the shirt around his arm and tied it.

"Fuck, watch it," he hissed and she sniggered at him.

"Stop being such a baby. Look, it was a freaking .22. Besides, Cynthia confessed it was Masters who killed Samuel. She has it on video on her phone, and she was able to save it from the car when they went over the embankment."

"But why? What the fuck did he have to gain by killing Samuel? Where is her phone? Masters is going to stay silent. We need to find the why. Who was he working with? Why did he do it? What could he gain from it? We hafta find something or the bastard will wiggle into a crack." Brock motioned to the attorney that several cops were lifting. The man was cuffed and surrounded by officers, and it was evident he was still looped from the punch Brock had delivered. "Make sure no one talks to him until he's read his rights." He pushed at Kallie, "Go make sure they do it right."

Kallie slapped away his hand. "Stop trying to boss everyone around. You're kinda an ass when you get shot."

"Well, yeah, because, hello? I'm shot!" He pointed to his arm with his good hand.

Kallie pointed to the gun that he'd dropped beside him. "It's a .22!"

She was laughing at him, and damn it, he couldn't help smiling, too. "Yeah, but it's still a bullet in my arm."

"Oh, poor baby," she crooned, and a couple of the cops still lingering laughed.

Brock threw his good arm up in the air. "Finally! Some sympathy."

"Redman, get him to the hospital." Davidson held up his hand stilling Brock's rant.

But damn it, he was so fucking pissed. "Masters. A slimy fucking lawyer. What the actual fuck?"

"Good question. We'll get to the bottom of it." Davidson leaned forward and offered him a hand up.

Brock took it and needed the assist more than he cared to admit. It was a small fucking bullet, but it stung like a motherfucker, and he'd admit, he was dizzy as fuck when he elevated. Kallie was next to him in a heartbeat, and he wrapped his good arm around her, steadying himself.

CHAPTER 16

"Hospitals suck." Brock muttered under his breath for the fiftieth time.

"Stop whining." She was re-reading the texts from Bettis, Hansen and the occasional update from Davidson.

"What's happening? Where is my phone?"

"You're going to surgery. I called your brother Brody. Your phone is back at the station. Bettis has it."

"Fuck. That means the entire clan will be here soon. Tell me what's going on with the case before the horde descends. Ask Bettis to bring my phone, yeah?" Brock was loopy, they'd been in and given him something for the pain. Seemed the damn bullet had lodged next to the bone in his arm, and perhaps he wasn't as much as a wimp as she was accusing him of being.

"Bettis is busy at the moment." According to what she was reading, they were missing the aftermath, and it was one hell of a ride, but she wasn't going to tell Brock that. He already felt like shit having to come to the hospital. "Okay. They have Dawson's statement identifying Masters as being at the warehouse with Cynthia. Cynthia took Hansen to where she hid the phone. It was behind one of the dry-cleaning machines. No one would ever have found it. But the video does show Masters killing Samuel. The audio is shit, so tech is working it. Masters hasn't said a word. He's being held for Samuel's murder and attempted murder of a police officer..." She waved at him and winked.

"Why? What the fuck possessed him? That's what I don't get."

"Davidson and the DA have been popping warrants all over the place. We'll find it."

"You mean you'll find it. Seriously, this doesn't even hurt anymore. I need to get back to the precinct. Damn it, of all the lousy luck."

"Stop whining. You're alive. Be happy." She was. She was ecstatic and just a little more than choked up, but hey you don't tell your boyfriend of two days that shit, do you? No. Not if you wanted him as a boyfriend for day three.

"He worked for Miriam."

Huh? "Say what?"

Brock scrubbed his face. "Masters. He worked for Miriam. Make sure they check for ties to her."

Kallie chuckled. She'd told him Davidson was doing that, the last time he'd asked her for an update. The drugs were trying to slow him down, but the man was tenacious.

A knock at the door turned her attention.

"Brock?"

Kallie slid off the side of his bed. A tall older woman entered the room, her worried expression eased as soon as she saw him in the bed.

"Son, you really have to stop getting shot. I'm only going to do this with you five or six more times before I let you do it yourself." She glanced at Kallie and smiled before she leaned over Brock and hugged him gently.

"Hey, Mom. I'm okay. Little bullet. Just ask Kallie. She'll tell you I'm over-reacting."

"Kallie?"

She turned and Kallie saw the resemblance. Those eyes were the same eyes she loved. *Liked.* Liked a lot. Not loved. She rolled her eyes and extended her hand. "Hi, I'm Kallie Redman, Brock's partner."

"What happened to Jordan?" His mom stopped and grasped her hand. "No, that didn't sound right. Where are my manners? It is so nice to meet you, Kallie. I'm Hannah King, his mom. His dad will be here as soon as he can free up from the mess that is going on at Briar Hill. It is a feeding frenzy up there right now."

Kallie smiled. "I can imagine. Jordan is on temporary assignment with the FBI."

"Mom, tell Dad I'm fine. He doesn't need to come down." Brock yawned and waved his hand dismissively. "Damn drugs."

"Language," his mom reprimanded before she turned back to Kallie. "What happened? Please tell me from the beginning. I haven't talked to the doctors yet."

Kallie leaned against the wall. She gave Brock a quick glance. He waved his hand in a 'go ahead' gesture and dropped his head back on his pillow, closing his eyes. "Okay, well, he was shot taking down a murder suspect."

"Where?" His mom sat at the foot of his bed and put a hand on his foot.

"At the precinct."

"On the street?" Hannah's eyes rounded, huge with worry.

"No, inside the building."

"What? How did that happen? I have to have my purse searched to get past the front desk."

"That's something we're still working on." Kallie knew Hansen was all over the video feed trying to ascertain how Masters was allowed in with a weapon. "The doctors did an x-ray of his arm. The bullet is lodged against the bone, so they have to go in and get it out. He's signed all the forms, and they've given him some IV pain meds. The anesthesiologist stopped in and said they'd be back as soon as an operating theater became available. The surgeon said it would be a simple slice-pull-stitch thing, but he didn't want to leave the bullet in Brock's arm that close to the bone as it could cause problems."

"Well I should hope they wouldn't leave a bullet in him." Hannah sounded scandalized.

"Hell, Mom, he's still got metal in him from when he was a Marine. What's an ounce or two more?"

Kallie whipped her head around. The man who walked in was someone she'd watch closely if she saw him on the street, because he was one tough looking mother... but then she saw his eyes. The same light blue irises rimmed with a darker edge.

"Hey, you must be Kallie, his new partner. I'm Brody, his younger brother."

"The J-DET sergeant."

He walked over and hugged his mom. "That's right," he responded, but his eyes were on his brother. "How are you doing, dude?" He took Brock's good hand and leaned down to give his brother a hug.

"I'm fine. Shouldn't you be at work?" Brock asked as Brody moved away and stood.

Brody shoved his hands into the leather jacket he wore. He was probably as tall as Brock, but he was thicker through the chest. His hair was the same color but longer and not cut the same. The scruff Brody wore, the tattered jeans, the old biker boots, the heavy-metal band t-shirt and worn leather jacket, coupled with the chain that ran to his wallet, sold his bad-ass vibe, but it was the man's eyes that told Kallie Brody was one tough customer. "Nah, seems brothers getting shot in the line of duty get you a pass at work for a while."

"It was just a .22." Both Kallie and Brock spoke at the same time. Brock's eyes met hers and they laughed. He elevated his good arm, and she gladly slid across the small space to take his hand.

"Oh!" Hannah's small gasp diverted her attention from Brock.

His mother's hands clasped over her heart. "You have a girlfriend!" The smile on her face as her gaze shifted from Brock to her was endearing, if a little scary.

"Mom, please, God, don't embarrass me." Brock yawned again. The pain killers were trying their best to pull him under.

Brody snorted. "As if." Hannah slapped Brody on the arm. "Hey! It's the God's honest truth, Kallie, she has no boundaries. None."

"Truth." Brock squeezed her hand. "It's new, Mom, don't put any pressure on us, okay?" He closed his eyes but kept her hand in his.

Hannah winked at her and held up a finger pressing it against her lips. She cleared her throat, "No pressure, honey. I can call Clarissa over at the Grand Hall and see what she has open for next June. I love June weddings."

Brock's eyes popped open. He struggled to sit up.

"No, Brock, I was joking. Seriously, stop trying to get up from that bed." Hannah sidled up on the bed sitting by his hip. "I'm just happy for you." She stroked his cheek. "All any mother wants is for her children to be happy."

The door opened and a swarm of medical personnel entered. "Detective King, we're ready for you, now." The transfer from his hospital bed to the gurney was quick and efficient. She managed to squeeze his hand before he was wheeled down the long corridor.

Over the course of the next two hours, Kallie met every member of the King family, except the Commissioner. Brock's sisters were mirror images of their mother. Bekki held court. Her vivacious energy affected anyone nearby. Her older sister, Brianna, was content to let Bekki shine. Blay, the youngest brother, was on duty, so it seemed his entire fire station made the trek to the hospital with him. Hannah's friend, Sharon McBride, who she learned was Sean's mom, arrived along with her husband, Colm. Sean ducked in for a short time but was called away. The small waiting room was filled to bursting. She was definitely the odd duck out even though Hannah took great joy in introducing her as Brock's girlfriend. She wondered if Brock would even remember outing them to his mom.

During one of Bekki's particularly animated stories, she slid from the room and strolled to the end of the hallway only to hear a familiar voice.

"We are a lot to take in, aren't we?" Brody leaned against the wall next to the vending machines.

"It's good to have a support system." Her mind flitted back to when she was in the hospital in Houston. She'd never had one.

"True, although the nurses are threatening to call the riot squad if anyone else shows up."

Kallie chuckled at his comment and leaned back against the wall, too.

"Tell me you guys have put a pin in this case."

Kallie nodded. "Yeah, Lieutenant Davidson is on it. I'm not sure what is happening right now, although I do know we have Masters on video killing Treyson."

Brody reached in his pocket and produced a crumpled five-dollar bill. He pointed at the soda machine. He inserted the money and hit a button dispensing a large plastic bottle. "Want one?"

"God, yes. I need the sugar." He handed the one in his hand to her and hit the button again.

"You want it for the sugar? I'm all about the caffeine."

"That too," she agreed.

"Who the fuck is this guy, Masters? How does he fit?"

"That's just it. He doesn't fit. He wasn't even a blip on our map." She took a long drink of the soda and sighed. She glanced at her watch. Damn, four hours since they loaded into the ambulance. What the fuck was happening? She glanced at her phone again. There hadn't been a message from Davidson, Bettis, or Hansen, in over three hours. Her phone vibrated and she snapped it up. Damn it. Just Rich and his hatred. She pocketed her phone and sighed. Something was brewing. She could feel it.

"He was a lawyer?"

"Yeah, from what I've found on his company's web page, he was a founding partner at Langley, Shaw and Masters. We had brief contact with him when we questioned Miriam Treyson. He was a blustering blowhard, but she sat on him." She shook her head and stared at the floor trying to remember every detail of their interaction with the man. There was nothing of note. Nothing.

"Was he a family lawyer? I'm sorry, I know it isn't my case, I'm just..." Brody blew a lungful of air and let the comment hang.

"It's okay, and honestly, I dunno." She shrugged. "And no one has messaged me in a hot minute. I'm just as frustrated as you."

"Perhaps I can help with that." A deep voice carried from down the hall. Brody straightened off the wall, strode the short distance between them, and hugged the man who'd spoken. Kallie stood up and watched the exchange. A few mumbled words passed between them before the men separated. "Detective Redman?"

Oh, this was the Commissioner. Brock and Brody's father. The man extended his hand. "I'm Chauncy King."

She took the hand offered. "Sir." She nodded.

"Is there someplace we can... oh, here." The Commissioner pointed to a small room across the hall. Both she and Brody stepped into what looked like a doctor's lounge and the Commissioner shut the door behind them. In the small space, the King men seemed to fill the room.

"How is he?" The Commissioner's voice reminded her of Brock's.

Brody answered, "Still in surgery. The medical team said there was a trauma that put his case on a slight hold. They started about thirty minutes ago." Brody flipped a plastic chair away from the table and slid it toward her. He did the same for his father and then dropped into one himself. "What's up, Pop?"

"A lot of information has come to light since we got a warrant and started following not only Masters' financials, but Samuel Treyson's."

Kallie leaned forward. "What have you found?"

"Unexplained deposits from the same shell company to both men's bank accounts. Random dates and times, but the deposits occurred on the same day and within minutes in both accounts."

"How much money are we talking?"

"Millions." The Commissioner took his son's soda and drank half.

"I thought you were supposed to be off sugar and caffeine."

The man winked at his son. "As far as your mother knows, I am."

Kallie shook her head. Two and two were not equaling four in this situation. "Wait, Treyson is rich..."

"No, he wasn't. Seems the heir apparent had run through his trust fund and even though he was functioning as the head of Treyson Enterprises, his father held the purse strings. Every time he needed money, he had to go to daddy. We can see deposits scattered erratically, usually before a big expenditure."

Kallie nodded. "That fits Sebastian's hallmark. He's a control freak. If he had a way to control his son, he'd use it."

Brody nodded and turned to his father. "So, what's the game here? A grudge? How does Masters just show up and kill Samuel Treyson?"

The Commissioner handed Brody his soda back and unbuttoned his suit jacket, leaning forward. "I called in a favor." He glanced at Kallie before he looked at Brock. "Guardian was able to trace the shell company to an umbrella organization that has a whisper of ties to the Fuentes Cartel. They can't confirm it... yet."

"Drugs?" Brody ran his hand through his hair and cussed under his breath.

His father nodded. The air crackled with tension. "Okay, so we can assume they aren't foot soldiers." Brody exhaled and shook his head. "This is a hell of a leap, but do we know if Treyson and Masters had ties to import/export companies?"

"Treyson Logistics is a global company," Kallie said and thumbed through her notebook. "I listed the companies that Samuel oversaw somewhere. Yep. Treyson Logistics. Global. He also was on the board for Treyson Shipping & Storage, and Treyson Parcel Delivery."

"But this information... is it admissible?" Brody glanced between his father and her.

Hell, she had no idea, but anything from Guardian was credible. That much she did know.

"I have initiated the paperwork. When the DA signs off on it, we can move forward with an official request. At that time, it will be actionable. Right now, we are gathering facts and starting to plan. Your team and probably several federal entities will be involved in the follow up of this mess," the Commissioner said to Brody.

"Yeah, I assumed."

Chauncey King stood. She and Brody did the same. The Commissioner then turned to her. "You and my son Brock are the rock stars that broke this case open. It was a powder keg and you handled it exceptionally well. Davidson has told me he plans on putting both of you in for Service Commendation Medals."

"We were just following the evidence, sir."

"Which could have ended in a wall of lawyers and no answers. Instead you two used the law to build a solid case. Well done."

"Thank you." She could feel her face heat at the compliment.

"Now on to other business. I understand you and my son are an item?"

"An item, Dad? What are we, stuck in the fifties?" Brody ducked the swat his father sent his direction.

"Whatever, boy, I will end you." Chauncy laughed when his son started bouncing on his feet and tucked his fists up like he was a boxer. "Such a scrapper." He turned his attention to Kallie. "The paperwork has been filed with HR, correct?"

"Yes, sir."

"Good. We do things by the rules, no exceptions." He turned to open the door. "Welcome to the insanity, Kallie. I wish you luck, but I have a feeling my wife has plans for you."

"I've been warned, sir."

"Ah... good. She means well, but she..."

"Has zero boundaries." Brody tossed his capped, half-empty soda bottle in the air and caught it.

"What he said." Chauncy winked at her and left the room.

Kallie sat on the chair and rifled through the information the Commissioner had just dropped their doorstep. "This is going to be a mess for you and your team."

"We're used to messes. I'm going to find a place with reception and privacy and give my Lieutenant and Captain a heads-up call."

Kallie nodded. "I'll go tread where angels fear." She nodded at the small waiting room where people now overflowed into the hall. She started down the hall following the Commissioner but stopped when Brody called to her.

"You and Brock? You make sense."

"Is that you giving us your blessing?"

"Fuck, no. I'm not that type. It's just me saying I can see why he likes you. Got any sisters?"

"Nope. Only child."

"Ain't that just my luck." Brody chuckled, spun on the heel of his biker boot, and headed down the hall.

Kallie smiled and glanced at the waiting room. Being close to Brock King meant she was taking a plunge into a world that involved family. She heard a roll of laughter come from the waiting room. All things considered, that was okay.

CHAPTER 17

Waking up after surgery sucked. Yeah, he was pro at it, but damn it, the disorientation followed by the drugged laced *'you know something's not right, but you can't remember what the fuck it is'* confusion blew. Brock blinked, trying to get his eyes to stay open. He watched the nurse at the foot of his bed. She was busy tapping at the computer on the rolling table.

He shifted. "Fuck." *Note to self. Use the other arm.*

"Ah, you're with us again."

What? "Where did I go?"

The woman laughed and shook her head. "Nowhere. You're in recovery right now. How are you doing? Are you in pain?"

Brock blinked at her. He should probably be

able to answer that, but for the life of him he wasn't following the dots. She walked up the side of the bed. "The doctor will be in shortly. In the meantime, are you in pain?"

Brock shook his head, for no other reason than that was what he assumed she wanted him to do.

"Good. There are a lot of people waiting to see you." She futzed with the tubing attached to him. "I'll go let the doc know you're awake. We'll be transferring you to a room after you wake up a bit more."

Brock nodded and then closed his eyes.

"Detective King?"

Brock roused. Damn, there was a different nurse now, he rolled his head... and his doctor. *Surgery. Right.* He cleared his throat. "How's my arm?"

The doctor smiled. "You'll be fine. A few weeks recovery and a PT stint is in your future, but you shouldn't have any lingering problems. It was a textbook extraction."

"Good."

"We're going to transfer you to your room soon, but there is quite a crowd waiting. Hospital policy will limit your visitors while you're here in recovery. I can authorize up to two." The doctor tapped the keys on the computer at the foot of the bed. "Is there someone special you want back here?"

Brock chuckled. "My partner, Kallie Redman, and you better let my parents in or there will be hell to pay."

The doc chuckled. "That's three, but I heard your father is the police commissioner, wouldn't want to make an enemy."

"Yeah, but let me tell you, he's a marshmallow compared to my mother. That is one person you do not want to piss off." Brock rolled his eyes so hard his brain hurt.

Both the doc and the nurse laughed.

"Go ahead, laugh. I'm telling you the woman looks meek and mild mannered, but it's an illusion. You've never had her guilt cannon leveled at you."

"Sorry to tell you this, but most moms are that way. I'll go get them." The nurse's laughter followed her from the curtained off area.

"I can go straight back to desk duty, right?" There were so many questions that needed to be answered about the case, his mind was already churning. What the fuck did Masters have to do with Treyson?

"Home for at least three days, then limited

duty," the doctor answered, although his attention was fixed on the computer screen.

He could hear his mom talking to the nurse. "Really, dear, I think since he's been out of surgery for almost an hour, we could have been brought back sooner. Are you a mom? No? Well, you'd understand if you were a mother. No matter how old they get, a mother's heart will forever be with her children."

The doctor glanced at him and chuckled. Brock pointed a finger at the opening in the curtain and mouthed, *'guilt cannon.'*

His father pushed the curtain wider and ushered in his mother and Kallie. Kallie slid to the side and shoved her hands into her hoodie as if she didn't know exactly what to do. His mom and dad moved toward his bed.

"You look pale. He looks pale. Is he supposed to be this pale?" His mother pushed his hair from his face and stared at the doctor, waiting for a response.

"He's the picture of health considering he's just undergone general anesthesia and surgery. His color will return. I'm happy to say everything went exactly as anticipated, and he'll be back at work with minimal down time."

"Good. Honey, you can come stay with us while you get back on your feet."

Brock blinked and shifted his worried glance toward his father. "Dad..."

"Now, Hannah, I'm sure Kallie will be able to watch over Brock. He's a grown man and doesn't need his mother to... hover."

"Hover?" Hannah straightened and glanced from him to his father. "Chauncey King, I *do not* hover."

"Yes, dear. Of course not." Chauncey gave her the smile he reserved only for her.

Brock took the opportunity to glance at Kallie. He mouthed, "I'm sorry." She smiled and looked down, trying to hide her amusement.

Brock took advantage of the rare moment of silence and jumped in. "Mom, I'm fine, really. Dad, what's happening with the case?"

"Oh, are we really doing this now?" his mom grumped and put her hands on her hips.

"Mom, I have to know what is going on." Brock wasn't going to let his mother derail him this time.

"Fine, I'll tell everyone you're doing well, although you're a bit pale. And thin. Kallie you need to take care of that. He doesn't eat well. I'm not pleased it took so long to get back here." She glared at the doctor before she dropped a kiss on his head. The doctor opened the curtain for her and departed when she did, leaving the three of them behind the curtain.

"This isn't the most secure location." His father glanced at the curtain walls.

"Then whisper, but damn, Dad, don't leave me hanging." Brock needed to know what was going on. He also wanted to offer his hand to Kallie, but unfortunately, he remembered her boundaries initiative. He was pretty certain talking about the case with his father fell somewhere in that work-slash-professional realm she mentioned. He could plead drug induced memory loss, but he wanted to be what she needed.

His father glanced around and grabbed a small plastic chair. After taking a seat he leaned forward and in a low, concise, manner brought Brock up to speed. Brock used his uninjured arm to rub his face. "Masters and Treyson are being paid by the Dominican Cartel."

His father nodded his head. "That's what it looks like. We have hoops to jump through before that information becomes official, but if Guardian is certain, I'll take it as gospel."

"Has Masters said anything? How did he get a fucking gun into the building?"

Kallie left her post by the curtain and moved closer.

"Masters has invoked his right to an attorney. He hasn't said a word. As far as how he got a gun into the building…" His father glanced at the curtain surrounding them. "We knew we had rats who'd found holes to hide. Seems Masters knew where to look. The sergeant working the floor stepped away to break up an altercation and one of the patrolmen in the lobby took Masters through. It's all on film. The patrolman was one of the few that Internal Affairs couldn't bring charges against in the East Side riots."

Brock sighed and dropped his head to the pillow. "What was he going to do? Kill Cynthia? I don't understand the concept of bringing a gun into a secure area."

"Desperation can make you do almost anything." Kallie spoke for the first time since they'd walked into the room.

"True." His father nodded and leaned back in his chair. "It also makes strange bed partners."

"Oh no, don't fucking tell me you're going to let the DA flip Masters. I mean I know it is the right thing to do, but damn it, Pops, he'll be getting away with murder. Literally."

His father shrugged. "It will further the investigation. The DA is very interested in getting Masters into Wit-Sec. But, he'll have to play ball, and I don't know if he'll go for it. Sebastian Treyson is pulling favors right and left trying to block the DA's intent, which has Larry fit to be tied. He has rats in his organization, too."

"Masters'll go for a plea bargain. The murder charge and attempted murder charge are slam dunks." Kallie said the words he was thinking.

"The motherfucker killed Samuel Treyson in cold blood and then torched the warehouse to try to cover his tracks. The fucker would have succeeded if Dawson hadn't talked to us."

Kallie grasped the silver rail of his bed. "The receipts to the cleaner, the tie in between Dawson and Samuel, and Cynthia's greed paved a perfect set up for Masters, except Cynthia wasn't a push over. I think Cynthia called Masters and threatened to out him. That's why he needed to get to her and to silence her."

"Wait, how did Samuel get the perc on his face?" He was still fuzzy, but fuck him, he needed to know what was happening.

Kallie filled in the blanks for him. "From the initial report I got from Davidson, she admitted to slapping him and telling him she was going to have Dawson beaten. That's when she said Sam dropped to his knees. To beg her not to hurt Dawson. She said she took his car keys and the cash from his wallet when he offered it to her and then left him still on his knees, thought better of it, and circled back. She saw Masters with a knife. She said the men were talking, Samuel started to get up, and Masters slit his throat. She'd videoed the entire thing."

His father stood up and stretched his back as he spoke. "If he takes the deal, we'll have all the answers, if not, well, we may never know. It is one of the hazards of the job. We do what we can do and let the system take it from there. But, if our suspicions are true and the cartels are in bed with some of the companies Treyson and Masters had access to… life just became more difficult for all of us."

His father winced as he straightened. He'd aged since he'd become the commissioner. The grey in his hair was more pronounced, but it was the ever-present exhaustion that worried Brock the most. High blood pressure and a high stress job were breeding grounds for a heart attack. His father had always seemed invincible to him, but today, he looked worried, tired, and stressed. Granted, his oldest son in the hospital probably didn't help, but...

"I need to get back to Briar Hill, but before I go, I'm going to spend a couple minutes with your mom. She's worried about you, so cut her some slack." He headed to the curtain. "Oh, and if you are released tomorrow, your butt will be at Sunday night dinner. It was only a .22 for God's sake." His dad raised a hand and ducked through the curtain.

Kallie managed to hold her laughter in for about two tenths of a second. "See, even your dad agrees."

"Har, har, har. I'm still not amused." But he did smile and then laugh. Kallie's mirth was infectious. "How was my mom? Did she make your life miserable?"

"No, she was very gracious. I met your entire family."

Brock closed his eyes and groaned. "You need these drugs more than I do." He motioned to the arm with the IV in it.

"No, really. Bekki is a force of nature. She's on Channel 2, isn't she?"

"Yep, my little sister, the investigative reporter. Brianna owns Horizon. It is a nice restaurant close to Briar Hills. She's quite the businesswoman."

"Your brother Blay brought the entire fire station with him."

"Yeah, if he was on duty, they'd all travel together. Did you meet Brody?" Brock hoped like hell she had. Brody was the sane one of the bunch, and he was closest to Brody.

"I did. We had a nice conversation, and your dad briefed me and him at the same time. Sean was here for a moment. He said he'd call you tonight or tomorrow morning depending on how his case played out."

"He's a good guy." His best friend was more than that, but he wasn't about to go into all the shit they'd done together. Things like sharing their first kiss experience… they'd kissed the same girl under the bleachers. Yeah, not material to share with your new girlfriend. A smile tilted his lips. His girlfriend. A damn good thought.

Her phone vibrated, and she glanced at it quickly.

"Is that from Davidson?"

She sighed and shook her head. "No."

"The ex?"

"Yeah."

"Kallie, how many times has he texted you today?"

She shrugged. "Enough to be annoying."

"What is he saying?"

"That he is going to get to me, and I'll be sorry for putting him in jail. Bla, bla, bla. Paraphrasing, of course."

Brock drew a deep breath and gaged his words carefully. "Let me help."

She gave a humorous laugh. "How?"

"I have contacts in Guardian. I can have them put eyes on the guy."

She took his hand. "I'm keeping a copy of the texts. Right now, they're generic threats. I'm a big girl. I know he's out there. When he comes after me, I'll be prepared."

"We'll be prepared." He squeezed her hand.

Her phone vibrated again. She glanced at the face and rolled her eyes.

"If those threats change, promise you'll tell me?"

"I can do that."

His nurse slipped back between the curtains. "Detective King, we have a room ready for you. I've told the masses in the waiting room where to find you, but I also told them no more than two visitors at a time." She glanced at Kallie. "We can let your..." The nurse looked from Kallie to him waiting for someone to fill in the blanks.

"Girlfriend," Kallie said before he could.

"Right, girlfriend, come with you as we move you up."

"Thank you." Kallie smiled at the woman and stepped back when three more people in scrubs entered the area. The IV was connected to the bed. He was disconnected from the monitoring machines, and the brakes were released on the bed. He hated that he couldn't walk to the room, but in all honesty, he'd make it about twenty feet before he'd have to rest. Those damn drugs really took it out of him.

Down the hall, up the elevator, and into a new room, Kallie stayed right beside him.

"I'm going to be back shortly. We'll keep an eye on your vitals and as soon as you eat and use the bathroom, we'll take that IV out. According to your family, you know the drill." The nurse laughed when he groaned. "Anyway, the doc will stop by tonight before he goes home. Do you have any questions?"

"When can I go home?"

"That's up to the doctor." The nurse checked his

IV, hooked the oxygen monitor back on his finger, and took his blood pressure again. "When do you want me to start sending in your family?"

Brock reached his hand to Kallie who slid hers into his. "Can you give us a few minutes? Delay my mother's entrance, please."

"That I can do. I'm on it." She whisked from the room and the door closed behind her.

He squeezed Kallie's hand. "Seriously, I know my family is a lot to take. If they get to be too much, you'll let me know, right?"

Kallie took her hand from his and sat down beside him. The vibration from her phone, a sound that had become all too familiar, filled the space between them. She didn't even look at the phone. He fucking hated her ex.

Kallie leaned forward. "I'm not going anywhere. Your family is wonderful. If whatever this is between us doesn't work out, it won't be because of your family, so stop worrying about them, okay?"

Brock reached up and palmed her cheek with his hand. The IV tubing tangled with her hair, but he didn't give a fuck. "I'm not going anywhere. This thing between us is new, but I'm all in, so stop expecting me to be like your ex, okay?"

Kallie's eyes widened. "I... you... How did you know?"

"I'm a detective, remember? You're giving me an out if this thing between us doesn't work. I'm not looking for an out. I'm looking for a way in. Let me in, Kallie. I know he is texting you, and I know you're trying to keep it from me. Don't do that. I'm not going to give up on us because of him."

"Fair enough. On one condition."

"And that is?"

"Stop getting shot."

"I can't guarantee it, but I'll try."

"I'll take it." She leaned into him, and he touched his lips to hers.

"Oh! Isn't that sweet, Sharon?"

Brock groaned at his mother's words and complained to the nurse, "I thought you were going to give us a few minutes." Kallie dissolved into laughter, and her head hit his shoulder. He opened his eyes and found the nurse sending daggers in his mother's direction.

"I'm sorry, sir, have you *met* your mother? She wasn't going to be delayed." The nurse shrugged and left the room. *Traitor.*

CHAPTER 18

Kallie opened the door to her apartment. She thought she'd make it back first, but every light in the apartment was on. Brock must have had a hell of a day. He'd milked the gunshot for three weeks of desk duty but had been back on the street for over a month. Davidson had semi-permanently assigned Brock as the side car to Bettis and Hansen's team. Being the third in a two-man team took some getting used to, but from what she'd seen, they were making it work. She hadn't heard of any fucked-up calls today... Something must have happened.

"Yo, Detective King, what are you, made of money?" She shut the door, turned the deadbolt and reached over to flip off the light in the kitchen.

She immediately turned it back on.

The oven isn't on. That's strange.

Whoever got home first always put dinner in the oven.

"Hey? How was your day?" She shouted down the hall and waited for a response. Nothing. *Is he already in the shower?* Damn, it must have been a total bitch of a day.

She opened the fridge, retrieved the casserole dish, and shoved it in the oven before she snagged two rocks glasses and poured each of them a finger of the good stuff. She dropped two ice cubes in each and used one hand to pinch the glasses together. With her free hand she cut off the lights in the kitchen and hall.

"What the fuck?" The living room was a disaster, cushions flipped off the furniture and her throws tossed over plants. She blinked, taking it in and scanned to the television, which was muted, but on. Old footage of her and Brock exiting Masters' trial ran in a six second loop. Her focus shifted to the stickie on the screen. "**Found you, bitch.**"

She dropped the glasses, drew her weapon, and palmed her phone. The glasses shattered against the hardwood floors. Training backed her against the wall to protect her six. She scanned the hall. Lights were on under the bedroom door and it was closed. A shadow slid past the door. The fucker.

Brock laughed when he answered. "Hey, did you miss--"

She hissed, "Shut up and listen. He's here."

"Who? Rich?"

"Yes!" Her eyes jumped from the hall to the hall closet and further to the small utility room. The motherfucker was In. Her. Home.

"Where are you? Are you safe?"

"Home. In the living room. I saw movement in the bedroom. A shadow against the light. There and then gone."

"Babe, don't be a fucking hero, get out." She could hear him snapping orders at someone.

"Fuck that. Call backup." She wasn't going to allow Rich to take her life away from her again.

"Bettis is doing that now. We're almost there. Wait for me. I'm your fucking backup!" The commanding tone in his voice rang over the connection.

She stood and edged her way to the front door. She cleared the hall to the rear and backed down the hall in the opposite direction. She kept her eyes on the bedroom door, pinned the phone to her ear with her shoulder, and reached back to dislodge the deadbolt.

"Front door is unlocked."

"We're a block away. Get the fuck out. He can't leave without coming through the front door or the fire escape. Bettis and Hansen are taking the rear." She heard him yell at Hansen to pull over and use the next turn to the right to access the rear of the building. "I'm on my way up."

"Standing just inside the door."

Brock's breath panted as she heard him climb the stairs. "Babe, I'm on the floor below you. I'll be there in thirty seconds."

At the sound of him in the hall, she placed her phone down and stepped forward. The front door swung open slowly, and Brock moved behind her. He pointed to the kitchen and living room. She mouthed, "Clear".

They advanced, her weapon pointed down, his up. He'd take high and she'd take low on any entry. She moved past the closet with Brock. There wasn't even enough room for sheets and hand towels in the small space; no one could hide in there. Silently, they moved down the hall. The laundry room was next. Positioned outside the door, Brock held up three fingers, and she nodded.

He lowered his fingers one at a time and yanked the door open. She lowered to her knees with him standing over her. Rich had strewn the cat litter all over the washer and dryer, and the bag of cat food was shredded, the kibble everywhere.

They recovered and moved to the bedroom. Brock stared at her. She knew what he was asking. She nodded. She was ready. He held up three fingers. They repeated the entry, but this time she moved right, and he moved left. Her clothes, and Brock's, were shredded and draped from every surface. All the drawers in the dresser had been pulled out and dumped, and the mirror over it read, "**Die, bitch!**" in her lipstick. He'd taken a sharp blade to her mattress and pillows and their guts littered the floor. The room stank of urine.

She ground her teeth together and did her fucking job.

Clearing the bedroom, Brock leveled his gun on the closet, moved in front of it with her as overwatch. Nothing. The bed was on a solid pedestal; no one was getting under that thing.

She nodded past the bed to the bathroom. As they slowly and silently inched forward, Fester issued a screeching meow and ran toward them.

Fuck! She stepped around the crazy cat and

moved to position in front of the bathroom door. Brock opened the door, and they moved as one to clear the small bathroom.

"Clear." Brock turned around at the same time she did. Fuck, what a mess. Fester weaved himself around her legs. She holstered her gun, reached down, and scooped him up. "What the hell?"

"He shredded all of our clothes. The motherfucker is dangerous, Kallie. How did he find you?"

"I don't know. Maybe the news coverage?" She smoothed her fingers through Fester's thick coat, stopping when her fingers hit something. "Oh, the sick bastard." She pointed to the small noose that was fastened around Fester's neck.

"Is he okay?" Brock's hand rifled through the cat's fur.

"I think so. Yeah. Purring like a motorboat."

Brock's gaze snapped to the twine. "Is that the string from the kitchen?"

"Probably."

"We need to get the crime scene techs in here." Brock wrapped her in a hug, nearly suffocating poor Fester in between them, but neither she nor the cat protested. "I'll call Bettis and Hansen and bring them in."

"You'll probably want to call Lieutenant Davidson, too." He nodded, his chin brushing her hair.

"I'm not going to let him do this. He can't have my life."

Brock made a sound of agreement, kissed her temple, and moved away. "Let's get this scene processed, and we'll worry about what happens next."

She gave her statement for the third time while sitting in the kitchen, and that's where she'd stayed. She'd turned off the oven over two hours ago when their dinner had started to burn. The crime scene techs had processed her entire apartment. Fingerprint dust covered absolutely everything. Both she and Brock gave sample prints for exclusion. They wouldn't find anything. Rich had been a cop. He knew to wear gloves. The stickie on the television and the homemade DVD with the looping footage were taken as evidence, as was the small noose that Rich had fashioned from butcher's twine. The sick son of a bitch. Fester had been rattled, or he sensed her unease, because he hadn't willingly left her lap and launched back into it as soon as she'd let him.

"Where are they?" Davidson plodded into the kitchen and dumped his body into one of the four chairs.

Brock followed him into the kitchen after closing the front door behind the last crime scene tech. Kallie slid her phone across the table and hit the messages icon. The men huddled together and read the latest vitriol from her ex-husband. It was nothing new. Nothing that indicated he'd found her. No uptick in the threats.

Brock gazed at her. She shrugged. "They are all the same. I told you I'd let you know if the tone changed."

Davidson started to scroll. "How many are there?"

"Hundreds." Probably closer to a thousand. Rich was prolific.

"This is going to a judge. Restraining order and hopefully a warrant to pick up this motherfucker. Then we need to determine what to do with you." Davidson looked up from his phone at her snort.

She shook her head. "Nothing. I'm not going to let this guy scare me into leaving my job. I've told Grant about Rich. I'll keep him informed on what happened tonight. Brock has known from the start. I'm not ducking out. I have a life here. I'm not letting him take that from me."

"At a minimum we should move you to another precinct." Davidson leaned back in his chair.

"May I ask you a question, sir?"

"Shoot."

"If this current situation was in your lap, if you had a nut job threatening you, would you move to another precinct? Would you demand it of Brock? Of Bettis? Of Hansen?" She shook her head. "You wouldn't. You'd talk protective measures, officer safety, intelligent decisions by them and their partners. I am a damn good cop. I'm not backing down. I'll get better locks and use them. My situational awareness is on high alert. Moving me would only delay whatever the fuck he has planned, and it would give me a false sense of safety which I cannot afford."

Davidson rubbed the back of his neck. "I'm taking this to the Captain, and we'll end up talking to the department's lawyers, but you're right. Cops operate under threats all the time. Knowing you're a target is an advantage, but I fucking hate that one of my officers is being stalked."

Kallie nodded her acknowledgment.

"King, you're on this woman's six when she's not with Grant."

Brock stared at him. "That's fucking guaranteed."

"I don't need a babysitter."

"No, you need backup. Insanity like this isn't something to fuck around with. I can put your ass into protective custody." Davidson stood and nodded at the door. "Both of you have a day off tomorrow. Get those locks changed, and for God's sake, use the damn deadbolt."

Brock followed him and shut and locked the door behind him. He leaned against the door frame, his hands in his jeans pockets.

She ran her fingers through the cat's fur and cooed, "He can't order me into protective custody."

Brock shook his head, his face a mask of seriousness. "Not the time to joke."

"Yeah, well if I don't, I'll snap. I don't want to give Rich that power. I take my personal safety seriously. There wasn't anything to indicate he'd found me."

"I understand that. When was the last time he texted?" Brock came over and put his hands on her shoulders and started to work the tense muscles.

"This morning."

"None since then?"

"No."

"Is that unusual?"

She opened her eyes and tipped her head back to look at him. "Yeah. Four or five bullshit threats a day."

"He hasn't texted or called to gloat. Why do you think that is?"

"I don't know. Maybe since he found me, the thrill of the chase is over?" She closed her eyes and leaned back against him.

Brock bent down and kissed her lips. He whispered against them, "Let's load up Fester and head to my apartment."

Her eyes snapped open. "No. I'm not letting him win."

"There is no contest here. The apartment is a zoo. We have no place to sleep. We'll come back tomorrow, clean up, and get the locks changed. Tonight, I want to hold you."

She blinked up at him. "I don't even know if I have clothes for tomorrow."

"We can wash what you have on." He moved from behind the chair and extended his hand to her. "Let me take care of you tonight, Kallie. You can be a bad-ass cop tomorrow."

A tired chuckle fell from her. "Yeah? I have your permission?"

"Definitely. You as a bad-ass cop turns my crank."

"Turns your crank? Hello, there's my Boomer." She stood, keeping Fester with her.

"Not a Boomer." He kissed her quickly before he left the room.

"If it walks like a Boomer and talks like a Boomer." She walked to the doorway and raised her voice as he went to get Fester's carrier.

He popped his head out of the utility room. "I do not walk like an old man."

"Sorry, you're right. If it thinks like a Boomer and talks like a Boomer..."

"Smart ass."

Kallie chuckled at the reply that she wasn't sure she was supposed to hear.

Sleeping with Brock was a guilty pleasure. Waking up to his touch? Amazing. A treat she'd learned to love since she'd started sleeping with him. Granted, waking up early enough to leisurely make love was rare. Those mornings were few and far between, but when they shared them, they were spectacular. She smiled. Even the mornings they had to hurry were incredible.

His fingers trailed up and down her thigh. She hummed and pushed back into his morning wood. He dipped down and trailed kisses along her neck. The pads of his fingertips meandered over her hip and up to her breast, all while dotting every inch of exposed skin on her neck with small, tender kisses.

Aroused and awake, she shifted her top leg and moved it up toward her chest. It was all the invitation Brock needed. He nipped her shoulder as he slowly worked himself inside her--sans condom. After Brock had been released from the hospital, they'd both been tested and had decided to forgo condoms because she had birth control. It was a luxurious sensation of freedom enhanced by their mutual trust. The emotion that engulfed her when Brock made love to her was impossible to deny. He was her true north. He was the direction she'd travel, no matter what. Everything in her life now pointed to him. He was her best friend, her lover, an intellectual stimulant, sparring partner, and couch potato soul mate. The ease and speed that her life had absorbed into his should have scared her, but there were no doubts. None. This man supported her but didn't stifle her. He encouraged her, applauded her efforts, laughed at her silliness and accepted her for who she was. Every damn time. Brock was her constant, her true north, and that realization soaked into every fiber of her soul.

He wrapped around her, spooning her against him, their bodies connected, touching, reassuring. With Brock she felt cherished. His fingers teased her nipples as he languidly moved forward and retreated. There was no rush, only sensation. He weaved his fingers through hers, while still moving in that perfect tempo that would shatter them, eventually.

"I could have lost you last night."

She turned her head and kissed him. "You could have but you didn't. We know the risks."

He took her lips and dipped inside with his tongue, the kiss just as controlled as his pace. "It doesn't mean I have to like it. I hate it. Promise me you'll be careful. Promise me."

"I will. You know I will. For you. For us."

His body sped up, his urgency shown not only by his words. Heat curled at her core, growing in intensity. She closed her eyes and let Brock take her to that wonderful peak. She squeezed his hand when her body rolled over the summit and held him tight through his climax.

"You have to make some changes. Small things to make sure you're covered. Not because you need a babysitter, but because you're the most important thing in my life." His words were whispered. They were a plea.

She reached back and hugged him closer to her. "I'll make sure."

CHAPTER 19

Brock stared sightlessly through the window of Casey's diner. Kallie was late, which given their profession wasn't unusual, but he worried. Rich had been conspicuously absent. No texts, no calls. He and Grant had talked and had worked out a system. The woman remained in one of their lines of vision. She didn't like it, but they didn't care. Since the top blew off the Treyson case, they'd both been busy working different cases. Grant Couch was a good partner for Kallie. They jelled, which fucking irritated him, but that was his baggage. The jealousy thing was new to him. The fucking little green monster trotted front and center whenever he thought of Kallie working late nights with Grant, but she didn't need or want that type of attitude. With her past, it wasn't welcome, and he'd shoved that little green monster into a box and shut the lid, for the most part keeping the gremlin at bay. But the specter of Rich never left him alone. The bastard was always around, distorting their normal actions, altering their lives in little ways. Irritating and offensive, but unavoidable.

After the break in at her apartment, Kallie finally started to open up to him about Rich. She'd given him her phone, and he'd scanned over four hundred of the most horrific texts he'd ever read. The man went into detail about how he was going to kill Kallie.

"Hey." Sean pushed into the seat across from him.

Brock blinked and sat up, pulling his foot off the banquette seat, giving his friend room. "Dude, what are you doing down here?"

"An apartment fire on Halstead around noon. The fire chief thought it went up too fast, so they called me in."

"Arson?"

"Nah, just a fuck-ton of code violations. I

figured I'd grab some food to go while I was here. Harper is working another case, and I don't feel like cooking. Where's Kallie?"

"Still out." Brock stopped talking when the waiter showed up to top off his coffee. Sean ordered two specials to go, and they were alone again.

"Saw both you and Kallie on television about a week ago, and every night since. That Treyson case is some serious shit, isn't it? That courthouse is a fucking zoo. Media everywhere. Sebastian Treyson has made the circuit on every talk show and then some."

"You don't know the half of it." He held up a hand, stilling the questions he knew Sean had. "When I can talk about it, I'll fill you in, suffice to say this is the case that keeps on giving."

"Fuck, no shit?"

"No shit." By not saying anything, he'd told Sean more than he'd told anyone else not directly connected to the case. Sean could read him like a fucking book, and he knew his best friend just as well.

"When's Jordan due back?" Sean leaned back in the booth.

"No idea. The feds lost Grappelli, again."

"So why is Jordan still gone?"

Brock drew in a long breath. He knew why, but it was classified. The feds were using Jordan. In order to smoke Grappelli out of the woodwork, they were milking information and instinct from Jordan. Instead of saying anything, he just shrugged.

Sean narrowed his eyes for a moment. "Can't say, huh?"

"Something like that. In the meantime, Bettis, Hansen, and I have a pretty good working relationship. I'm still the third wheel, but it works. The communication is heinous at times, but we get shit done."

"How long until your Lieutenant finds you a new partner, permanently?"

"Don't know. Davidson will keep me unattached as long as possible, but life happens, right?"

"Man, you got that right. On another subject, what do you have planned for Valentine's Day?" Sean's smile told him his friend had plans, but for what woman?

Brock gave him the same shit eating grin right back. "It's only the middle of January."

"True, but you got to plan things like this, my friend."

"I'm prepared. Eagle Scout, remember?" The ring he bought Kallie was tucked in that black velvet box, tucked into the inside pocket of his coat. "What about you?"

"Working it." Sean winked at him as the waiter brought two Styrofoam containers to the table bundled up in a white plastic bag.

"Do you need another refill?" The waiter wiggled the coffee pot in his hand.

Brock shook his head. Sean gave the man two twenties and told him to keep the change. "Not like you to turn down more coffee." Sean chuckled as he scooted from the booth.

Brock motioned toward the window. Sean's eyes followed. Kallie stood on the far side of the street, her hands in her pockets as she looked down the avenue waiting for traffic to clear. Brock did a quick scan of the surrounding area. *There.* Grant stood at the entrance to the parking lot waiting for Brock to see his partner. The man had their backs.

Brock stood and headed to the door with Sean.

"Ah, well that explains it. Coffee can't compete with your girl. Hey, why don't we get together for the Super Bowl, drink too much, and eat a shit-ton of food?"

"Perfect. Your place?"

"That works. You bring the food; I'll have the drinks covered and the spare room made up in case it goes into overtime."

He opened the door and held it so Sean didn't have to juggle the take out containers. "Make sure you have two pillows, my man."

"Pfft. I was an Eagle Scout too, remember? Always prepared. Speaking of which—" Sean glanced at his watch "—you'll be late for dinner."

"Mom lets *her* get away with it." Brock chuckled at Sean's stupefied gape.

They moved to the sidewalk together. "Holy hell, she must really love that woman."

"Yeah, they cook together on weekends when Kallie isn't on a case. They've bonded." Kallie had fit into his family seamlessly. She and Brianna were tight. Although Bekki and she were friendly, they weren't as close. Kallie gave no quarter to his brothers, which he fucking loved.

"So, if this doesn't work out, they're keeping Kallie, and you're booted to the curb?" Sean laughed and dodged the elbow Brock threw his way.

"Asshole. Tell me your mom wouldn't keep a fantastic woman if you ever brought one home."

"Probably, but I'm not there just yet, so no worries on that point."

He nodded to his woman. "I did something right to get her."

Kallie stepped off the curb when the light turned and was halfway across the street. He and Sean stood at the curb waiting. She saw them, he waved, and a huge smile parted her face. Grant waved to him from behind her and turned toward the parking lot, catching his attention. He heard Sean say something at the same time as he saw a man dart off the curb behind Kallie. She waved back, but all he could see was the man's face. It was screwed into a snarl. Brock dropped his hands and ripped the snaps of his coat open to access his weapon. Kallie must have noticed the action because she jerked her head and looked behind her.

There are some moments that seem to stretch into eternity. This wasn't one of them. Brock saw the gun as the man lifted it. Instinct, training and terror catapulted him into action. With the butt of his gun already palmed, he yelled for Kallie to get down. She dropped like a fucking rock and his gun kicked in his hand. The lunatic behind Kallie jolted backward and crumpled to the ground. He ran forward and held his gun on the man, but lowered his weapon and sank to his knees when he reached Kallie. Sean, who'd been at his side the entire time, held his automatic on the bastard.

"Babe, fuck... Kallie!"

"I'm okay." Her voice shook as she grabbed his hand and let herself be hauled into a crushing embrace. Sean was on the phone and barking orders to the cops who flew from the precinct offices.

"Who the fuck?" Brock glanced at the man when Sean toed him over and cuffed the bastard.

"Rich. That's Rich."

Her fucking ex-husband. The man looked nothing like the mug shot he'd seen of the bastard. The bastard on the street had filthy matted hair and a full beard. "Are you sure you're okay?" He ran his hands over her face. Her color was shit; she was so damn pale. He watched Sean kick the gun the asshole had drawn on Kallie, moving it from the son of a bitch's reach.

"I... ah... yeah." Down filling fluttered to the street and his gaze fell to her jacket. There was a bullet hole just under her left arm. "Wow, that was kinda close, huh?" She grabbed his arm, steadying herself.

"How the fuck did he find you?" He stood and helped Kallie up. Rich moaned and they both turned to face the man who'd tried to kill her.

"My bet is on the newscasts from the Treyson case. Both of you were front and center and the media hasn't stopped talking about the case." Sean stood when Rich was flipped onto his back. Cuffed, the bastard wasn't going anywhere, and several officers worked on stemming the blood loss from the gunshot wound to his thigh. The fucker would live to go to court. Again. Brock had been shooting at a moving target while running. His bullet went low and left and hit the bastard just below the crotch on the outside of his leg. He clutched Kallie tightly.

"You good here?" Sean asked.

"Yeah, sorry, but I think you'll have to reheat your dinner." Paperwork took for fucking ever, especially when a weapon was discharged.

"No worries, and besides, the way this place is covered with video surveillance, we won't be here long. They can confirm our account without problem." Sean holstered his weapon.

"You fucking bitch. I'll kill you!" Spittle flew

from Rich's mouth, hanging in a string down his cheek.

Rage seethed under his skin. That bastard had tried to kill the woman he loved, the woman he was going to ask to marry him. The motherfucker didn't deserve to draw air into his lungs, and yet there he was, spewing vitriol and hate. "Come on. Let's get inside." Brock nodded, acknowledging one of the officers who escorted them into the precinct.

"You bitch! You ruined my life!"

Brock spun on the bastard. Her ex sneered at him. "She'll ruin you, too."

"Brock, let's go inside." Kallie moved in front of him, blocking his view of the bastard. "He's taken too much from me already. He can't hurt me anymore. Let's go do the paperwork and put him where he belongs, for good."

He dropped his forehead to hers and held her. "He almost took you from me." He couldn't fathom his life without her in it. She'd become his cornerstone, his foundation. Finally, he leaned away, "Let's go."

He didn't know who was going to do the investigation, but when some bastard tries to take down one of their own, whoever had the case would be doing it by the numbers. Letting someone get off on a technicality wasn't going to happen. He surrendered his weapon when asked and helped Kallie back into their building.

Davidson stood at the top of the stairs. "The video has already been downloaded. I'm not the DA, but it looked like a justified shooting. His gun bucks and discharges before yours. IA has been called. You'll both need to give statements, and I'm going to have to separate you until that's done. You sure you're good, Redman?"

Kallie nodded. "I'm over the shock, and I've moved on to pissed-the-fuck-off."

"Then let's get this shit over with and get everyone home before midnight." Davidson caught Brock's eyes and motioned to Kallie as if asking if she were actually good or fronting. Brock nodded. She was more squared away than he was, and that was a testament to her internal strength.

Kallie tugged her boots off and nearly stumbled over her own feet. She could hear Brock in the bedroom. He'd headed there right after they'd gotten home.

"Kallie?"

"Kitchen."

"Do you want a drink?" Brock leaned against the door jamb.

"Yeah, something strong, please?"

"You got it." He leaned in and kissed her gently on the lips. When she opened her eyes, he was staring at her.

She smiled at him again. "I'm fine." She'd reassure him as many times as it took. Having him watch over her was a priceless gift. He'd been hovering since Rich had tried to kill her. Her smile froze in place, and she blinked that thought away. She didn't want him to see the shattered web of nerves underneath the veneer. Instead of releasing her, he wrapped his arm around her waist and walked with her to the kitchen.

She knew she'd been quiet on the ride home. Brock had just held her hand and let her have the time, his quiet strength there for her should she need it.

She sat down at the small table and waited until he'd poured them both a two-finger measure of bourbon. She downed the liquor in one go… and the flames of hell scalded her throat. "Oh, fuck," she rasped with the infinitesimal amount of air her lungs managed to claim. Tears filled her eyes and her nose clogged. She coughed and managed to suck in some air only to cough again and again. A paper napkin was shoved into her hand, and she gratefully used it to blow her nose. "Whoa, fuck, note to self don't do that... again." Kallie blinked at Brock who was on his knee beside her.

He opened his fist, displaying a small black velvet box. He slowly reached up with his other hand and opened the lid. "I was going to wait until Valentine's Day, but today made me realize I didn't want to wait a minute longer. I almost lost you. It terrified me. I need you in my life. I need you to be my wife, my partner, and my friend. With our careers, I can promise you more fucked up shit than you should have to deal with, and you'll have to put up with my family, too." Brock dropped his hand, taking the ring from her view. "Fuck, that's not selling this very well is it?"

Kallie laughed and ran her hand down his arm to the hand that held the ring. "You had me at the first murder investigation. The fucked-up shit and family balance each other out. Good with the bad."

Brock's brows drew together. "The family's the good part, right?"

Kallie threw back her head and laughed. "The best part."

Brock held her hand and slid the small round solitaire onto her finger. It was absolutely perfect. "So that's a yes? You'll marry me?"

She leaned forward and kissed him. "Yes, I'll marry you."

"You know what that means, right?" Brock stood, still holding her hand in his.

She blinked and shook her head. "Ah... no."

"Proposal sex, acceptance sex, and then fantastic engagement sex." He helped her to her feet.

"Oh, *that*..." She laughed as he nodded his head, a cheesy smile plastered his face.

"Yeah, that." He dropped her hand and cupped her face. "Let me make love to you until what happened tonight is a distant memory." His smile faded as he stared into her eyes.

She couldn't help the shiver that ran through her at their intense connection. She sighed and leaned into him. "That could take a long, long time." The emotion she'd been trying to fight cracked through and her eyes filled with tears. Happy tears, but it was a crack in the dam.

His thumb wiped away a fat drop that pushed

over the edge of her eyelashes. "I'm not going anywhere. I'll be here, and I'll love you the way you deserve to be loved." He stood and brought her up with him. He lowered and placed a tender, almost-there kiss on her lips. Kallie burrowed into his arms, and he wrapped her up, cocooned her in safety and, most importantly, love. What she'd had with Rich had never been this.

Brock led them through the small apartment. He carefully removed her shirt, kissing the exposed skin of her shoulders. His fingers traveled over her skin, raising goose flesh in their wake. He unfastened her holster from her jeans and placed her service weapon on the nightstand before he unfastened his secondary weapon and placed it beside hers. The fact he didn't have his primary weapon jolted her from the moment. Rich's actions hit her again, stealing all her joy.

"No, this time isn't about him. It's about you and me. Our lives together. He doesn't have a place between us. Not now, not ever." Brock kissed her until she was breathless. He didn't dominate her, but led her higher than she ever dreamed she could go.

His fingers trailed over her skin and cast off her bra. Brock lowered her to the mattress, his strength holding her when her balance no longer could. He'd never let her fall. She knew that as surely as she knew she'd pull oxygen into her lungs with the next breath. Brock was a constant, a rock, and he was hers.

When he slid inside her, the unsheathed heat of his cock felt delicious. She cradled him in between her legs, holding onto him as his hands and mouth made her feel like a princess. If this was a fairytale, she never wanted to wake up. She'd met her prince. He wasn't perfect, but then again, neither was she. He was a man-child, coarse and foul-mouthed at times. He also worked too hard, drank too much coffee, slept fewer hours than any person she'd ever met, and had problems being civil to her new partner. Brock King wasn't perfect, but he was hers and hers alone.

Thoughts of anything but Brock seeped from her mind as he played her body like a master musician plays a fine instrument. He knew how to touch her to make her insane with desire. He'd learned just how much pressure to apply to her nipples to send waves of pleasure through her body. His breathless kisses peppered with erotic whispers of love and forever pushed a tidal wave of prickling sensitivity through her.

"Oh, God, yes," she sighed after he moved her leg and thrust deeper inside her, the connection between them as profound as it could be. Her body tightened like a bow pulled to the breaking point. This was the moment she'd needed, the cresting accumulation of all the sensations sitting at the precipice of an explosive crescendo. He thrust again, his body pushing into and against hers, the friction, inside and out, launched her into orgasmic bliss.

"You're beautiful." His breathless words snapped her eyes open as she gasped for air. "You are the most beautiful thing in the world. I love you." His thrusts became erratic and she felt him climax. The corded muscles of his neck and shoulders showed in deep striations. His arms bulged as he held himself up, careful, even as he lost control, not to crush her under his weight. His head dropped to her shoulder where his breath cooled her heated skin with hurried pants.

When he finally lifted his head, she smiled up at him. "I love you, Brock. I love you for who you are with me and for the man you are when you are at work. I love that you are a grown ass, foul talking, aggravating and demanding detective and you're still a momma's boy. I adore the way you treat your friends, and I'm proud to be yours."

"I'm not a momma's boy." His brow furrowed as he looked down at her.

"Really, *that* is what you took away from what I just said?"

He couldn't hide the smile, even though she knew he tried. "Well, no, all that other stuff was cool and all…"

Kallie reached for the man's ribs and dug her fingers into his sides. He shrieked like a teenage girl and jumped from bed. "Stop!" He held up his hand when she rose to her knees and crawled toward him. "Tickling? Really?"

"Getcha ass back in bed, Detective." Kallie stopped at the edge of the bed and licked her lips. "We've done proposal sex, but we still have acceptance and engagement sex to celebrate."

"Oh, yeah… *that*." A cocky grin spread across his face, but he stalled just beyond her reach. "Tickling is not sexy."

"Tickling is very sexy, but I promise not to use it again tonight."

"With great power…"

"Yeah, I know. Great responsibility, now getcha

ass in bed before I decide to take you to the floor and tickle you again."

"Damn, that threat shouldn't be that hot." Brock eased into bed and rolled her on top of him.

"Why's that?" She leaned down and licked up his neck, stopping at his earlobe, taking that into her mouth.

"The fact that if you tried hard enough you might be able to take me down." Brock shuddered when she nipped his lobe.

"We'll experiment sometime." She straddled his hips and pushed against his cock. "Right now, I want my fiancé inside me."

"Fiancé." Brock smiled and lifted her hand from his chest. He kissed the ring and then tugged her down to his lips. "I'm sorry in advance for the mistakes I'll make."

"Mistakes happen. We'll figure it out. Together." She leaned down and kissed the man she was going to marry and spend the rest of her life with. The realization settled deep inside her, became part of her, and solidified her knowledge that Brock King was hers, forever—a forever that would be earned with hard work and determination to be what each other needed. Forever.

Kallie stretched and sat up in bed. Brock had left their bed early, called out. She'd rolled over and promptly fell back into an exhausted sleep. Grant wasn't picking her up until about noon tomorrow. They had interviews scheduled for later in the day, but Grant would handle them alone. They couldn't stop the world, and crime didn't take a break. She glanced at the engagement ring on her hand. It was perfect. A small round diamond. Nothing flashy, she wouldn't have worn anything flashy and Brock knew that about her. He knew everything about her.

Rich was behind bars. Again. She could breathe easier, for now. The court system was good, but fallible. Knowing he was behind bars gave her a semblance of peace. What Rich's actions had torn from her, Brock had repaired.

She got out of bed and pulled on a t-shirt and pair of shorts before she padded to the kitchen and Brock's collection of coffee pots. She had time to make a full pot and drink it. A luxury. As she was pouring a cup of coffee, she heard keys jingling from the hall. "Kallie?"

"In the kitchen." She lifted a mug the size of a salad bowl to her lips and sipped the fresh brew.

Brock's head and only his head appeared in the door. She blinked and frowned. "What are you doing?"

"I... ah... I did a thing."

"A thing? Is this thing female, sexy and single?"

Brock's eyes enlarged. "Ah... female and single, yes. Sexy? No."

Kallie put her coffee cup down and crossed her arms over her chest. "I haven't had a full cup of coffee, King. Stop fucking around and spill it."

"Okay." He stepped into the doorway and held out both hands. "You know Jordan is going to come back eventually. I know how much you love Fester and I thought maybe..."

"Oh, Brock..." She moved across the floor as she stared at the small, fluffy white kitten lying on her back in his hands. She had a green bow tied around her neck and was bending into contortions trying to get at the ribbon.

"Bettis' cat got knocked up. He was describing the kittens yesterday. I thought maybe... Awww... damn it. You weren't supposed to cry."

Kallie wiped at her cheeks. "Happy tears." She

reached out and stroked the kitten's pudgy belly. It twisted and batted at her fingers. "Oh, she's sassy!"

"She's got tons of attitude." Brock extended his hands and she took charge of the tiny fluffball. "Is it too soon for us to get a pet?"

Kallie shook her head and pulled the ribbon from the kitten. It rolled onto its back and swatted at the satin. "No. Not too soon." She smiled up at him. "Thank you."

"I got all the stuff for her downstairs in the car. I wasn't going to lug it up here if you didn't like her."

The kitten meowed and batted at Brock's fingers when he reached out to pet her. "What are you going to name her?"

She lifted the kitten and looked up at the little furball. Her green eyes were wide, and she meowed her discontent––loudly. "She's got a ton of attitude, doesn't she?"

"A ton." Brock moved behind her and wrapped his arms lightly around her waist.

She lowered the kitten to the floor and watched as she reared up and attacked the green ribbon that had fallen to the floor. "How about Sassy?"

Fester poked his head around the corner and

the kitten arched her back and hissed before she skittered after the bigger cat.

He chuckled and rewrapped his arms around her when she stood. "I think that's perfect."

She leaned into him and closed her eyes. "Brock?"

He gave her a small squeeze. "Yeah?"

"I love you. If this is a dream, never wake me up."

"We're real, babe. We're strong. We're together, and we'll last a lifetime. Together."

EPILOGUE

Brody jogged into the building that the Joint Drug Enforcement Team used for its operations. Brock and Kallie's wedding had started late and ended late. The *reason* the wedding started late was because Brock and Kallie didn't subscribe to the superstition, they shouldn't see each other before the ceremony. So... his entire family and the McBride family waited while the post-nuptial activities got a kick start. If his mother ever found out, she'd give birth to a cow. A full-grown, horn-toting, ring-in-the-nose, bull-type, beef critter.

He wondered how long it would be before the rumor mill made it through the family and back to his mother. He so wanted to be at that family dinner, but with the information and leads they'd been accumulating from Masters' deal on the Treyson case, he'd been lucky to pull four hours off for his brother's wedding. The web of criminal activity alleged was massive and the FBI and DEA had been called in to help his task force, brandishing federal authority when the big guns were needed. They were moving at a snail's pace. It was frustrating as fuck, but they had a ghost of a trail, and they were following the money. For that, they'd requested and received permission to work with Guardian. Thank God.

Now that his brother and wife were on their way to their honeymoon, he had to get back to work. He envied them a long weekend in New York City, but they were celebrating their wedding *and* Rich's sentencing. In Maryland the maximum sentence for attempted murder was life and that was the term the judge handed down.

He opened the back door to the briefing room and slid inside. He nodded to his lieutenant and captain. He'd sent them a text and let them know he'd be running late. They tipped their chins at him, and he leaned against the back wall, taking in the team in front of him. His other lieutenant was at the front of the room talking to someone he didn't recognize. The rest of the team was cutting up or ignoring the fuck out of everyone and tapping on their phones.

He glanced over at Captain Terrell. The man was a straight shooter and a hands-on type of guy. He went into the field with his team, which was unusual and controversial, but that was Terrell in a nutshell.

"Nice tux," Terrell grunted. Brody flipped him off. He had work clothes in the office, he'd change later.

"Did I miss anything?" They were expecting the DEA to come in and brief them on a new twist to the flow of drugs into Hope City.

Lieutenant Anderson shook his head. "Nah, the feds made a switch up mid-stream. This guy is waiting for the agent that will be assigned here on a permanent basis. He's fielding questions about a current surveillance they are working with the port authority."

"So, the DEA is actually agreeing to permanently assigning someone to the task force? What do they want in return?"

"Nothing, yet," Captain Terrell grunted. "You can be sure they'll want a favor in the future."

The front door to the briefing room opened. The air in his lungs disappeared. *Fuck me.*

His lieutenant leaned over. "You know her?"

Shit, he must have said that out loud. His eyes drilled holes in the back of the woman's head. He knew that walk. Knew how soft her long red hair was. He knew she could kick ass and knew that she was wicked smart. "Yeah, I know her."

A lifetime of events flashed through his mind. Middle school, high school, prom, college, that damn apartment. He blinked hard and stared at the woman again. She'd grown her hair longer, and the clothes were more elegant, but...

"Gentlemen," The DEA agent in front of the room addressed the suddenly silent squad room. "May I present Agent Amber Swanson."

The woman turned and scanned the men seated in front of her. He saw it when she recognized him. For a moment, she hesitated. Only for a moment. But then again, what did he expect?

Captain Terrell leaned forward. "How do you know Agent Swanson?"

Brody swallowed hard. "I asked her to marry me. She said no."

For the next Hope City Book, Click here:
Rory
Killian

Read all the Hope City Series by Kris Michaels and MaryAnn Jordan

Brock - Book One

Sean - Book 2

Carter - Book 3

Brody - Book 4

Kyle - Book 5

Ryker - Book 6

Rory - Book 7

Killian - Book 8

ALSO BY KRIS MICHAELS

Hope City

HOPE CITY DUET - Brock and Sean

HOPE CITY - Brody - Book 3

Hope City - Ryker - Book 5

Kings of the Guardian Series

Jacob: Kings of the Guardian Book 1

Joseph: Kings of the Guardian Book 2

Adam: Kings of the Guardian Book 3

Jason: Kings of the Guardian Book 4

Jared: Kings of the Guardian Book 5

Jasmine: Kings of the Guardian Book 6

Chief: The Kings of Guardian Book 7

Jewell: Kings of the Guardian Book 8

Jade: Kings of the Guardian Book 9

Justin: Kings of the Guardian Book 10

Christmas with the Kings The Kings of Guardian

Drake: Kings of the Guardian Book 11

Dixon: Kings of the Guardian Book 12

Passages: The Kings of Guardian Book 13

A Backwater Blessing: A Kings of Guardian and Heart's Desire Crossover Novella

Montana Guardian: A Kings of Guardian Novella

Guardian Defenders Series

Gabriel

Maliki

Guardian Security Shadow World

Anubis (Guardian Shadow World Book 1)

Asp (Guardian Shadow World Book 2)

Lycos (Guardian Shadow World Book 3)

Thanatos (Guardian Shadow World Book 4)

Tempest (Guardian Shadow World Book 5)

Smoke (Guardian Shadow World Book 6)

STAND ALONE NOVELS

SEAL Forever - Silver SEALs

A Heart's Desire - Stand Alone

Hot SEAL, Single Malt (SEALs in Paradise)

Hot SEAL, Savannah Nights (SEALs in Paradise)

ABOUT THE AUTHOR

USA Today and Amazon Bestselling Author, Kris Michaels is the alter ego of a happily married wife and mother. She writes romance, usually with characters from military and law enforcement backgrounds.

Made in the USA
Las Vegas, NV
08 December 2020